Max and the Space Pirates

Mark Blackwell

This book is dedicated to our daughter Rebecca.

Contents

Chapter One

The Dream

Bang, a direct hit, the Vanquish shuddered. Max felt the vibration rattle through the ship, sparks flew from the instrument panel, and smoke began to fill the bridge, stinging his eyes and nostrils. Other than the faint glow from the sun, which cast an eerie light through the asteroid belt, and his high intensity lights, it was pitch black out there. He swung the controls to the left and weaved through chunks of floating debris. Suddenly there was another bright flash directly in front of him, a small chunk of rock exploded, a great burst of orange and white light lit up the surrounding area, briefly illuminating dozens of smaller fragments. He threw the ship into a steep turn, but some of the debris scraped along the hull, creating a loud clanging noise that vibrated through her.

Speeding up, he weaved in and out of small chunks of rock, going as fast as he could. At times he just missed them, at other times they clanged off the ship's hull. As they ducked under another chunk, the lights of the Vanquish picked out a large asteroid closing in fast. Max accelerated again, the lights picking out a steep valley, turning the scene into a surreal landscape of dancing shadows.

Going as fast as he dared, he entered the valley with the pirate ships close on his tail. There were explosions on either side of him as they fired their laser cannons off in volleys, briefly illuminating the barren crater-ridden surface. Wrestling with the controls he had the Vanquish swerving from side to side, dodging the incoming fire, as streaks of blue light shot over him and to the sides.

Suddenly, the instruments sounded a warning: up ahead a steep wall of rock was approaching, the surface was streaking past in a blur beneath him. He pulled back on the controls as hard as he could and felt the ship groan as he managed to put her into a steep climb. Thankfully, and with inches to spare they shot back into space. He could see the whole Milky Way stretching out in front of him. Swerving again, he just narrowly missed another small asteroid that appeared as if from nowhere. Out of the corner of his eye he caught a flash of light and realized one of the marauders had not been so lucky.

One down, two to go. His heart jumped as his instruments then found two more marauders were closing in to join their comrades, with another six of them, five hundred kilometers away.

Bang! Again, flashes of sparks and smoke erupted from the instrument panel. The shields were holding, but only just.

Max had to think of a plan and fast. The Vanquish would not be able to take too much more of this punishment. He decided to head deeper into the asteroid belt while thinking of a solution to get him out of this mess.

After a while he decided that the best thing to do was to hide from the Pirates. What better place than on an asteroid? All he needed to do was find a suitable one and fast.

Eventually a big enough one appeared on his monitors about one hundred kilometers away. Firstly, however, he needed to get some distance between the Pirates and his ship to give himself the time needed to hide.

For the next hour he weaved in and out of the asteroids, all the time being pursued. Every now and then bursts of cannon fire straddled him, as he tried to throw off his pursuers. They kept up the chase, but his speed and agility were beginning to show. They were now about three hundred kilometers away. Feeling the time was right, he changed course and headed towards the asteroid that he had seen earlier. As he approached, he accelerated, descended, and skimmed the surface, scanning the asteroid's surface for somewhere to hide, and at the same time putting the asteroid between him and his pursuers, hoping their sensors would not see what he was up to. Shooting past and coming around its blind side, he put the Vanquish into a steep U-turn and headed for the surface. Slowing down, his lights skated across the surface with shadows dancing in their wake, looking for somewhere to hide

He checked his sensors: he could not detect the Pirates, which meant in turn they could not detect him.

.....

"MAX, MAX, MAX!" someone shouted. Opening his eyes, he saw his friend Ben standing over him. They had met on their first day at school and now, aged eleven, were as close as brothers. Although they could not have looked less like brothers, Max with brown hair and eyes, lanky and tall for his age, and Ben with a messy shock of blonde hair, grey eyes, chunky, fit and healthy looking.

"You must be deaf; the class bell went five minutes ago. Come on let's go, it's the end of term." With that Ben headed off towards the door with his school bag following on behind him.

Rubbing his eyes, and seeing stars, Max got up from his desk and, taking one last look around the classroom, he followed Ben out to the school corridor. As usual he had been dreaming about fighting the pirates. However, little did he know that his school holidays would be anything but normal, and that his dream would become a reality.

His school was in Citadel One, on Ganymede, one of Jupiter's moons. It was a vast city of three million people, who all lived and worked within its huge walls or commuted to the various mining camps. There were other smaller citadels on the planet which were mainly outposts. He caught up with Ben who was standing by a huge window looking out over the surface far below. However, all you could see was the planet Jupiter filling the horizon: it was so big that you could only just see the blackness of space beyond. The big swirling storm was visible on the planet which was moving quite fast even at this distance. All different shades of reds, browns, whites and oranges, the surface just kept changing. At least half a kilometer below, on the surface, you could make out the skyway trams moving through their translucent tubes, heading off to other citadels or to the Space Port across the frozen landscape.

All around them were hundreds of students heading back to the dormitories, chatting excitedly about their holidays, and getting ready for the evening meal.

"Are you looking forward to tomorrow?" Ben asked with a sideways glance, his scruffy blonde hair hiding half his face.

"Yep can't wait. I'm looking forward to speaking with Dad tonight to find out what we are doing," Max said turning to watch two boys playing chase down the corridor on hover boards. "" hope we will be going further than the solar system now they have bought a new space freighter."

Ben laughed and said it would be better than his trip as they always did the same thing every year, which was to go and see his aunt and uncle who lived on New York 2 which was in orbit around Earth. With that the two friends went back to their rooms to get ready.

Chapter Two

Journey to Jupiter 2

Max woke up early, excited about the day ahead. The conversation he had had with his Mum and Dad the night before was playing on a constant loop in his head and had been all night. They had already arrived at Jupiter 2, the orbital space station for the Jupiter system. The most surprising news was that the new ship they had bought was a brand-new Boeing star freighter. Although he knew they had bought a new ship, it was a surprise to him that it was one of these. These were massive delta-winged ships that were designed to carry huge amounts of cargo throughout the galaxy. Also they had taken on a new first officer by the name of Patriq, a big jolly chap from Mars. Even better he had a son who was his age, called Steve, who although disabled, got around on a hover chair, and he would also be on the ship for the holidays. All of a sudden the summer holidays were looking up.

The buzzer went on his door, breaking his thoughts. Who could that be so early in the morning? Opening the door, Ben stood there, his blonde hair all over the place, with a big grin spreading from ear to ear. Before Max could say anything he charged through and nearly tripped over his travel case, which fortunately got out of his way just in time.

"Guess where I'm going on holiday?" he yammered excitedly.

"Do you realize how early it is? I haven't even showered yet—" but before Max could finish his sentence Ben carried on,

"I'm going on a space cruise to the Rier's system. Dad told me last night, he wanted to keep it a secret till I got to Jupiter 2, but he couldn't wait to tell me, how cool is that?" He was so keen to tell Max that he was now out of breath with excitement.

"Well, that's brilliant, isn't that the one that Hope Wiseman is going on?"

"Yes, I can't wait to see the look on her face when I see her."

They both laughed, but secretly Max was a little jealous. With that Ben left and Max finished getting ready and grabbed his shower.

.....

Max left his room with his bag following behind. The corridors were a hive of excited activity, with people rushing around chatting loudly about their summer holidays. He arrived at the Grav lift and waited in the queue.

With Grav lifts you just selected your level, stepped into the shaft and the gravitational beam locked onto you and carried you to the level required. Stepping out he had arrived at the school canteen. At one end of the canteen was a huge floor-to-ceiling window looking out over the planet. Jupiter was not in view yet, but on the horizon you could see the lights of a mining station flickering away, and across the surface a web of tram tubes connecting the citadel to the rest of the planet. He looked around and saw Ben waving. Threading his way through the tables Max got to where he was waiting. Hope was also there with another friend called Sarana, with her very long red hair and green eyes.

"Morning everyone,'" he said taking a seat.

"How are you?" Hope asked whilst slurping on a fruit drink into which a lock of her long, blonde, curly hair fell, without her noticing.

"Great thanks, has everyone got their luggage all packed?"

"Ours is in the luggage area," Sarana said.

Just then an automated waiter came over and hovered over the table to take Max's order. He ordered a hot fruit tea. The waiter silently rose and flew away. Max asked Sarana if her parents had arrived at Jupiter 2.

"They arrived last night, hopefully we will be leaving for Titan this evening." You could hear in her voice that she wished she was going with any of them rather than spending time on Titan. Her green eyes, unusually, avoided his gaze.

Titan was a moon of Saturn and her parents were scientists working for one of the big corporations that made and repaired space ships. It was supposed to be beautiful if rather rugged, with vast oceans, and fantastic views of Saturn and its rings.

The waiter had arrived back with his drink, and while the others sat there chatting away about school, Max sat back and thought about his holidays. Now that his parents had bought a star freighter, it could mean only one thing, rather than moving cargo around the confines of the solar system as they had to do in their old ship, hopefully they would be travelling further, using the intergalactic pathway to travel to other systems and planets. The entrance to the pathway was positioned near Pluto, and guarded by Kyiv 2, a service space station. He had been to Pluto once when he was eight, to deliver supplies there. Although they were not allowed to land on the planet because it is a high security prison, he remembered looking out of the windows watching the robotic transit shuttles arrive, opening up their hatches and releasing their teams of android workers to empty his Dad's ship of its cargo.

"Max, time to drink up."

He looked around the table, he had been so lost in his thoughts that everyone had got up and was patiently waiting for him. Standing, he took one last gulp of his drink and followed them through the crowds and noise to the baggage area, their bags following on behind them, and headed towards the skyway station. It was hectic as all the students were heading in the same direction.

The skyway station was set in the heart of the citadel. From here they could catch the electromagnetic trams, which could either take them to other stations within the citadel, or travel further across the surface to mining outposts, or in their case to the shuttle station to catch the shuttle to Jupiter 2.

Eventually they arrived. From the walkway which took them there, they all stood in silence to soak in the atmosphere of the giant hall. Looking down from where they stood, they could see at least thirty platforms spread out below, with thousands of people milling around. The noise was intense. At each end of the platforms were tunnels from where the trams came or went on their journeys. Gliding above them and the platforms were three-dimensional holographic advertising cubes, promoting anything from clothes to new and used spaceships for sale. Other cubes fighting for space were ones with the station's timetables on.

"Blimey," Ben said excitedly, "there must be a million people down there."

"Stop exaggerating," Sarana said as she started off towards the escalators.

Looking up, Max looked for the timetable to see which platform they would be leaving from.

"Hurry up you two, we're leaving from platform 15," he said, rushing after Sarana, with Ben and Hope close on his heels.

Pushing their way through the crowds they made it to the platform. Looking up again, Max saw an advertising cube promoting Virgin Galactic's latest cruise ships going to the Rier's system.

"Hope, Ben, look up, they are advertising your cruise," Max said.

He smiled as he saw his friends with heads bent back looking up at the cube as it passed overhead.

Just then a tram silently arrived at the platform. As it came to a halt the sides of the tram's carriages slid up. When the arriving passengers had got off, the friends found some seats, while their bags stored themselves in the luggage compartments. Once seated, the doors slid closed and sealed themselves with a faint hiss. The blue comfort lighting lit up the carriage, and they could feel a slight change in pressure as the tram's atmosphere and gravity system came online. After a short while the tram vibrated, ever so slightly and started to move off and entered the tunnel

Max watched his friends who were looking out of the window. Each one of them had an air of excitement about them as they were lost in their thoughts about what lay ahead for them during the holidays.

"Max, how long until we leave the citadel?" Hope asked. She sat there with her head resting on the window looking out at the pitch black of the tunnel, her blue eyes looking dark in the reflection.

"Don't know, I think we have another station to go yet," he replied.

Just then they came out of the tunnel and came to a stop. This station was a lot smaller, on the other platform a tram was just leaving. The platforms were not too busy and only half a dozen people got into their carriage. The doors hissed shut, the carriage repressurized and the tram pulled away back into the tunnel again. After another ten minutes Max noticed a reddish glow ahead, which was slowly getting brighter.

"Hey, I think we are coming to the end of the tunnel and about to enter the tubes," he said excitedly.

"Brilliant!" Ben said, jumping up and down in his seat.

"Stop behaving like a big kid," Hope said, although she said it jokingly with a smile on her face, trying to look down the tunnel. An automated voice came through the speakers warning all people to remain in their seats as they were about to exit the citadel. With that the atmosphere in the carriage changed again, and the gravity field intensified. Without this everyone would have been hurled around

Suddenly they entered the translucent tubes. These were designed to protect the trams from the elements of the planet. The tram immediately took a sharp right and followed the outer wall of the citadel. Looking up and down, the wall stretched as high as they could see, looking out of the other window the surface of the planet stretched off into the distance. On the horizon was Jupiter, which filled the view. They felt as though they could just reach out and touch it. Rolling across the surface of Jupiter were some large storms. The tram went into a dive and was now heading towards the surface which was at least half a kilometer below them. Out of the window then they could see other tubes coming out of the citadel, and if they looked closely they could see trams in some of them. The tram was now near vertical, as it descended down the outside wall of the citadel towards the surface of Ganymede below them. The friends could see the surface below. All of a sudden the tram changed direction again and they were now travelling above the surface towards the shuttle station. Looking back, the citadel was shrinking into the distance. Max pointed out a mining station to the others, silhouetted against the backdrop of Jupiter in the distance. They were now travelling at such a speed that anything near them was just a blur.

"Look everyone!" Ben shouted excitedly, pointing out of the window.

All eyes followed where he was pointing. Coming into view was a shuttle: it was huge and they could see the small windows along its side with little faces looking back at them. It slowly passed by the tram and then disappeared from view with the bright red pulsar engines glowing behind as it headed towards the shuttle station to land. Eventually the tram turned again towards the station and started to slow down. Another ship was hovering over the station, its engines glowing bright red, then building up speed, it headed towards space and either Jupiter 2 or another moon. Eventually they entered a tunnel and came to a stop at the platform in the shuttle station.

"Here at last," Hope said as she got up.

The friends waited on the platform, and once their bags had caught up with them they joined the crowds of people and headed off towards the terminals.

"Which way?" Sarana asked

"Terminal 10 is where we fly from," Max said looking around, eventually spotting a sign for the terminal. "This way, follow me." With that he headed off towards the check in.

"It's a shame you're not coming with us on the cruise. It looks fun. Do you think there are any pirates out there Max?" Ben asked without pausing for breath as he caught up with him.

"I doubt it. Even if there were, they wouldn't try and attack a cruise ship. They are more likely to go after small freighters so they can sell on the cargo," Max said with a hint of envy in his voice, adding, "I wish I was going with you though. You never know, we might be headed that way ourselves," he added with a grin and a little nudge.

"That would be cool," said Ben.

They checked in and followed the crowd of fellow travelers through the security gate, and then went over to the windows to look at their shuttle. There were maintenance droids flying around it cleaning off the dirt and checking for any damage. It was painted red with a large Z in a darker red on its side, the emblem of the Zeuss Corporation. They got onto the shuttle without too much delay and took their seats. Max checked his wristband to see if his Dad had sent a message. He had not. He had butterflies in his stomach, not only in anticipation of the flight ahead, but also of seeing his parents for the first time in months. Due to the nature of their work, he boarded at school during term time. He was looking forward to seeing and exploring the new ship, plus he was looking forward to meeting Steve, which sounded like fun, he traveled around on a hover chair, and hopefully he would let him have a go on it.

An announcement was made thanking everyone for flying with the Zeuss Corporation and wished them a safe flight to Jupiter 2. There was an excited buzz around the cabin as everyone waited for lift off. Max was hoping that he would see his parent's new ship, which was in a stationary orbit around Jupiter 2. Looking at his friends, he noticed they were in deep conversation about their space cruise, while Sarana was telling them about Titan and the huge orbital factories that made the spaceships.

By now they could feel the vibration as the engines powered up. Everyone had gone quiet as the shuttle started to climb vertically away from the terminal. Looking out of the window he could see the space port shrink away as they gained height. Suddenly the shuttle picked up speed and headed towards open space. Everyone was now glued to the windows as Ganymede disappeared below them. They could see the curvature of the planet and Jupiter beyond. As quickly as it had begun, they were slowing down on their approach. He tried to see if he could see the ship, or the cruise ship but he could not spot either. This meant that they must be docking on the lower levels.

As they approached the docking arm, he could see all sorts of smaller craft flying around, from small one-man craft to small freighters. Jupiter 2 was a massive space station which had four hundred levels. It was also home to a Treaty Defense Force, which not only protected this area of space from pirates, but also different elements in the mining and cargo industries who were always feuding with each other. Once docked the friends made their way through the docking arm and into the main terminal for this level, all the time being pushed this way and that by eager people hoping to find those waiting for them.

"Look there's my Mum and Dad," Hope said as she ran towards them.

"Hello Mr. and Mrs. Wiseman, I'm Max, and this is Ben and Sarana."

"Nice to meet you. Hope has told us so much about you all. I believe one of you is going on the cruise?" Mr. Wiseman said.

"That's me," Ben said excitedly.

"Well I'm sure we'll see you on the ship," he replied, ruffling Ben's blonde mop of hair. Ben took a step back shaking his head. Everyone laughed as Ben hated anyone messing up his hair, although it always looked a mess any way.

"You two, stay in touch with us over the holidays. Ben and I will keep you informed of our adventures," Hope said, giving Max a wink and with that they disappeared into the crowd.

Just then Ben's and Sarana's respective parents came over. After saying their goodbyes, they too disappeared, and Max was left standing on his own as the arrivals area slowly thinned out.

Max felt a tap on his shoulder and looking around he saw his Dad standing there. He gave him a big hug, lifting him off the floor.

"Good to see you, son. Come on, let's go, I have a few things to do here before we get going." With that he put his arm around Max's shoulder, and they set off.

Chapter Three

Onwards to Mars

They made their way to the shopping levels. As they stepped out of the elevator they headed towards a café in the middle and found themselves a table. Looking around, the shops must have been doing a good trade as the level was packed with people. An automated waitress glided over and took their order for two fruit teas.

"Dad, when are we going to the ship? How big is my room? And are we going somewhere exciting this time?" Max asked excitedly, without even pausing for breath.

His Dad sat there and looked at him with a smile on his face. His dark-brown hair was cut shorter than usual, and the scar on his cheek was a little redder than normal. Although no one knew how he got it, Mum said it was probably in a fight with some trader on a distant planet. Although she said that the story changed somewhat when he got together with friends.

Just then their drinks arrived. Taking a sip, his Dad said, "Well, I'll answer some of your questions, before you badger me to death, but then I need to go to the administration level to sort out some registration matters."

As his Dad was talking away Max noticed two men take the table next to them. They were both big men and one of them had a hooded robe on that covered his face. The one without the hood had a grey face and looked at Max with cold deep-blue eyes that sent a shiver down to the base of his spine. He quickly looked away and back at his Dad.

"Have you been listening to me?" he asked.

"Er, yes. Where did you say we are going again?"

"Obviously not. We are going to Mars to pick up Steve. Then we are off to Phobos to pick up our cargo. But before you ask, as yet I don't know where we are delivering it," he said finishing his tea.

Max noticed the men trying to listen in on their conversation. He looked away quickly thinking they were just being nosey, but he did not like the look of them.

"What you mean is, you just won't tell me," Max replied with a hint of frustration in his voice.

Putting his hands up in mock surrender his Dad replied, "Honest, Captain, I don't know, but you will be the first to know when I do." He put on the silly accent he used when playing around. "Now I have to go, don't forget, be here in an hour."

"Ok see you then."

.....

As his Dad left he noticed the man in the hood lean over and say something to his friend, who nodded then got up and left, going in the same direction as his Dad. He wondered if he was following him. He looked over at the hooded man, but he was just looking down at his drink. He thought if he got up and left the hooded man might follow him as well. Getting up quickly he headed off through the crowds to the shops. He got to a shop called Riley's Galactic Clothing, and turning around, tried to see if the hooded man had followed him, but he was nowhere to be seen. Feeling a bit annoyed that he had not been of interest to the hooded man, he spent the next hour looking around the shops, soaking in the sights and sounds. There were many different races here, all dressed in different styles of clothes, and more than anything he noticed that there were so many different languages being spoken, most of which he didn't understand.

As he got back to the cafe he noticed that the hooded man was still sitting at the same table. It was hard to see what he was looking at as his face was covered. He took a seat at a table, a waitress came over but as he did not want anything she glided off to find someone else to serve. Overhead an advertising cube floated by, advertising businesses on Jupiter 2. Looking around he noticed the hooded man looking in his direction. As soon as Max caught his eye he looked away. Why was he looking at him, and why had his friend got up and followed Dad? Just then his friend came back to the table and they immediately started having a heated conversation. Feeling a tap on his shoulder, which made him jump, he looked up to see his Dad standing there.

"Bit jumpy, aren't we?"

"Sorry Dad, I was watching those men over there. When you left one of them followed you."

"I'm sure that they have better things to do than follow me around. Anyway let's get going; I want to get to Mars as quickly as we can."

.....

The shuttle deck spanned the whole diameter of the station. In the central column was the operational and command center, plus waiting lounges and cafes for those waiting to depart. It was not too busy. Looking down from one of the lounges Max could see about 300 shuttles of varying shapes, sizes and colors parked below. Looking out beyond that he could see Jupiter in the distance. The shuttle deck did not have doors, instead it had a force field that covered the whole circumference of the deck. This allowed craft to enter and exit, but also kept the atmosphere in.

There were a lot of people either walking to their craft or carrying out any maintenance the ships required. Also, there were quite a lot of service droids flying around, or doing maintenance on ships, or in the hanger. Added to this quite a few smaller craft were slowly moving around the hangar either departing or going to their parking bays.

He then noticed the hooded man and his friend heading towards a small, blue, two-seater vehicle. It looked sleek and very fast. It was only good for short journeys so they must have had a bigger ship parked nearby. They climbed aboard, and almost immediately their ship rose vertically and started following the green chevrons leading them to the exit. Once through the force field it sped off.

His Dad called and he ran over to the lift and they made their way down to the flight deck.

"What were you looking at so intently?"

"I was watching the hooded man and his friend leaving."

"Still playing the espionage game then?"

"I didn't like them, that's all. Where is our shuttle?" he asked.

"Soon enough, you will like it though, it's a new family class cruiser. Your mother and I chose it for when we are away in new systems so we can all take time out and explore new planets, including the crew."

The doors opened and they stepped out onto the flight deck to be greeted by two security robots who took them over to their consul to book their departure flight. After checking their details, one of them led Max and his Dad to his hover car. These robots were about seven foot tall and dark blue in color with a gold badge on their breast plate. They talked in a friendly manner but were able to change the pitch according to each situation.

The hover car glided silently around the hanger in between neat rows of shuttles parked either side of take-off strips which were illuminated with chevrons pointing in the direction of travel. When they got to where their shuttle was parked the chevrons were red. When they were cleared for departure, they turned green. The shuttle bay was huge and through the exit you could see open space. In the distance Max could see another one of Jupiter's moons moving slowly as the station revolved. People were walking along the walkways by the shuttles. Not just from the solar system, but also aliens from faraway places who had either just stopped off to rest or were doing business here.

Just then a small freighter came through the force field and glided over their heads before it found its berth and reversing in, came to halt.

"Here we are Max, what do you think?" his Dad said.

As they came to a halt next to their shuttle Max felt his heart pump with excitement. Jumping out of the car he stood there and looked up. It was the color of sand and nice and shiny. It had a rounded front end with big dark cockpit windows. Along the sides were several windows on two levels. It was long in shape with two pulsar engines at either side at the rear. At the back the ramp was lowered. Without even looking at his Dad, and with a big grin on his face he ran round the back and up the ramp. Stopping at the top he saw a corridor and on either side were two doors, probably to the bedrooms. At the end was a set of stairs, halfway up were the doors to the flight deck. On the top floor was a living room and galley with a door at the end to the engine room. Above, the roof had panoramic windows. Looking up he could see the roof of the flight deck some 150 meters away. Breathless, he made his way to the flight deck where his Dad was getting ready to depart.

"It's brilliant Dad."

"Ok, take a seat we are now cleared for takeoff," his Dad said as he started moving his hands rapidly over the control panel.

Max felt a slight vibration as the engines came online. Looking out he could see the chevrons glowing green. They moved off and followed the take-off lights. Accelerating slightly the ship passed through the force field and then came to a stop. Craning his neck, he looked out to see the vast structure of Jupiter 2 disappearing below them out of sight. In front of them in the distance was Ganymede, which in turn was silhouetted by the sheer size of Jupiter. A small freighter passed in front. Once it had gone past they built up speed, and banking to the left, sped off towards the freighter.

"There she is, doesn't she look beautiful?" Dad said with a hint of pride in his voice.

They were approaching the star freighter fast. Its massive delta wings looked as though they took up the whole of space. All the cargo was stored in these, while the central rib housed the bridge, engineering, and accommodation decks. They came in underneath it and then ascended up into the shuttle bay, once the shuttle bay doors closed, the shuttle came to rest.

As they came to a rest Max noticed his Mum standing there with a big grin on her rosy cheeks, and next to her stood another man who looked big, even from where he was. That must be the new first officer.

The rear ramps lowered, and he went charging out straight into his Mum's arms, who gave him such a big hug she nearly crushed him.

"Missed you, little one," she said holding him at arm's length, looking him over. "Although not so little anymore," she added.

"Missed you too," came his excited reply.

Looking around he noticed the first officer towering over him.

"You must be captain Patriq?" he asked.

"That I am," he replied, offering Max his hand. Max's hand just disappeared into his huge fist. He had a reddish face with a big mop of grey spikey hair. He took an immediate liking to him.

"Just call me Paddy, nice to meet you. I've told Steve all about you and he is looking forward to spending the summer here with us all."

"Paddy, are we ready to get going? I need to stop off at the Los Angeles' service station. Will this take us too far off our route?" Dad asked as they all made their way to the lifts to take them up to the bridge.

"No, not too much. The station should only be ten minutes from the space way route," Paddy replied. "I'll log our new route change with control before we leave."

The doors to the lift opened and they all got out onto the bridge. It was semi-circular in shape, with big control panels flashing away on the back walls. In the middle were stations for engineering and the pilot controls with the crew sitting there awaiting instruction. Other people were manning other stations getting ready for the journey ahead. In front of all this was a big window where in the distance Max could see Jupiter 2 lit up in all its glory. Behind it was Jupiter, its glow illuminating all around it.

"Look Max, there's the cruise ship your friends are on," his Mum said from behind him. Coming from behind the space station the Sagaris came into view. She was huge and as bright as the sun, all lit up as it made its way towards the space way control gate. She then sped up and disappeared from view.

'Right everyone, let's get going. Sandy, slow ahead and take us to the gate."

Sandy was the ship's helmsman and on Paddy's command started to move them towards the gate. To travel around the solar system there were a series of space ways along which all ships traveled. These were patrolled by the solar police to help protect travelers from attack by pirates. Spread along the routes were service stations named after great cities on Earth. Others travelling outside these routes were not protected, although many did so to try and speed up their journeys.

Looking through the forward view-screen, the ship had started to turn and Jupiter 2 had now slipped from view. They could see other smaller craft travelling around them, and crisscrossing in front of them. In front they could now make out the tower of the gate. Around the tower were a series of lights, which were glowing red. When they went green they would have permission to enter the space way. Over the audio system the controller wished them a safe journey, and with that the lights turned green. Picking up speed they quickly accelerated to cruising speed. Just in front was another smaller ship which they quickly overtook.

"Let's show you to your new cabin," Mum said and with that both of them headed off to the lifts.

.....

The accommodation deck was on level 12 and when they got there Max saw that his room had his name on it. Pressing the button on the control panel to unlock it, the doors slid open.

"I'll let you get sorted out. All your things are in there. If you need me I'm only next door."

"Thanks Mum. Will you let me know when we get to the station?"

"Sure, see you later." With that she gave him a kiss on the cheek and left. The doors slid shut behind her.

His cabin was big and split into two with the bedroom off to the right.

The lounge was big and had a big cream-colored sofa in the middle.

It also had a 3D holographic viewer and a food processor which would make drinks and food. The windows overlooked the cargo wings and beyond that the blackness of space, with stars strangely elongated because of their speed. He relaxed on his sofa and sent his friends a message telling them about his cabin and the ship.

He had been dozing, dreaming of the hooded man and his grey friend. He had been chasing them on a space scooter, firing at them with his laser pistol, when the communicator stirred him. It was his Dad saying that they were approaching the LA service station. He quickly got changed into a one-piece blue jumpsuit and got to the bridge just in time to see the service station in front of them. It had a tall central column, with big docking arms stretching out around the circumference. Some of the arms had ships of various sizes already attached. Their ship was automatically guided to an empty one by the station's control room. Creeping forward slowly the nose of the ship connected to the arm and came to a stop.

He could see signs on the sides of the station, advertising hotels and restaurants, and one caught Max's eye, The Anders Spaceship Company. It said that it was located on the lower shuttle deck.

"Paddy, I'll be gone for about an hour. If you let the control know we will be leaving in an hour and twenty that should speed things up for us. Max, do you want to come or stay?"

"Right behind you."

"Come on, let's go."

…..

They went through the security gates where the security robots checked their ID. The main area of the service station was in the middle where all the bars and shops were located. High above was a clear roof. It was totally black out there but every now and then Max could see a streak of light from other ships travelling along the space way.

"I've got to go to the command center, and before you ask you can't come, so I'll meet you back here. And don't get up to any mischief."

"Ok," he replied, relieved, because he wanted to go and explore The Anders Spaceship Company and play around with what they would have for sale.

As his Dad disappeared into the throng of people he found a layout of the station and locating Anders he set off in the direction of the lifts and went down to the shuttle deck. Exiting, he stood there looking around him. The place was bright and seemed almost deserted. He saw to the left of him what could only be Anders. To the right it was empty, other than in the far corner was what looked like a mountain of junk. He looked up and saw a sign over to his left and made his way over. Sure enough there were about fifty craft for sale. They were mainly the family type which could be used for travel within the solar system. They were all different shapes and sizes, with most of them looking as though they had flown their last mission many moons ago.

A large alien from the Tagon system suddenly appeared from behind a shuttle, making him jump, and came striding over. Tagons were generally very large and had a greyish skin color, and bright orange eyes. They also had a reputation for being shrewd businesspeople who were to be found throughout the galaxy. Although their system was a member of the Treaty, there were rumors that they would deal with anyone if it meant making a profit. They were a peaceful race who did not like conflict, but always seemed to create trouble because of the way they would sometimes conduct business.

"Hello there, little one, how can I be of service to you?" rasped the Tagon in his deep voice.

Max took a step back. "I'm just having a look round to see what you have," he said puffing his chest out, trying to look confident.

"Well, you are a bit young to be buying one of these but have a look round and be careful." With that he turned and set off back to the office. Just then another Tagon appeared.

"Everything ok?" he boomed.

"Just a kid having a look 'round," said the first Tagon.

"Well hurry up because they want to get going." With that they both disappeared back into the office.

Max heard voices coming from in there, but could not hear what they were saying. Deciding to sneak over and listen, he crept up as close as he dared to the office door. His heart was pumping with excitement. Just as he got near the door he heard footsteps coming from within. Quickly looking around, he saw a small one-man space hopper and ran over and hid behind it. Just then the door opened and the hooded man stepped out, closely followed by his friend who was with him on Jupiter 2. He held his breath, and shrank further down behind the scooter, frightened to breathe in case they heard him. They both got into a lift, the two Tagons watching them silently before going back into office where it sounded as though they started having an argument.

"What are they doing here?" Max thought. It seemed they must be up to no good. Although shaking slightly he felt excitement welling up inside him. He had to find out what they were up to so, with his heart racing he ran over to the lift. The doors slid open and he asked for the main deck. As the lift stopped he ran out and stood there looking for them, however the place was busy with people rushing around and there was no sign of them. He wondered where they could have gone. Just then he saw them on the upper ring heading towards the docking area, and they disappeared down a corridor to what could only be their docking station. Running as fast as he could, pushing people out of his way, and getting a few comments thrown at him, he eventually got to where he had last seen them. But the corridor was empty. They must have got onto their ship.

Oh no, he thought, puffing slightly after his charge across the station. All he could think was that they must be up to no good. But what were they up to? His communicator bleeped; it was his Dad telling him to meet him at the docking station.

"There you are, you look out of breath, where have you been?" his Dad asked as they made their way back to the ship.

"I went down to see Anders Spaceships but when I got there they were having a meeting with the hooded man."

"Who's the hooded man when he is at home?" came the reply as they entered the entrance to the ship.

"You remember that creepy looking man we saw on Jupiter 2?"

"Oh him, he must think you are following him," his Dad said with a laugh as they entered the bridge.

.....

Through the view-screen Max could see the station slowly moving into the distance as the ship reversed away from its docking arm. As it disappeared from view they built up speed and were back on the space highway.

"We will be passing Earth in thirty minutes," Pat said as he concentrated on the controls.

Max's Mum had also joined them on the bridge and sat next to him as they watched their journey through the view-screen. Every now and then they could see streaks of light coming towards them from ships travelling in the opposite direction, and other ships as they overtook them. Eventually Earth started to come into view, slowly growing bigger. At first they could see the lights of cities as flew round the dark side, then as they moved round the blue of the oceans, white cloud fronts and the landmasses were becoming clearer. Then the Earth's moon appeared, crescent-shaped, high above Earth. They could now clearly make out the continents, as due to their speed everything started to get big very quickly. The great orbital cities, New York, London, Bombay, to name but a few, were also now becoming visible. The moon was still too far away to see any of its cities. There was a hush on the bridge as everyone soaked up the view.

Also far below them they could see hundreds of space craft slowing down and coming to a virtual stop as they left the space highway and started to join the thousands of other craft heading towards earth and the cities.

Just as quickly as Earth had come into view it disappeared, as they now made their way towards Mars. At their present speed they should get there in five hours, so Max went back to his room to tell his friends of his adventure.

…..

He was woken up as he felt the ship slowing down. Getting up he could see Mars filling his window as they came into orbit. The red planet looked exciting; he could make out the light from some cities as they started circling the planet. He was looking forward to seeing Steve, and hopefully getting a chance to have a go on his hover chair. It would be nice to have someone his own age to mess about with. Getting dressed, he left his room and made his way down to the shuttle bay, where his Mum and Dad were waiting for Paddy to return with Steve.

"I guess you are looking forward to meeting Steve, he has bags of energy, you should both get on well together," his Mum said. Looking at his Mum, Max could see that she was happy that he would have a new friend to play with. "I can't wait. Do you think he will let me have a go on his chair?"

"I am sure he will," she replied with a smile.

Just then the warning alarm sounded, the shuttle bay doors slid open and the shuttle slowly entered. Silently it came to a rest and the shuttle bay doors slid shut. The rear ramp opened and Steve shot out on his hover chair and stopped in front of Max who had taken a step or two back in shock.

"You must be Max?" he said, hovering in front him.

He was bigger than Max, with dark-brown skin, common for Martians, with a mop of jet-black hair that was all over the place, but short at the sides. Without waiting for a reply, he turned to Max's parents and said hello.

"Good to see you again, how was your journey?" Dad said.

"Cool, I like the new shuttle," came the reply.

Max coughed, and as he got everyone's attention said, "Yes, I am Max, nice to meet you."

Just then Paddy who had been shutting down the shuttle joined them.

"Mum, can I show Steve to his room?"

"Of course, you can, but please don't get up to too much mischief."

"'Come on, Max, jump on," Steve said excitedly.

Not wanting to be asked twice Max jumped on the back of the chair. With that Steve sped up, the doors opened and they both charged off through the ship and explored.

Later Max was lying in bed thinking that he had not had so much fun in ages. Steve was great and he could not wait for the next day.

They had picked up their cargo from Phobos. After passing through the gateway they were now headed for a planet called Thuell, which according to Dad was a Treaty base. Leaning over he set the lights in his room to dim and went to sleep looking forward to spending the next day with Steve.

Chapter Four

Captain Black

Captain Black stood looking out of the window of his office. In front of him he could see asteroids moving past, occasionally bumping into each other. In the distance he could see the sun which cast a faint glow over the asteroid belt.

He had had this base on an asteroid for as long as he could remember, and although the Treaty ships came looking for him, and many times they had come close, they had still not found him.

He felt nervous about the visit of Nino Bassi. The Carpathians were a ruthless race of people who had been waging a war with the Treaty way before the solar system had been discovered. It was ironic perhaps, in one way that the solar system owed its survival to the Carpathians, for had it not been for the fact that they had built a Galactic Gateway to attack the solar system, the Treaty would have left them alone to develop further, until it was felt that they were advanced enough to join it. The Treaty helped defeat the Carpathian's attack on the solar system. They then retreated back to their system and continued in their efforts to undermine the Treaty.

The gateway was now used for ships to travel throughout the galaxy, to other systems and build trade routes. In turn this meant that Captain Black and his band of pirates had even more rich pickings to steal, then trade to the highest bidder.

Captain Black had first come across the Carpathians three years ago. He had been captured on the planet Nahi by Treaty Police Troopers. The planet was a renowned trading outpost, where black market goods were traded to the highest bidders. The planet was one of thirty in the Tagon system. The Tagons were famous for being astute business men who liked a good deal and a good profit. They were also known to keep their mouths shut, which benefited many a trader. He had landed at the planet's main city of Lon, to try and sell some engine parts that he and his men had stolen from a cargo freighter a month before. Lon was a bustling city with every kind of villain known from all over the galaxy. Everyone who went there only had one purpose: to buy and sell as quickly as possible then leave. However, unbeknownst to Captain Black, the engine parts were for military ground attack tanks and hidden in the cargo was a galactic tracking beacon.

As he was sitting back in a bar drinking with a Marryat trader, about twenty heavily armed police, in full battle armor, had burst in. The bar had gone deathly quiet, except for the scraping of chairs and tables as everyone had reached for their guns. It soon became apparent that they were there for him, so everyone relaxed and carried on doing what they had been doing before.

Tagging him, they had taken him back to their ship and thrown him into a cell. He was not alone, sitting in a corner was a Carpathian. He was not too happy at being caught, and least of all he did not like one little bit the idea of spending his time with a criminal called Tee Baa, who was not only wanted by the Treaty, but also by his own people.

The police ship had lifted off and set a course for the nearest military base.

Black had looked at his surroundings, the cell was small and had two benches which doubled up as beds. Tee Baa just sat there looking at him. Being tired and resigning himself to his fate, he had decided the best thing to do was wait. He knew his crew would know that he had been arrested, so hopefully they might be planning his escape. With this in mind he had stretched out and grabbed some sleep.

He was awoken after he did not know how long. The ship had come under fire, the lights were flickering and smoke had filled his cell, and Tee Baa was pacing up and down with a worried look on his face. Black was hoping his crew was coming to set him free. The doors to the cell block had opened and some Cyclops troopers had entered, Carpathians. Things had now gone from bad to worse. They had rushed into the cell and grabbed hold of Tee Baa. They had taken the Carpathian away. Then, returning with blasters leveled at Captain Black, they were about to kill him. Thinking fast he pleaded with them that he was an enemy of the Treaty and that he could help them. After talking on their communicators, they had then grabbed him and had taken him to their ship.

On the Carpathian ship he came to meet a man who made his blood run cold. His name was Nino Bassi a Carpathian spy. Carpathians were smaller than humans but were very strong and had black scaly skin, with yellow eyes. They also had an army of soldiers called the Cyclops who were bred for fighting and were feared throughout their part of the galaxy. He had never seen one as black as Nino Bassi. He was also taller than most and frighteningly, you could feel the power radiating from him. Nino had looked at him and told him that for saving his life that day he would one day be called upon to help him or suffer the consequences. Three years later that time had come.

As he stood there looking out at the asteroid belt he caught site of Nino Bassis' ship making its final approach to his base. Escorting it were two single seat attack ships no doubt piloted by the dreaded Cyclops troopers. Ten minutes later his first officer Rolfe entered his office, closely followed by Nino. Nino had a big smile on his face. Black turned around; a hand extended said. "Hello, my friend, I trust you had a good trip."

"I don't like pleasantries Black, you humans try to be so nice, when all the time you are devious. But as you mention it, my trip was fine. Now, down to business," came the cold reply. With a final stare from those cold yellow eyes Nino took a seat.

Rolfe took his leave and left the two of them alone, although he knew that just outside were two Cyclops troopers, who were Nino's bodyguards. He was also happy that Rolfe, with his deep-blue eyes would be watching them like a hawk.

"It's been a long time Nino. I had almost forgotten you. How can I help you at such short notice?" Black asked suspiciously.

He had literally heard from the Carpathian that morning saying that he wanted to meet him. He had suggested a meeting place but was not prepared when the Carpathian said that he would come to his base in the asteroid belt. When he told him that he did not have a base there, Nino replied that he knew everything about him, including where his base was. He was shocked and confided in Rolfe, who suggested they might have a spy in their crew. They had discussed it but they could not think who it could be.

"I have a mission for you. As I said three years ago when I need you I will call." He sat there looking right through him with those yellow eyes. Although his office was not hot, Black started to sweat, but remaining controlled, he sat there and stared back.

'My spies have informed me that the Treaty are preparing to move a secret cargo from Phobos and are taking it to the Planet Thuell." Getting up he continued. "This cargo is not to reach Thuell, because you and your crew of villains are going to steal it for me."

After a minute's silence, Black got up and walked around his office. Eventually he arrived back at his desk, which was a replica of one of the old president's desks in the oval office from centuries ago. Leaning on it with his knuckles whitening he looked Nino directly in the eyes. "And how do I manage that? I have never attacked a military ship. We wouldn't even get close before they blew us to bits." He had anger in his voice. Continuing, he said, "I owe you one for saving my life, but this is suicide."

"Firstly, it is not suicide, the military want this cargo moved silently, so they have hired a cargo ship to deliver it. We don't know the name of it, but it is a star freighter. We also know that it will be at Jupiter 2 tomorrow as the captain has to pick up an infant who lives on Ganymede. These ships are lightly armed but have heavy shielding, it will be no match for your marauders. And secondly, if you do not do as we want your existence here will come to an end." He had menace in his voice.

While he had been talking Nino had been walking up to his desk and was now leaning an inch from Captain Black's face. He had said this last part with such venom, that Black felt a burning desire to kill the Carpathian there and then. He knew he could not, but he secretly vowed that one day he would.

"What is this cargo you speak about?" he asked dryly.

"That is not for you to know. All you have to do is get it and deliver it to me," came the cold reply.

"And where would that be?"

42

"I will contact you to tell you where. To make sure that you do as I ask, and don't double cross me, I am leaving you with a squadron of Cyclops troopers, they will help you on your mission. When you have got the cargo they will then tell you where to deliver it."

For the first time he thought he saw the Carpathian smile. "And where are these Cyclops?"

With that he pointed out of the window. Just coming into view was a Carpathian cruiser. "How the hell has that bypassed our defenses?" he thought angrily. Five minutes later Rolfe entered the office followed by a Cyclops trooper dressed in his red and black battle suit. He stood at least eight foot tall with his long green eye wrapped around his forehead. He stood there and greeted Nino in a metallic sounding voice.

"This is leader Mu, he will be assisting you on this, mission. He has been told to take orders from you. But if he thinks you are going to betray me, he has orders to kill. Do I make myself clear?" This was said very calmly and with a noticeable grin on his face.

"Perfectly."

"Excellent. I'll be off, good luck till me meet again."

With that Nino turned and left with his guard following him, leaving Rolfe, Mu, and him alone in the office.

. . . . .

Captain Black ordered Mu to leave. When he had gone he asked Rolfe if he had heard everything. He replied, "It doesn't leave us much time to plan this. I don't like having them around either, they give me and the men the creeps."

Rolfe had been with him for ten years now. He was a tall man with grey skin, a large nose and his eyes were a deep, dark blue. He was also totally trustworthy and loyal.

"Me too, what do you suggest we do?" Black said with a frown on his chiseled face.

"I've already got the men ready. I think we need to get to Jupiter 2 as quickly as we can to see who this captain is, check out his ship and see what we are up against."

"My thoughts exactly, well done. We leave in one hour," said Black.

As Rolfe left the office, he turned round just in time to see Nino's ship leave. He had a bad feeling about this mission. The Carpathian was a dangerous man, and he would have only hunted him down to do this mission for one reason and one reason only: it was extremely dangerous. He had to be very careful and perhaps plot an escape or alternative plan if it all went wrong.

Chapter Five

Hijack

Max woke up with a start, his heart was racing. He had a feeling in the pit of his stomach that he always got when something frightened him. He could not put a finger on it, but he thought he felt the ship shake. Sitting up in bed, the lights came on, casting a warm yellow glow around his room. Looking around, he heard everything was quiet. He could just make out the hum of the engines, but apart from that, nothing. Looking out of the window, he could see stars moving past slowly and in the distance he could see the pinkish glow of a nebula nearby. Perhaps it was just a dream, although he could not think of anything that he had been dreaming about.

Getting out of bed he looked around again, his heart now beginning to calm down. Everything was as he had left it before he went to bed, clothes on a chair, the holographic consul was off so it could not have been that. Nothing had moved. "Strange," he thought aloud. So, he got back into bed. The lights switched themselves off and his room was now cast in a reddish glow from the nebula. Looking at the stars he slowly went back to sleep. Then the ship shuddered again, more violently this time, throwing him from his bed. Getting up from the floor, he felt panic flowing through him, his heart was now trying to jump out of his chest. Putting on his clothes he ran over to the intercom and called his Dad. "What happened?" he yelled.

"Not now, Max, stay in your room and don't move from there!" came the reply.

He could hear panic in his Dad's voice, there was also a lot of shouting going on around him before he cut off the link. This sent a cold chill down Max's spine. He had never known his Dad to panic before. This sent his mind racing, thinking of many things that could have happened. Had the engines blown up? Had they hit an asteroid? What should he do?

"Calm down and think rationally," he said to himself. He finished getting dressed and strapped on his controller. Just then he caught a movement out of the corner of his eye. Looking round he saw a small craft fly past the window with blue flashes coming from it, followed immediately by the distortion of the ship's shields. Again, the ship shook. Running over to the window he saw another four ships firing at them. They were under attack but from whom? Max immediately thought of pirates.

What should he do, stay put in his room or try to find his parents on the bridge? He did not want to stay in his room in case they boarded the ship. He would be vulnerable separated from his parents. The pirates were obviously after the cargo. Just then the ship shuddered violently again.

Making up his mind, he left his cabin.

Standing there in the corridor, he looked each way but could not see anyone. The place was deserted. Turning to his left he went to his parents' cabin and banged on the door. There was no response and he could not open it. He ran towards the lifts, on either side of him all the doors to the other cabins were firmly shut. If anybody was in them they had decided to stay put. As he was running he tried to contact Steve on his communicator but had no luck. Hopefully, he was thinking the same thing and was heading for the bridge.

Panting slightly, he pressed the button to request the lift. Looking around he could now hear the alarms and looking back down the corridor the emergency lighting had come on, lighting up the walls and floor to guide people to the lifts and stairwells. Hearing the hum of the lift he realized it had come to a stop and the doors opened. Looking around he stood there frozen with fear. Standing there in the lift was a Pirate. He had never seen anything like it. It had red and black body armor on and stood so tall Max had to lean back to look at it. Looking into its one green eye he also noticed that it had a blaster in each hand.

Still frozen with fear, and with sweat running down his back, his first thought was the stairwell next to the lift. As the pirate came for him, he dived to the right, just missing the swipe of the blaster that nearly hit his head. The doors opened and he shot into the stairwell. Not having time to think, he went down the stairs as quickly as he could. Behind him he heard the pirate ordering him to stop. Going as fast as he could and gulping in air, he carried on. His feet felt as though they were made of lead. He could hear the pirate giving chase clanging down the stairs behind him. He passed level 10, then 9, then 8. He was going in the wrong direction but had no choice. As he got to level 8 the doors opened and he dived in. Leaning against the wall trying to catch his breath, he was shaking violently, although this was more from the effort of running than from fear of his pursuer.

Looking around he saw that he was in a cargo bay. The area was vast and to his surprise seemed empty. On closer inspection he saw something, but in the light could not make it out. Just then he heard his pursuer on the other side of the door heading down the stairs. He could hear him talking but it was fading as he carried on down. Max decided to take a look and as he headed further into the cargo bay lights came on and went off as though they were following him. He started to feel excited, and turned to the matter in hand as he went further into the hold, even forgetting about pirates and that the ship was under attack. It was strange that such a huge cargo bay held something so small. As he walked up to it, it was no more than three meters square. It was just a metal box. Walking around it he looked for markings, anything, but there were none, nothing, no catches, locks, or seams. He could not even see how to open it. Feeling it, it felt ice cold and he recoiled. Remembering that they stopped off at the Treaty station on Phobos, he knew it must have something to do with them. He recalled watching a cargo being loaded onto the ship. This must be what the pirates were after. It must be some sort of weapon he thought.

Just then his controller buzzed, looking down he saw that Steve was trying to get hold of him.

"I tried to get hold of you, are you on the bridge?" Max whispered.

"No, I tried to get there, but I ran into pirates. I escaped but they are all over the ship looking for something," came Steve's calm if excited reply.

"I'm on level 8 in the cargo hold. There is something strange here, which I think they are after, but I don't know what it is. I was chased but managed to shake him off," Max replied.

"Wait there, I'll join you. We have to get off the ship and the shuttle is our only hope." Before Max could reply Steve cut him off.

He sat down and waited for Steve. His thoughts soon turned back to the situation he was in. Waiting for Steve seemed the logical thing to do as he knew the ship better than Max did. He did not like the idea of abandoning ship though, as he wanted to be with his parents.

Max tried to get his Dad on his controller to discuss this, but all he got was static. Perhaps this was a good thing as he did tell him to stay in his room. Not knowing what was happening with his parents and the crew worried him. Perhaps when Steve arrived they could come up with a better plan, although he had no idea what. Max decided that while waiting he should go and explore. So, he headed off further into the cargo hold to see what else was there. Suddenly he heard the hum of an elevator. Looking around the doors opened and four pirates stepped out wearing armor and atmosphere helmets and looking different to the one who chased him. Their black armor glowed menacingly in the light. They spotted the cargo and went and took a closer look. He hid behind a pillar, hoping they would not see him and watched. They walked forward cautiously, not really paying attention to their surroundings. One of them touched it and quickly drew back his hand, putting his glove back on.

"Is that what we are looking for?" one of them asked.

"Yep, it's cold and fits the description. You had better tell the Captain we have found it."

"Captain, this is unit five, we have found the cargo. It's on level 8, what do you want us to do?"

Immediately a voice came out of his controller, shouting. "What do you think I want you to do? Stay with it and I'll send some more teams to help you move it back to the Cutlass. How heavy is it?"

They looked at each other. "Don't know," came their reply.

"Well, find out and let me know, you idiots! Hurry, we don't have much time!"

With that they all tried moving it, but it would not budge. The lift doors opened and another half a dozen pirates turned up. But between them they just could not move it, not even an inch.

"Captain, we have tried to move it, but it won't budge. What shall we do?"

"Are you sure?" replied the frustrated Captain.

"There are ten of us. It won't move," came the reply.

"We have no choice. We'll take the ship with us, leave a guard and…"

Just then Max's controller went off. It was Steve. They all stopped and turned in his direction. He frantically tried to turn it off, but his hands were shaking, Steve's voice boomed out.

"Max I'll be with you in two minutes."

"Steve hurry! I'm in trouble here. There are pirates here. If they didn't know I was here before, they certainly do now."

Two of them were heading in his direction, weapons ready, then the Captain's voice filled the cargo bay.

"What was that noise?"

"There's someone hiding in the cargo bay, we'll get them."

"They might have heard our plans. Don't let them escape. Let me know when you have got them and bring them up to the bridge."

"Yes Captain."

Max stood there, his mind racing. They were now heading in his direction. Walking backwards he tried to keep the pillar between them. Where the devil was Steve? One of the pirates spotted him. He fired off a shot and a beam of blue light went over his head and hit the far wall in a shower of sparks.

"Stop where you are!" one of them shouted.

Hitting his controller Max shouted. "Steve, I really need you here, where are you?"

"Nearly there"

Max stood there facing them. He raised his arms having no choice, it was that or immediate death. By now the pirates were ten meters away, the others had turned back to the cargo. It was then that a noise began filling the cargo bay. Everyone stopped what they were doing and looked at what appeared to be a light coming from the floor. The loading doors were opening up connecting the cargo bay with the one below. Steve suddenly appeared in his hover chair. This caught them all by surprise. One of them fired at him but he was too fast, he flew at the pirates nearest to Max hitting one of them and sending another diving to the floor.

"Jump on!" he shouted. Max did not need to be told twice.

The pirates started shooting at them and shouting at them to stop. There were flashes of blue light everywhere with sparks flashing around them as Steve swerved left and right dodging their fire. He got to the cargo bay doors and they disappeared through them into the lower bay. This bay was full of cargo from floor to ceiling. Steve was making his way down an aisle looking for a hiding place. Max spotted one about twenty feet up from the deck and Steve reversed his chair into the tight space with Max leaning over his shoulder. The two friends looked at each other and laughed.

"Whichever way you look at it, it was fun," Steve whispered.

"That was close. For a moment I didn't think you were coming."

"I had to escape from them myself. They are all over the ship. As far as I could see they took everyone to the bridge. Now that they have found what they want they'll probably be leaving soon. I doubt that they will look for us now, so we can sit it out here."

Trying to get himself a little more comfortable, Max replied, "I heard them talking to someone called the captain. I think it could be the notorious Captain Black. Anyway, they couldn't move the cargo, so he told them he was going to take the ship with them. But he didn't say where. You mentioned the shuttle. If we could find that we could escape and alert someone."

Steve sat there thinking for a bit, then replied with a grim smile on his face. "I know how to get to the shuttle. My Dad told me that it had an emergency program that once activated would make it take us to the nearest Treaty base…" he paused. "What a summer holiday this is turning into! My friends will never believe this."

"Mine neither. Let's go, and thanks, I owe you one," Max replied patting him on the back.

After a couple of narrow escapes and confrontations with the pirates the two friends finally reached the shuttle bay. It was exactly as they had left it when Steve had arrived two days ago. The rear doors to the shuttle were open.

"Can't see anyone, let's go," Max said.

With that Steve moved forward steering his chair into the shuttle. Max jumped off and went and sat in the pilot's chair. There were monitors and touch screens everywhere, illuminated in reds, greens, and yellows. "Now how on earth does all this work?" he thought.

"Well, let's get going," Steve said hovering close by to him.

"Great idea, but what do I press, any ideas?" Max replied with his eyes scanning the consul.

"I know how to close the rear doors. There, press that one," Steve said, pointing.

"Well that's a start." Max pressed the button, and with a hiss they closed. He also noticed one marked 'Shuttle Shields', so he pressed that too. As they were both so focused on the control panel they had not noticed the pirates entering the shuttle bay, until they stared firing. However, the shields just rippled and the shots deflected themselves sending them diving for cover as they ricocheted around the hanger.

"You said something about an emergency switch we need to find. Also how do we open the hanger doors?" Max asked with not a little tension in his voice.

"Look!" said Steve pointing to a covered button above his head. Pressing the button, they looked at each other as nothing happened. The pirates were now back on their feet just looking at them. Suddenly they just disappeared from view and looking up they saw the under belly of the ship receding above them. They were held in their seats through the sheer speed as the shuttle escaped the ship. As quickly as they started falling they now came to an abrupt stop. The shuttle's gravity system had now powered up so they did not end up floating around the bridge. Max looked up and thought his parent's ship was at least four kilometers away.

Steve was just about to say something but his mouth was just hanging open with a strange noise coming from him.

"Are you ok?"

He pointed out of the front screen. Looking out, Max was greeted with the view of two marauders that had taken up position in front of them. They were silhouetted by the pink cloud of the nebula.

Just as the marauders opened fire, the shuttle's pulsar engines opened up and they sped past them. Accelerating rapidly, they headed towards the nebula.

Max gave a huge sigh of relief, and looking at Steve said, "Where to now?"

"Who knows, I guess we sit back and enjoy the ride," smiled Steve.

Chapter Six

The Crash Landing

The happiness the two friends felt at escaping from the pirates was short-lived. The two marauders had given chase. They were about ten thousand kilometers behind but were starting to close the distance between them and their slower ship. The only chance they had was to hide out in the nebula which was still at least a million kilometers away. Once in the nebula their instruments would become useless but so would the marauders', giving Max and Steve the advantage of remaining undetected.

All they could see in front of them was the pinkish color of the nebula as they sped towards it at maximum speed. "How long do you think we have before they catch us?" Max asked.

"Don't know, but I think more importantly we need to worry about when they will be in weapon's range, because when they are we are in deep trouble." Steve sounded calm, but Max could detect a slight tremor in his voice. Looking at the display, traveling at their current speed they should reach the nebula in about two hours' time.

"How long do you think we have?" Max said.

"I reckon about an hour or two. Looking at the computer it is going to be close. However I don't know the range of their weapons," Steve replied. He was just behind Max at the computer consul working rapidly on the screens, making his calculations. He was also asking the computer to research any data on the marauders to see if any information was stored regarding their firepower and performance.

Max turned his attention to the problem of navigation and speed. They were both learning fast, their lives depended on it. The engines were running at maximum. Once in the nebula they both thought the pirates would give up the chase and return to their fleet.

Suddenly a warning alarm sounded. "What on earth was that?" Max thought. His heart was racing as he looked around to find out what it was.

"A missile has been launched from one of the marauders," Steve said, without looking up from his panels. "We have two minutes before impact. The rear shields are at maximum." He then switched off the alarm.

"What can we do?" Max asked.

"The missile is locked onto our engines. You need to try and evade it."

Max swung round and took control of the ship. He put the rear viewer on maximum magnification on a heads-up display. He could clearly make out the missile chasing them. Steve informed him that a second missile was now launched. He armed the forward lasers and a targeting grid appeared in front of him on the window. He could see the first missile closing fast, and the second one had now come into view. Max started to swerve and try to throw off the missiles, but they just kept following, tracking the ship.

"Can you man the lasers and try and blow them up? I can't do both."

"Leave it to me, you just fly the thing." Max heard stress in Steve's voice as he maneuvered his chair next to him.

Max saw the first missile which was right on their tail. At the last possible moment, he swung the shuttle into a steep right turn, the missile shot past them and it came into view through the front window. Just then Steve opened up with the lasers. There were streaks of red light shooting off all over the place except towards the missile.

"I think I'm getting the hang of this," Steve said with excitement in his voice.

"Good, just don't take all day. That one has started to turn round and the other one is closing fast!" Max said as he pulled back on the controls and sent the shuttle climbing vertically.

Steve was now firing with more confidence and as fast as he could, while Max carried on weaving around trying to disorientate the missiles. The view out was now totally pink as they neared the nebula.

Just then a big explosion appeared in front of them. The ship got thrown around as the shock wave hit them. By luck Steve had hit the first missile. One down, one to go but where was the second one now?

"Can you see it?" Max asked anxiously.

"No, I can't, but the marauders are about two hundred kilometers away. While we have been evading the missiles they have nearly caught up."

Suddenly a massive explosion happened underneath them. Max flew out of his seat, and Steve crashed into the side of the bridge. Smoke started to fill the bridge. Shakily, Max got to his feet and went back to the consul.

"No wonder we couldn't see it, it came up underneath us," he said with a slight quiver. He felt calm then, and more determined. He had cut his cheek just below the right eye and it was now running with blood. Steve threw him a first aid kit he had found. "That should have some synth skin in it, use it on the cut."

"Thanks."

Coughing with the smoke and his eyes watering, he tried to get the shuttle under control. The display panels were now flashing on and off.

"How far away are they?"

"I have no idea. The computer and the systems aren't working properly. That missile has done a lot of damage to the ship's power systems," Steve replied.

"I can just about use the steering controls, but I think we are losing engine power. I have no navigation, although that won't make any difference once we hit the nebula."

Just then the ship shook violently as it took a hit from a laser cannon, making Steve wobble in his chair.

"Look!" Steve shouted with alarm, pointing out of the left-hand viewing window. Pulling alongside of them was a marauder.

"There's nothing we can do. The power is draining fast, we are now losing life support. Once in the nebula we have had it. Perhaps we should surrender and take our chances with them."

"There is one thing that I'm not doing and that is surrendering to them." Steve retorted. Max raised his eyebrows and nodded in response.

.....

The pinkish mist of the nebula was getting thicker and the marauder was all but disappearing in the cloud. The control panel and cabin lights took one last flicker before they went out, leaving the bridge bathed in a pinkish light. The engines were still running but were slowing down all the time.

"Well, I think our decision has been made. As the old saying goes we are up the creek without a paddle," Max said. He even managed to give a nervous laugh.

After a moment Steve said defiantly, "Well, I don't know about creeks and paddles, but I think we are in deep trouble stuck here. But at least we didn't surrender."

"True. It was certainly not what I had planned this holiday. We need to try and fix the ship and get out an SOS, and we need a plan," Max replied.

"We need to think of something fast."

Max and Steve sat there staring out at the thick pink soup for what seemed like an eternity, talking about fighting the pirates. Steve had gone to the galley to get something to eat and drink, when Max noticed that they were picking up speed. With no instruments working there was no way of telling what was causing this. Just then Steve appeared with something to eat and a fruit drink he had found out the back.

"Are we speeding up?" he enquired.

"I think so. But I don't know what's causing it. The engines are just about running, but not enough to do this."

"Suppose we'll have to sit back and wait."

With that they sat there silently eating their food deep in their own thoughts and waiting to see what would happen next. Suddenly Max sat up alert.

"Steve, something's happening."

Steve noticed the alarm in Max's voice. He moved his hover chair next to him and looked out.

"I am sure the ship is building up even more speed. I saw something out there. I thought it was a planet. But you don't get planets in nebulas."

They were both straining to see through the cloud, which bizarrely was beginning to thin. All of a sudden a pinkish ball with black swirling clouds appeared in front of them.

"That's why we've been speeding up. We've been caught up in the planet's gravitational pull," Max said as he tried to get some response from the steering, but he had no success. "There is no way we can escape this. All we can do is hope and pray."

"The planet does not look too big," Steve said, more for something to say than anything else.

"No but I have never heard of a planet in a nebula before. We had better strap ourselves in and hang on, this could get bumpy."

Using restraining clamps Max helped Steve secure his chair to the floor. He then strapped himself in, just as they entered the upper atmosphere.

They started to get thrown around all over the place. As they cleared the upper atmosphere they could make out the planet below. The whole landscape looked red from that height. As they got nearer they could make out deep red oceans. The ship was vibrating quite strongly now as they descended even further into the atmosphere. They flew over the oceans and eventually came over the land mass. They then noticed that the land was covered in giant trees of different shades of red. Steve pointed out what could only be the ruins of very old cities that were overgrown in red and bluish foliage. The ship was getting knocked about with the speed of the re-entry, and also due to the high winds. They were literally hanging on for dear life. The tops of the trees were rushing past them in a blur of speed. Alarmingly, they were heading towards one of these forests with some trees towering above them even at this height. In the distance above the canopy was the top of a giant building that looked as though it was a pyramid.

.....

The ship hit the top of the canopy with such force that it flipped them upside down. They were both now hanging upside down in their seats, swinging violently as they crashed through the forest's canopy. The noise was deafening and although they tried to shout at each other, neither of them could hear. Eventually the shuttle started to lose momentum, thumped through the forest, and skidded to a halt on the forest floor on its side, coming to a halt. The two friends hung in their seats unconscious.

Chapter Seven

The Planet Trieg

The smell of the air first stirred Max. Although breathable, it made his nose sting and eyes water. Looking around he could see the windows had been broken and that there was a split in the hull letting in a red glow of light. Smoke was still floating in the air, and there were small flames coming from the control panels. He got out of his seat and climbed up the floor to where Steve was. He had just started stirring with a groan and was shaking his head trying to clear the mist that was engulfing him.

"Power up your chair. We have landed on our side. I'll release the clamps."

He released the clamps and he and Steve fell to the other side of the cabin. Steve powered up and righted himself and hovered there.

"Blimey, that air stings a bit," he said rubbing his eyes.

"I know. We need to get out of here. There are flames starting to build up over there. That building we saw before we crashed, I think it's only a short distance from here. We need to find it."

Max climbed through the broken window with Steve following behind. They then stopped there, absorbing what they saw. Looking back from the ship they could see a tunnel the shuttle had created through the dense foliage of the trees. At the end of the tunnel, they could just make out the reddish sky. Looking directly up they could not see the tops of the trees; they were too tall. The trees had to be at least a kilometer high. Looking around them, everything on the planet was red, the trees, the soil, and the strange looking grass. The tree trunks were at least forty foot thick, how they managed not to hit one was a mystery. Max walked up to a tree and touched it. It felt sticky and he noticed that his fingers had turned red. He tried to rub it but only a little came off. Meanwhile Steve had gone back to look over the ship, or what remained of it. Lying on its side, it had dug a furrow through the red soil. It was badly damaged with red dust already starting to coat it. Smoke was starting to come from the inside.

"Max, I think we need to get away from here, the ship is about to blow up."

Without even answering he jumped on the back of his hover chair and Steve accelerated away into the thick red forest. After a while they heard an explosion. Coming to a halt Steve said. "Well, if no one knew we were here after that landing, they surely will now."

"Who knows, can you hear anything?"

After a while Steve replied. "Nothing bar the wind whistling, it's deadly quiet."

"That's what worries me. Perhaps the whole planet has died out. We could be stranded here."

They moved off. The silence was quite frightening. They kept moving through the forest weaving in and out of these huge trees. Some of them had some bluish plants growing around them. Occasionally they went under or over trunks that had fallen down.

In the three hours since the crash they had seen or heard nothing. Max tapped Steve on the shoulder. Stopping, he looked in the direction that Max was pointing. Overgrown with the blue plants, but still visible, were the remains of a wall.

Steve steered his chair towards it and stopped. "What do you think it was?" he asked.

Max hopped off and stumbled over to the remains. Looking along it, he caught his breath as he saw in the distance that in places it stood as high as one hundred feet. In other places there were large chunks of wall lying around in the undergrowth. He could see where tree roots had grown underneath the ruins knocking them down.

"Well apart from a wall of some sorts I don't know, perhaps it was a city boundary or something, those bricks are huge.

Whoever built it were either huge beings or they had machines. I hope they had machines," Max replied with a worried look on his face.

"Do you think it was built to keep something out?"

"Who knows?" Max replied as he walked over to a bit of rock and touched the funny red grime that was coating everything. To his surprise underneath the grime the wall was made of a smooth material and it was black.

"Look. It looks as though it's made of some black material." He was now kneeling down. "Why do you think everything is covered in this red stuff? Do you think something happened?" Max asked rubbing more grime off to reveal more of the brick.

"I have no idea. Everything is odd around here. Maybe they moved to another planet having destroyed this one, like we nearly did with Earth. I have noticed that it hasn't got any darker or lighter since we've been here," replied Steve.

"I hadn't noticed that. This place gives me the creeps. Let's try and find that building and see what we can find that might be useful." With that Max jumped on the back of the chair and they set off to find the building.

It was hard because the forest was so dense but they eventually found it. It was huge, and again covered in red grime. But looking up at it, the walls just disappeared up through the canopy. In each direction it just went on as far as the eye could see. They went right up to the wall, Steve rubbed off

69

the red grime and revealed that the building was made of the same black material. They moved along the wall, first in one direction, then another looking for an entrance but could not see anything, not even a window. Looking closer the walls had been rubbed back to the black material by trees which had been scraping against the walls.

"What shall we do?" Steve asked with a hint of frustration in his voice. Max noticed that they were now both covered in the red dust that was everywhere. "We need to try and find an entrance. Someone or something lived here once. Let's go around the whole building. We need to find food and water at least."

They then started to travel around the building. How long they moved along it they did not know. But eventually Steve spotted what must have been the remains of a road heading directly for the building, but it ended at the wall with no obvious entrance. Max jumped down and started scraping away the grime and dust looking for any sign of an opening, but he could not find anything.

"I don't know what to think. I can't even find a gap."

"Stand back I'll ram it with the chair."

"No, if you do that and break it, we've really had it."

"If we don't try something we have had it anyway. Stand aside," Steve said defiantly as he reversed his chair. With that he shot forward, hit the wall and bounced off landing on the ground. Max ran over, but he got the chair and himself upright.

"Well, that didn't work," Steve said with a smile on his face.

"We'll have to—" Max started, but never finished. Behind him he heard a noise coming from the wall. Turning to face it, he saw a huge section of the wall starting to move inwards as if gliding on glass. Then it stopped and started to rise, followed by a great whooshing of air that blew them along the ground right into a tree behind them.

An entrance had appeared about fifty feet high and twenty feet across.

"Quick it's now or never!" yelled Max as he ran towards it. Steve was hot on his heels. Once inside they were greeted by pitch black and then the door slammed shut behind them. Steve turned on the lights of his hover chair and shouted hello at the top of his voice, which echoed around them.

"What now?" he whispered. This was then amplified and echoed around the building.

"I suppose we wait and see, yet again," Max said, resigned. They did not have long to wait. Lights started to illuminate the vast room they were in. They could not see any walls or the ceiling, everything just seemed to blend in. The floor was made of the same black material as they had found outside.

"Max, something is coming towards us."

"I can see it."

It was a large black disc that just floated up to them. It came to a stop and in the middle something raised, and a blue beam came out as if scanning them. Max touched it and pushed it away. It floated across the room and disappeared from sight.

"I don't know what that was, but it glided away as though on ice."

"Well, it's coming back," Steve said pointing.

Max looked around to see it coming towards him at speed. Before he had time to react, it stopped in front of him at exactly the same spot as it had been before. This time when he pushed it, it did not move.

"We can't wait around here all day. Let's take a look around." With that he went to walk around the disc, which moved sideways to block him. No matter which way Max went, the disc followed him and blocked him, even at one stage nudging him. When he went to stand next to Steve it went back to its original position. Steve found this funny and was sitting there in fits of laughter with tears running down his cheeks, smudging the red dust.

"If you think it's so funny you have a go," Max said angrily folding his arms.

"Ok then." So Steve moved forward and tried, but no matter what direction he went in or how fast, the disc just blocked him. Now it was Max's turn to laugh. "See, not that easy is it?"

"Oh shut up. It was funny though. Let's both try. You go one way, me the other."

"Good idea."

Max ran to his left, Steve to the right. The disc followed Max and blocked him. Looking to his right he saw that another one had appeared out of nowhere and was covering Steve. "Guess they don't want to let us in then."

"Whatever gave you that idea?" Max said sarcastically.

A funny noise started to fill the room. It seemed to surround them, but they could not figure out where it came from. Was it something trying to communicate with them? They looked at each other, then Max said, "If you are trying to communicate, we can't understand you?"

Two beams of blue light appeared again from the discs which swept over them. After that the discs moved back into the shadows and a voice boomed out. "What are you doing on Trieg?"

They both looked at each other in disbelief. "You speak," Steve whispered. "My name is Max, this is Steve. We accidentally crashed here. Can you help us?" Max said, looking around trying to find who he was speaking to.

"Trieg is a hidden planet, how did you find it?" the voice replied.

Max explained their story of how they were attacked by pirates and their escape and that his parent's ship had been hijacked.

"An unusual story. My name is Nyxam and I am the guardian of Trieg."

"Can we come and meet you?" Steve asked.

"No, I am a machine."

"What are you guarding against?"

"Anything that would bring harm to the planet."

"We mean you no harm," Max replied.

"I know."

"Can you help us?" Steve asked.

"I will have to ask the council of elders this question."

"Can we speak with them at least?"

"No. they will see no one. They do not even see themselves."

"How do they exist if they see no one?" Max asked with a puzzled tone to his voice.

"It is what you would call complicated. They only see their families. This is the way they have chosen."

"It sounds a strange existence," Steve whispered to Max, then to Nyxam, "Why do you guard the planet? Are they afraid?"

There was a silence for about ten minutes before Nyxam replied, "Many millennia ago, Trieg had a sister planet called Eeg. We were called by a different name then, Tri. Both planets were greedy, they were only interested in power. War followed war as one tried to be better than the other. All resources were being used to create better machines and weapons. Respect was lost. There was no value in life. Value was who had the better weapons and machines."

They looked at each other in shock as Nyxam continued.

"Tri eventually built a weapon that could destroy planets. Over time, our people moved into great cities like this one as each planet tried to destroy the other. Tri decided to use this weapon on Eeg. By this time our people had turned into savages. The day came and the great weapon was fired. People had turned out in their millions to watch as the weapon was fired. The light from the weapon was so bright and strong it created winds across the whole planet. It heated up the air around and caused great fires. People ran in panic. The planet started to burn as everyone hid with fear in the cities. Many millions were left to die as the cities locked themselves down.

However, it was too late to stop, and that night Eeg turned into a bright red ball of fire and exploded. Eventually huge chunks of the planet rained down in a firestorm destroying anything and everything. We had not only destroyed our sister planet, but ours as well. The destruction of Eeg created the nebula and it also contaminated our planet. That is why everything you see is red. Plants, soil, oceans, and the sky. Most of our wildlife died out. There are beasts that have survived in the forests. Nothing but they can live on the surface for any length of time…." he paused.

"The few million who managed to survive were so ashamed of what they had created, they vowed they would never seek to mix with any other race again. They created me to look after them and renamed the planet Trieg. My name comes from the person who created the weapon to remind future generations of what happened."

The two friends looked at each other. They were visibly shocked at what they had just heard. It was Steve who asked the next question.

"What's happened to the people now?" His voice was shaking.

"They live underground all over the planet. Underneath the ruins of the cities. They live in family units. They don't trust each other enough to do anything else."

"Do you think they will help us?" Max asked. "We need to leave the planet and find our parents."

"How can they help you? My helpers have seen your vessel and it is destroyed."

"Do you have a ship we could borrow?"

"If we have it will be old. I'll have to consult the elders. Your guardians will take you somewhere to rest and provide food. It might be a while before I get back to you."

.....

After eating some unusual food, exhausted, they rested in the room provided and fell asleep. After what felt like days they were awoken by the voice of Nyxam. Rubbing their eyes, Max helped Steve back into his chair and they sat there and listened.

"I have spoken with the council. They have agreed to help you, but there are conditions. Will you accept?"

Not having any choice, they agreed.

"You must not reveal where we are. When your mission is complete you must return the ship we provide."

"You have a ship?" they both said in unison, excited.

"We do. You must understand that it hasn't been used for a long time, but it is an advanced ship. We will program it to understand your language but you'll have to learn how to use it as there is no one to show you."

"You have a deal," they replied in unison.

…..

Thanking Nyxam for his help they followed their two guardians, which led them deeper into the city. Now and then they saw other discs gliding around as they were led higher and higher. Eventually they arrived at a giant door which slid open. In front of them was the ship they had been promised. Max's idea of a sleek ship like the Vanquish in his dreams was instantly blown apart. It was a dark green in color and looked a bit stubby. It was sitting on its landing gear. At the front were some stairs leading up steeply to an open door. There did not appear to be any windows. It looked as though there might be a ramp at the back which was shut. High up on the back was a wing-like structure which was obviously the engines. It looked very rugged and powerful though.

Nyxam's voice suddenly boomed out of the hanger. "Don't look too alarmed. That ship is a deep space exploration vessel, and very tough. It can cope with the harshest of environments. It is well-armed and shielded. It has been resupplied with food. In the back are two small planet hoppers for you to get around on should you need to."

Steve had since come alongside Max grinning like a Cheshire cat.

…..

Nyxam continued, "As promised the systems will understand you. Also, the computer has as much information about you as we could give it."

Thanking Nyxam again, the two of them went aboard. Finding the bridge, Max sat at one of the control panels which were everywhere. There were seats at the other panels running along one side. To their surprise there were windows to the front and sides, which you could not see from outside. The seats were quite big. Presumably the people from Trieg were as well.

"We have to give it a name," Steve said.

"Let's call it Huntsman, as we are going on a hunt of sorts."

"Good idea. Ship, we are going to call you Huntsman," Steve said.

To the friends' surprise the ship spoke to them. "I heard you the first time," came the rather huffy reply.

Max looked at Steve, who had gone bright red. Max asked Huntsman if it could fly them to where his parent's ship had been attacked.

"Do you have the location?" Huntsman asked.

"Yes I have it on my controller."

In front of them a door opened and the ship started to move out. As they cleared the door they looked out and were surprised to see how high up they were. Even so the giant trees were still high above them, and below them the wall of the building disappeared from view. They slowly gained height and once above, the canopy began to accelerate at such speed that in no time they had cleared the planet. Steve looked at Max and said as if in thought, or shock, "Blimey this thing is fast."

"I am not a thing; I am now Huntsman and that was slow. This is fast!"

With that the ship cleared the nebula and shot off into deep space on their mission.

Chapter Eight

The attack on the Sagaris

"Mayday, mayday we are under attack!"

The two of them sat up straight, alert.

"What was that?" Steve asked Huntsman.

"A distress call I have picked up from a ship called the Sagaris," Huntsman replied.

The boys looked at each other in disbelief. Since leaving Trieg, they had been circling the area where they had come under attack from the pirates. They had been unable to pick up the trail of the pirate ships or the star freighter. Huntsman had been sending out signals trying to contact any ships that might be close by, but they had had no luck. They had also heard nothing, until now.

"Huntsman, can you locate the Sagaris?" Steve asked.

"I will try."

Max turned to Steve. "What do you think?"

"It's hard to say. Surely it can't be the pirates? That would be audacious of them. I wish we could get hold of the star freighter. I'm worried about them."

"Me too. I also have friends on Sagaris, Ben and Hope. I've been trying to contact them," Max replied as he gazed out at the stars.

After a while Huntsman told them that he had found the Sagaris near a planet called Seroc in the outer Rier's system. He had plotted a course. It would take a day to reach them. Max told Huntsman to go as fast as he could. With a slight hum from the engines, they changed course and headed deeper into space towards the Rier's system. Max and Steve decided to get some rest and told Huntsman to wake them if anything happened.

…..

Max felt his wrist controller vibrate. It was Ben trying to get hold of him. Rubbing his eyes, he saw they had been travelling for eighteen hours and must now be nearing the Sagaris. He asked Huntsman if he had heard anything.

"They have been communicating with a military ship which is on its way to help."

"Why didn't you wake me?" Max asked angrily.

"It is nothing important, you needed to rest."

"That's for me to decide!"

Just then Steve appeared. "What's going on, what's happened?"

"There is another communication from the ship. Do you want to hear it?" said Huntsman.

"Yes,' came Max's sulky reply.

Huntsman played the boys the communication: "This is the Military Cruiser Ajax we are now about an hour away. We had trouble understanding what happened earlier. How is your ship, Captain?"

"As I said before, we were attacked by heavily armed pirates. Our engines are running at half power, and I have had to evacuate six levels due to damage" replied the Captain of the Sagaris.

"Do you know who the pirates were?"

"It was Captain Black. He was after a cargo. Although he wouldn't say what it was. He also had some Cyclops troopers with him, and strangely a new star freighter. I saw this ship at Jupiter 2."

"Are you sure?" came the reply from the Ajax.

"Positive. I need to evacuate some passengers who were hurt in the attack. Can this be done?"

"An evacuation ship is en route and should be with you in the next three hours."

"Thank you, Ajax, Sagaris out."

.....

With that everything went quiet. Max and Steve sat there in shock with Steve mumbling about how bad that was.

Max's mind was spinning. In some way he was relieved to hear his Dad's star freighter was in one piece but shocked to hear it was involved in the attack. However, this could mean only one thing, his parents and the crew were now fugitives and would be hunted down. His controller went off, stirring him from his thoughts. It was Ben again.

"Hi," was all he could manage. Steve had come alongside him and was listening.

"What do you mean, hi! Hope and I have been trying to get hold of you!"

"Hold on Ben. Huntsman, can you pick up this signal?" With that Ben's voice came through the ship.

"What do you mean hold on? Your Dad's ship has attacked us, he is a wanted man."

"Ben, listen! We were attacked by pirates. Steve and I managed to escape. The pirates captured my parent's star freighter and crew."

"Who's Steve?"

Max filled in Ben and Hope about their adventure and how they had got hold of Huntsman.

"What do you mean you crashed, and someone lent you a ship?" came Hope's voice.

Max smiled and looked at Steve who said that it did sound a bit farfetched with a shrug of his shoulders.

"Where are you both?" she asked.

Huntsman confirmed that they were two hours away.

"Who's that?" Ben asked.

"Huntsman."

"He can talk?"

"Yep. We are going to look for our parents, rescue them and prove their innocence. Do you two want to help?"

"Some holiday this. How do you plan to get us off? Land on the Sagaris?" Hope said sarcastically.

"Sounds about right, what do you think Steve?"

"Whatever," Steve said in a resigned tone. "Huntsman, can we land in the cargo hold?"

"If we have help it shouldn't be too hard. Your friends will need to open the security doors. I'll scan their systems and get the code for them."

Max asked Ben and Hope if they would help and they agreed to let him know when they got to the cargo deck.

….

Huntsman had slowed down. In the distance they could see the Sagaris. The ship looked badly damaged. There were flashes of light as the power was fluctuating throughout the ship. In the distance was the blue planet Seroc. It was an uninhabitable planet that had constant electrical storms rolling across the surface. They could see the lightning, even from this distance. Coming alongside the Sagaris was the military cruiser Ajax and a small shuttle left its bay and started to circle the stricken ship, obviously checking for damage.

"Huntsman, have we been detected yet?" Max asked.

"Negative. I have activated an anti-scanning device. It will hide us for the time being. But once near them we will be detected. We will need to be fast."

"How fast is fast? Steve asked, looking at Max with a worried look on his face.

"We will have no more than five minutes before they figure out what we are," replied Huntsman.

"That's cutting it fine," came Steve's reply.

.....

Captain Milos Bainbridge was a small man, but also a very shrewd one. He had been the Captain of Ajax for the past ten years and knew everything there was to know about her. She was an Olympus class cruiser, not only heavily armed but also carrying twenty heavily armed attack tanks. Standing at the scanning station on the bridge, he was trying to make out what it was that Lieutenant Jim Cross had seen. He had reported what he thought had been a ship approaching, but as soon as he had seen it the signal had disappeared again.

"What do you think, Jim?" Bainbridge asked.

"I can't make it out, Sir. There was definitely something there. We have tried to magnify the frequency in that area of space but can't trace anything. It must be too far away for our view screen to pick up."

"Seems strange to me. Can't be pirates again, not with us here. Even they aren't that stupid. Keep an eye on it." Turning, Captain Bainbridge headed towards the command center.

"Why would pirates attack a cruise ship?" he asked the officer in charge of the helm.

"Don't know Sir, but I have the ship on high alert after that blip Lieutenant Cross found," came the reply.

"I agree. Keep the engines powered up as well in case we need to move fast."

Taking his seat, he looked out at the Sagaris, deep in thought. This situation troubled him. The target was surely too risky for the pirates unless the cargo was so valuable that they were prepared to risk it all. Just then the communications officer shouted out that he had picked up a signal coming from the Sagaris.

"What did it say?" Captain Bainbridge asked leaning back in his seat.

"It said we are in the cargo hold Max. It seems a strange message Sir."

"What do you make of that Captain?" Lieutenant Cross said. "Do you think they have left someone on board?" he added as if in afterthought.

"Maybe, go to high alert and notify the Sagaris that they might have visitors in their hold."

The communications officer, who was an Ovrie by the name of Zic, told them of another communication and put it through the Ajax's audio system.

"Ben, Hope, we are coming in. Open the doors now!"

"Zic, what is going on? Jim, tell me something, have you seen a ship yet?"

"I have detected a ship. It is now going so fast I don't know if it will slow down in time. I haven't seen a ship like it before. It doesn't resemble anything in our data base. I've put it on the view screen Sir," came Jim's reply.

There was now tension on the bridge as everyone concentrated on their tasks, trying at the same time to understand what was going on.

They sat there and watched as the ship approached the cargo hold of the Sagaris. It rapidly slowed down and disappeared into the cruise ship.

"Jim, can we get a lock on the ship with the weapons?"

"Negative Captain. It moved too fast and caught us out. If we fire now we could hit the Sagaris. We can try again when it leaves."

"Very well. Helm, move the Ajax and try and block them in the hold."

With that they started moving forward. The Sagaris started to grow in size as they built up speed and headed towards it. But it was too late. The ship left the hold, swerving drastically, nearly hitting the Ajax, and then it then disappeared.

"Sir, the unidentified ship has just hit light speed."

"Thanks Jim. I need answers fast. I need to know what was taken. Who are these Ben and Hope? And most importantly what was that ship, where has it come from and can we track it? Once help has arrived we are going to go and find it. I want that information ASAP. Do I make myself clear?" With that Captain Bainbridge stormed off the bridge. If he hated one thing it was being outsmarted.

…..

Max and Steve were worried about the operation to get their friends off the Sagaris. Huntsman had told them that the Ajax had detected them. It also informed them that Ajax was in a high state of alert and that any mistake could prove deadly.

After giving Ben the password, Huntsman set off at great speed hoping to catch the Ajax off guard. As they sped towards the Sagaris which was still having sporadic flashes from the damage caused from the pirate attack, they could see the massive bulk of the Ajax. It was stationary and looked menacing. The good thing was it had not moved, which hopefully meant they had not been detected just yet.

They entered the cargo hold, coming to an emergency stop. There was cargo lying around, stacked neatly, until they crashed into it, sending containers flying everywhere. Lowering the rear ramp Steve and Max went to the rear and standing on the ramp looked for Ben and Hope. It was no good shouting for them as the noise from the engines was so loud their ears felt as though they would explode.

Seeing their friends, they started waving at them frantically. They came running, jumping over boxes, and weaving between the bigger ones, and managed to get to the ramp just as some of the ship's security guards entered the hold and started firing at them, with red beams of light exploding on the hull of the Huntsman. Diving in, the ramp came up and they were safe.

Everyone sat on the floor panting for breath. Steve said a quick hello, then shot off in his chair to the bridge. Max yelled "Huntsman, get us out of here, and quick!"

The others arrived on the bridge as the ship banked wildly to avoid hitting the Ajax that had been moving in to try and block them. With that, distant light seemed to pull towards them as the Huntsman hit light speed and sped away.

Chapter Nine

The Lost Cyclops

Captain Black was sitting in his office on board the Cutlass. Rolfe was pacing up and down with his arms behind his back in deep thought.

Ever since Nino Bassi had come to see him about this mission he had had a bad feeling about this. However, he had not realized how bad. Apart from the fact that they had captured a ship and its crew, the attack on the Sagaris had gone terribly wrong, and for what who only knew. They were now seeking refuge in a cluster of planets called the Carweg system. This was a new planetary system and was basically a collection of lumps of molten rock circling a sun. The static created in this system would hide him and his ships from anything that would pass this sector of space.

"What are you thinking, Rolfe?"

"I don't like it. The cargo on the star freighter gives me the creeps, and that crate we got from the Sagaris is strange. How did they know that was on board?"

He was referring to Nino Bassi's communication telling them they had to get the cargo off the cruise ship. He continued, "We can't open it, the cargo on the freighter won't budge and everywhere we go those Cyclops troopers want to start shooting at everything that moves."

"We were defending ourselves and the mission!" Mu retorted.

"Well, you didn't do a good job, because those kids escaped to who knows where, and the Sagaris is floating around space with big holes in it," Rolfe replied angrily, staring at Mu with his deep blue eyes.

"Calm down you two. Mu can you contact Bassi?"

"No, he said he would contact us. Any way there is too much interference from the system we are in."

"Well, we will keep the ships here. I'll take the Cutlass to the planet Kalin and see what I can learn. Rolfe you stay here. Mu you come with me."

"Is that wise?" asked Mu. "Kalin is a bad place to go."

"I agree, Captain," Rolfe added. "There are some bad people that go there. If they find out you have stolen military hardware they might try and procure it for themselves."

"If they did find out they will link us to the Sagaris. They do not like the military sniffing around. We could be trouble for them. I'd like to bring some troopers with us for protection," Mu said.

"As much as I don't like the idea, I think it would be wise Captain. Also, I'll get a troop of our men together," replied Rolfe nervously, keeping an eye on the Cyclops.

"Mm… I think that's fair. Mu, we leave in fifteen minutes."

….

Meanwhile far away, the Ajax was patrolling, looking for any clues as to where the pirate fleet had gone and also where the ship that had taken two kids off the Sagaris had gone. A fleet and a ship cannot just disappear.

Captain Bainbridge was standing in front of his chair, deep in thought, looking out to space. He had found out that there was a secret military cargo on the Sagaris, and also on the freighter that had been captured. His mission was to recover these cargoes. These were top secret and they had to be retrieved at any cost. It was still daring of the pirates to steal these, especially as they also attacked a cruise ship, knowing the military would hunt them down.

"Captain, we think we have something," Jim said breaking his chain of thought.

"What is it?"

"We have picked up a ship's signal leaving the Carweg system."

"How far away is that?" came the excited reply.

"At least a day away. If we are lucky we should be able to track it," Jim replied.

"Helm, full speed, let's see where this ship takes us."

....

The Cutlass sped out of Carweg system and set course for Kalin, unaware they were being followed.

"Klad, have you picked up anything on the sensors?"

Klad was Captain Black's operations officer. He was a small man with very wrinkly yellow skin and came from a planet called Yth. No one knew how old he was, including himself. "I thought I did, but it was too far out. I'll keep an eye out though."

Captain Black stood there with a frown on his face. He watched Mu who was standing next to Klad looking at the monitors. Through the view screen all he could see was the blackness of space with distant stars strangely elongated due to their speed. He was worried that they could have been spotted leaving the system but decided not to say anything. If there was anything following them he had faith enough in Klad to detect it. Turning around he headed off to his quarters and told Klad to call him when they arrived at Kalin.

.....

Captain Black got to the bridge in time to see the planet come into view. The planet was yellow and very bright due to its proximity to its sun. If they were to travel across the surface they would need to wear radiation suits and special goggles to protect them from the harsh atmosphere of the planet. Kalinians were immune to the planet's conditions. Their skin was almost white and rubbery to the touch. They were a tall race and had many eyes enabling them to see 360 degrees. Because of their height and slender frame, it made travelling to other planets quite an arduous task for them. Due to this, anyone who wanted to trade with them had to come here. However, they were a dangerous race, and although they did not like to travel, if crossed they would travel anywhere to settle a score.

Captain Black did not like them or trust them, however if you needed information this was one of the best places to come. There were only two cities on the planet that were adapted to allow other races to feel comfortable. Anywhere else and you were not only in danger from radiation but also from the Kalinians themselves as they did not like strangers. The planet was guarded by drone attack ships that would destroy any unwelcome visitors. They had to get clearance from the planet to guarantee themselves safe passage.

…..

Standing at the helm he could see at least four hundred ships in orbit. Being too big to land on the surface the crews would have taken their shuttles to the surface. The Cutlass, however, was able to land on most planets and after getting clearance they descended through the cloudless atmosphere to the smaller city called Waveney. Their descent took longer than normal due to a radiation storm which threw the Cutlass all over the place. They eventually made the surface and were guided to a docking port.

Leaving Klad in charge of the Cutlass, he instructed him to keep the ship ready in case they needed to leave quickly. Captain Black, Mu and two Cyclops troopers made their way through the city to a bar called the Ten Eye. This was the main meeting point for anyone coming to the city, not just for outsiders but also for the Kalinians wishing to do business. At the doorway stood two Kalinian guards who were checking people to make sure no weapons were being taken inside. Knowing this, Black and Mu gave their weapons to the two Cyclops troopers who were to remain outside. If any trouble happened they would come to their rescue.

As they entered the bar the first thing they noticed was the noise. There must have been at least three thousand people in there, ranging from the odd human through to people like the Tagons, and the Baas. Baas had no heads. Their eyes and mouth were on their chest and they had four legs, two small ones at the back, and larger ones at the front, which also acted as arms. As they forced their way through the crowd of people towards the bar, some turned round and scowled at them. However as soon as they saw Mu they shut up and let them pass. Not many people had seen Cyclops troopers, but their reputation preceded them.

The Kalinians did not like much about anything, especially serving people, so the bar was run by Tagons who liked nothing better than making money. When one came over Captain Black asked Mu if he wanted anything.

"No," came the curt reply.

"I'll have a Kalinian beer," he said, "and make sure it's cold." Leaning on his elbows against the bar he surveyed the scene in front of him. His beer had arrived and taking a sip from the bottle he asked Mu, "What do you think we should do?"

"I think we should split up and try and find out what, if anything, the story is on the Galactic vine."

"Good idea. Let's give ourselves an hour and meet back here."

....

The Ajax had been following the vessel for some time. Although they did not know anything about it, its course towards Kalin was suspicion enough. They were confident that they had not been detected and had taken up a position close to the surface of Kalin's volcanic moon called Fodil.

"Jim, is there any way that we can get onto the surface of the planet?"

Bainbridge's voice had an excited ring to it. He was never happier than when there was a mission on, and this one intrigued him.

"The problem we have is that they don't like strangers. Also, as we are a Treaty cruiser they will be angry that we have got this close to their planet without revealing ourselves. If they found us here we would probably have a fight on our hands. I suggest we wait till this ship leaves again and follow it."

"I agree, although I don't like it. I think we should move back out of their system and wait for the next move. Take us to the outskirts of the system."

With that the Ajax sped up and headed for deep space.

Captain Black had managed to get some information about the attack on the Sagaris, and what he had learnt did not make him happy at all. In fact he was angry to boiling point. This mission for Bassi had turned into one disaster after another. From what he'd learnt, the Sagaris was in a bad way and was being towed back to a Treaty station called Nero for repairs. On top of that he had learned that another ship had arrived at the scene and taken two children off the Sagaris. This unidentified ship had nearly rammed the Ajax whose Captain believed it belonged to the pirates and the Ajax was now in hot pursuit. Things could not get any worse.

He saw Mu at the bar and joined him. Telling Mu what he had learnt, the trooper confirmed his story saying that he had heard the same thing. However, he also said that others had heard about the cargo that had been stolen being military hardware, and that other people were now looking for those responsible in order to steal it for themselves. They decided that they had probably better leave before anyone put two and two together.

Pushing their way through the crowds towards the exit they found their path blocked by a group of Mours. These were a race of people who were known as roaming traders but were in fact no better than the pirates themselves. They had deep blue skin, verging on black, and had four arms and were about the same height as Captain Black. He had come across them several times before and generally gave them a wide berth, as wherever they were, trouble tended to be not far behind. He had also seen one of them before who went under the name of Tolet. "Can I help you?" Captain Black asked him.

Tolet smiled at him showing his sharp blue teeth and laughed in his deep guttural voice. "Aar, Captain we meet again. I have heard that you and your friend here have been asking questions about the attack on that cruise ship. Now my friends and I have been thinking, why would he be here on this forsaken planet asking questions about that, unless of course he was the person who had attacked it? Now if that is the case you must have a very valuable cargo which you need to dispose of. A cargo that I would very much like." Tolet finished this last bit in a low menacing voice, pointing four fingers at him.

Looking around him the whole bar had become silent as everyone watched what was going on at the entrance. Mu was getting fidgety and Black put a hand on his arm to warn him not to do anything.

"Good to see you again Tolet. However, we were just passing through and stopped to look for some engine parts. We had heard of the attack and just wanted to find out more," he replied trying to keep his voice calm.

"I don't believe you, what have you done with the cargo?" Tolet replied angrily.

"I was going to ask you the same question. Taking on the Treaty is too dangerous for me. However, it is more in keeping with the type of thing you might do. So my question to you is what have *you* done with it?" Captain Black replied boldly.

This caught the Mours off guard and they started talking amongst themselves waving all their arms around.

Eventually Tolet turned round. "Don't blame us. I think we would like to come with you to your ship so we can see for ourselves that you haven't got the cargo."

"Not possible. We need to go now, so let us pass."

The situation was getting dangerous. Some more Mours had arrived now, totaling fifteen of them. The guards at the door had also taken an interest and had drawn their lasers. One of them came and stood between Black and Tolet.

"We don't like trouble on our planet. Break it up and leave," he said looking at all of them in turn. Mu tapped Black on the shoulder. Just coming into view were the two Cyclops they had left outside. Now everyone was quiet, the atmosphere was tense and something was going to happen. Black whispered to Mu to signal the two to stay put and not do anything.

Looking back, the guard stood his ground, Black also noticed that three of the Mours had gotten lasers out that must have been hidden in their thick garments. Just as he had noticed it so did the guard, who spun round and raised his laser, but it was too late, one of the Mours shot him. As he fell to the ground the other guard fired. A blue laser beam hit one of the Mours who screamed out grabbing one of his arms where he had been hit. Another Mour shot the other guard hitting him in the shoulder. By this time panic had set in at the bar and there was a great surge of people heading for the exits. Black and Mu found themselves in a sea of bodies. He had lost sight of Tolet and his crowd which was the only good thing to come out of this. Mu grabbed hold of Black and pulled him towards the exit where they were met by the two troopers. Above all the noise he could hear lasers being fired and saw some more guards pushing their way through the crowd towards them.

"Quickly, this way!" one of the troopers yelled. Pushing through the crowds they made their way along the corridor towards the docking ports. Suddenly a laser beam hit the roof above them showering them in sparks, this caused more panic around them. Looking back, Captain Black saw Tolet and his band in the crowd behind him. They were firing in their direction and behind them, even further back were yet more guards were giving chase. They got to the docking port and through the windows he could see the Cutlass. People were now trying to get to their ships. Guards were trying to stop them, but there were just too many people for them to control.

The laser fire from the Mours had intensified and the two troopers had stopped by the gate to the Cutlass and were returning fire. The noise was deafening. People were screaming and shouting, there was laser fire everywhere.

Black got the door open and he and Mu dived through. At the other end the doors to the Cutlass opened and two of his crew came to help them. As they looked back one of the troopers took a hit and fell to the ground. One of his crew went to try and get him but Mu stopped him. "Leave him we need to get out of here before it's too late." With that the doors to the Cutlass slid shut just as a laser beam hit the corridor above Mu's head. Black and Mu ran to the bridge. They could hear the engines powering up as they eventually got there.

"Klad, get us out of here and fast!"

"We're on our way."

Looking out of the view screen all they could see were hundreds of ships leaving the surface and heading towards space. The Cutlass started to overtake smaller craft as they built up speed.

"Keep an eye out for any Mours ships. We might have company. Try and stay with the crowd for as long as possible as it will be harder to find us."

He then turned to Mu. "Thanks for grabbing me back there. Sorry we lost one of your crew."

"It was nothing. I had no choice but to leave him or we would all have been killed. And I need you alive," he replied with no sign of emotion.

"Klad get us back to the fleet. And make doubly sure that we are not followed. I do not want those Mours paying us any surprise visits."

....

Captain Bainbridge was sitting in his office just off the bridge of the Ajax.

He had been reading the reports from the Sagaris incident. The Sagaris had now reached the Space Station Nero and after being patched up was en route to the repair yards at Titan. The parents of the two missing children whose names he had now got, were puzzled as to why they would leave the cruise ship aboard a spaceship, although the girl had left a message to say they would be okay and that she would explain to them later. Understandably, the parents were worried.

Just then he got a call through the intercom to come to the bridge urgently. As he entered the bridge all he could here was hundreds of voices all mixed up, coming through the intercom from the radio scanners.

"Can someone please tell me what on earth is going on?" he asked as he took his seat, "and please turn that noise down, or off," he then yelled.

Jim took the seat next to him as the bridge crew headed to their stations as they were now on high alert.

"From what information we can gather there has been an incident on the surface. Two groups started firing at each other, they wounded two Kalinian guards. Everyone is heading for their ships and leaving the surface through the panic this has caused. The Kalinians are hopping mad and are trying to lock down the system. However with the volume of ships fleeing this will prove impossible. All the ships in orbit have powered their engines getting ready to leave the system. Any other information is hard to get just yet because of the volume of radio traffic and languages," Jim said looking at the Captain.

"Will we be able to track the ship we are looking for?"

"If all these ships leave at once, it will be hard, as we estimate there to be at least one thousand ships getting ready to leave," Jim replied.

"Captain, look!" came a startled shout from the helmsman.

Everyone went quiet and looked at the view screen which had been magnified. They could see small ships coming up from the planet. Some of them were either docking, or going into their parent ships in orbit, while larger ones were just accelerating quickly and making their way into outer space. The ones that had taken aboard their shuttles had also started to depart orbit and were speeding up. At least one hundred ships were now heading their way, like one great stampede.

"Helm, turn us around and get us away from here, and fast, before we have a collision. Radar, see if you can find our quarry amongst that lot," Bainbridge shouted.

They could feel the engines powering up and slowly the Ajax started to move. Turning in a tight arc she built up speed and the view in front of them moved away to just catch a glimpse of the small asteroid they had been near slide from view. Just then a massive cargo ship that had overtaken them came into view and with a bright green glow from its engines it went strangely elongated as it hit light speed and suddenly disappeared. "There isn't a chance to find our quarry, Sir, there are just too many ships."

"Put the rear viewer on, and let's see what is going on behind us, and keep filtering the radio signals, we might just pick up something," Bainbridge said with frustration in his voice. Looking through the rear view there were ships everywhere. They saw two ships collide with a big explosion crippling them. They just came to a stop with smoke and flames coming from their sides, with one of them floating on its side, like a giant dying fish gasping for air.

"Jim, come with me to my office. Helm, plot a course back to the Carweg system. Let us see if we can find anything there." With that he headed off with Jim hot on his heels.

"I am getting frustrated with this mission Jim. It seems that every time we get near to something important we get foxed. I hope we can find something at the Carweg system, what are your thoughts?" Bainbridge said, shuffling from foot to foot with his hands behind his back.

"I think there is more to this than meets the eye. For a start we have these pirates, the military cargo they have stolen and the two kids and the strange ship they disappeared on. I don't understand where they fit in to all this. But my guess is that if we find the pirates they won't be far behind. Also the ship they were on does not match anything the Treaty has seen before, which troubles me."

"It certainly is a strange situation. What puzzles me though is that Star Freighter that was with the pirates. Intelligence informs me that it was chartered to take a cargo for the Treaty. But are they working with the pirates or were they captured? Time will tell I guess," he replied as he stood looking out of the window in his office with a slight frown on his face. The view out of it was dark, which mirrored his mood.

Chapter Ten

The Rescue

Max was sitting in the pilot's chair on the bridge of Huntsman looking out at the comet they had been hiding behind. Every now and then there was a twinkle of light as bits of the comet hit their shields. Since their escape from the Sagaris and the near collision with the Ajax, Huntsman had hit light speed plus, and put as much distance between them as possible. They had been hiding behind the comet for two days whilst they decided what to do. The trail from the pirate ships had long since disappeared and they needed to come up with a plan. After many a discussion of good and bad ideas, it was Huntsman who said that they should head deeper into space and sit silently monitoring the radio waves to see if they could hear anything that might be of interest. After what felt like a lifetime of sitting there, they finally picked a signal from the Ajax to Treaty command saying that they had followed a ship to the Kalinian system and that they were waiting in orbit to see what the ship was up to.

Departing the safety of the comet and as fast as they could they headed towards the system to see for themselves what was of interest to the Treaty ship.

However, en route they picked up communications about the incident on the planet, and more importantly they also discovered that a wounded Cyclops trooper had been captured. This changed their plans. Also heading in their direction, apart from the odd fleeing ship was the Ajax, flying to a system called the Carweg which they had passed near to some time ago. Not wanting to be detected they decided to hide behind yet another comet for a while. Just then Steve, Ben and Hope joined him on the bridge.

"Have you seen the Ajax yet?" Ben asked as he took a seat next to Max.

"Not yet, Huntsman says it will pass by us in the next few minutes. Are the hoppers ready?"

"Yep," replied Steve in his usual nonchalant way.

"Hope, are you ok with what you have to do?" Max asked, as he fiddled with the controls.

"Of course, I am. Huntsman and I will come to your rescue. We have worked out a plan to disable the planet's defenses should we need to. But it will only give us a small window so you need to be quick once the alarms go."

The plan sounded simple but after the incident on the planet, the Kalinians would be on high alert. They had decided that the best way to find the pirates was by capturing the Cyclops trooper held there. As they were not from any system near here it was probable that it was something to do with the pirates. They had obviously gone there to trade, and perhaps that had gone badly wrong for them. Good news for them however!

Through scanning the radio waves, they had discovered that the Cyclops had been taken to a prison deep in the Kalinian desert. Just then Huntsman informed them that Ajax would be passing them now. The Huntsman powered down and the bridge descended into darkness apart from the eerie glow coming from the comet. Magnifying the view screen, they could now see the Ajax travelling at speed. Its sleek shape looked menacing as it flew over the top of the comet and disappeared on its mission.

"Huntsman let's go to Kalinian and get ourselves a robot," Hope said excitedly, and a big smile lit her brown face, her blue eyes twinkling. With that they peeled away from the comet and with a hum of the engines sped off on their mission.

Arriving at the planet they slowed down and Huntsman started to scan the surface looking for the prison, while Ben had started to map the positions of the drones that guarded the planet. Huntsman had distorted the ship's signal so it would be hard to detect them unless someone saw them, but they did have that back up plan Hope mentioned. Steve was down below getting the hoppers ready for when they landed. They would have little time on the surface due to the radiation. Although they would be wearing radiation suits that they had found, they did not know how effective they would be, due to their age, although Huntsman reassured them that they would be fine. Ben eventually found the frequency the drones used to communicate with the surface and prepared to jam it when everybody was ready. They were now in a giant orbit around the planet. In the distance they could make out other ships that had either just arrived or had remained after the previous mass exodus after the incident on the planet.

The planet's surface was bright yellow. Although they could not see them, there were radiation storms on the surface which would make landing all the more difficult, but everyone had every confidence in Hope and Huntsman landing as near to the prison as possible. Max and Ben wished Hope good luck and headed off down to get their suits on and join Steve.

The suits were exceptionally light and in no time they got them on and helped Steve into his. The helmets had large dark visors, but once on they could see clearly.

The hoppers were flat-bottomed as they had anti-gravity engines that made them glide over the surface. There was room for three people on each and you controlled them with handle bars. They were quite big for them, and they had to stretch but only because the people of Treig were big, so they said to themselves. They also had a couple of lasers mounted on the front which would help them should the need arise. After getting themselves ready they took a laser pistol each. Ben and Max helped Steve onto one of the hoppers, Ben sat behind him and Max got on the other one. They sat there and waited for the ship to land and the rear ramp to open.

…..

Hope meanwhile was having a fight of her own. The radiation storm gripping the planet had started throwing the Huntsman all over the place and it was proving hard to keep them on track. They were still thirty miles up and the winds were at least three-hundred miles per hour, gusting in pockets to five-hundred. Huntsman was finding it hard to track the winds because they were so erratic. Between them they managed for the best part to keep on course to the area where the prison was. The surface was bright yellow as was the sky around them. The windows and view screen had been dimmed so the brightness would not harm Hope or the others should they look out. As they neared the surface she told the others to get ready for landing. Looking out she could see a mountain range in the distance and could now make out the prison compound where the Cyclops trooper was being held. The structures were made up of single-story buildings in a circle and meeting in the middle, where a tall building rose with a dome. This had to be the control tower for the complex. There was no fence around the complex, probably because if any one escaped they would not last more than an hour or two in the harsh environment. The winds had died down as they neared the surface which made navigating a lot easier. Spotting a small gully about two miles from the complex, Hope instructed Huntsman to land and lower the rear door. She looked out of the side window in time to see her friends disappear on the hoppers over the rim of the gully in a cloud of dust. Now all she could do was sit and wait.

.....

The journey to the surface was far rougher than Max and the other two had expected. Max had been thrown to the side of the ship bruising himself in the process, so they decided the best thing was to sit on the hoppers and hold on. As they neared the surface they felt the ride getting better and just sat there waiting. No one really said anything as they were all feeling nervous and a little frightened. Max went over the plan again with Steve and Ben, who then told Max to stop worrying and leave it to them to create the diversion. The plan sounded simple: Steve and Ben were to attack the control tower and try and get the security guards to give chase, and cause havoc and disorientate the guards. While doing this, Max would enter the compound and go directly to where they had pinpointed where the Cyclops was being held.

Just then they felt the ship land and the rear door opened. The brightness from outside caused Max to blink, but just as quickly his visor darkened to filter out the light. Wishing each other luck they sped out of the Huntsman and made their way towards the complex. Max slowed down to a hover and watched as Steve and Ben raced across the surface towards the compound. As they got nearby, a high-pitched siren went off, Max could then see them open fire with their laser cannon at the control tower and watched the sparks and flashes coming off the building as it got hit. He could see the guards coming out of several buildings looking around to see what all the fuss was about. They started running around when one of them pointed out the hopper firing at the control tower. Those who had weapons started firing erratically and wildly in the direction of the hopper. Just then Max saw a couple of guards come out of a hanger on small, one-man, anti-gravity style bikes.

"Steve, Ben watch out behind you, there's a couple of guards on bikes heading towards you!" Max called out over the intercom.

"Thanks for that. We are off, over to you now. We will go in a big loop and head back once we have shaken them off," came Ben's excited reply.

With that Max saw them head off over the desert with six bikes in hot pursuit.

He powered up and made his way slowly towards one of the yellow buildings, all the time keeping an eye out for any guards. Looking at his control screen he moved along the wall looking into each cell until he came to the one which held the trooper. Reversing back he set the blaster to two bursts and blew a hole in the side of the building. With rubble and dust everywhere, he drove the hopper through the hole in the wall and stopped by a bed, on which sat the Cyclops trooper. His red combat suit was covered in blast marks from his battle earlier on, and was now covered in yellow dust. Max yelled at him, "If you want to live, get on the back and make it quick!"

Without moving he replied. "Who are you and why should I trust you?"

Max had turned the hopper around; he had no time for this question-and-answer routine and said again, "I have no time to explain, get on now or they won't ever let you go after this!"

Reluctantly the trooper stood up and went to look out through the hole in the wall; he was huge. After a while he came back and climbed on the back. With that Max shot out through the hole and came just as quickly to a sudden stop. Encircling him were about twenty guards, dressed in their turquoise one-piece suits, with laser rifles pointing at him; their white faces seemed to shine in the light and their many yellow eyes seemed to be boring holes into him. One of them walked forward and stood in front of the hopper.

"Dismount from your machine or I will order them to open fire!" The voice was loud and sounded menacing.

Max sat there feeling hopeless, he could feel the trooper shifting behind him but he said nothing. If he sped off they would open fire and with that many guns aimed at them they would not stand a chance. He looked out across the yellow surface towards where Huntsman was hidden in the haze of the planet surface. Looking to his left and right he could see other guards coming out of buildings watching the standoff. He felt hot in the suit and could feel himself sweating as he thought of anything that could count as a plan of escape. He tried calling Steve and Ben but their signal had to have been jammed. They had agreed beforehand that if anything went wrong then the remainder of the group must leave the planet and continue on the mission. The guard leader again ordered them to dismount from the hopper or they would open fire. Even if Max opened fire with his lasers they would not stand a chance so he had no choice but to dismount.

He climbed off and stood by the hopper's side and the trooper also got off and stood on the other side.

The guards started making their way towards them when Max noticed something moving fast close to the ground in the distance towards them. As it got nearer he could see that it was the others coming at speed, churning up a dust cloud behind them. The leader of the guard saw him looking beyond him and stopped and turned to see what he was looking at. With alarm in his voice, he pointed at the oncoming hopper. His guards immediately turned and started firing their weapons. Long beams of red light shot forward towards Ben and Steve who had started weaving around dodging the fire. While they were distracted Max jumped back on the hopper. Without needing to be asked the trooper did the same. He opened up the throttles and they shot off hitting the guard leader and sending him flying. The guard leader opened fire, with laser cannon rounds being fired far off into the distance, just missing them. Max fired at the guards sending them diving as he shot off over the top of them. The guards were now in panic as they were under fire from two directions. They were shouting at each other and were totally disorganized. Making the most of this he headed off towards a building and turning sharply, disappeared around the corner. They nearly hit three guards who were in front of them, but managed to miss them and with red laser beams flying passed them, they made it into the desert. Eventually Max felt they were a safe distance away and he slowed down to see if he could see where the others were. Eventually Steve and Ben pulled up alongside him with Ben pointing dramatically at Steve. Max could see that Steve was slumped over, there was a dark burn mark on his suit. He heard static coming through and then he heard Ben's voice coming through.

"Max, can you hear me?" came his frantic voice.

"I can, how bad is it?"

"I don't know!"

"Let's get back, Hope can you hear me?" Max called as he opened up the throttles and sped off towards Huntsman.

"I can, what's going on?"

"Steve has been hit; I have the trooper, but we got into trouble. Get ready to take off before we get into anymore. Try to find out what we have in the way of medical supplies, and hurry!" Max shouted.

He heard a moaning in his helmet and was relieved to know that Steve was still alive.

In what seemed like ages they eventually saw Huntsman in the distance. Hope had the ship hovering over the ground with the rear doors open. They flew into the back and the doors shut. Max jumped off the hopper and ran over to where Ben and Steve were. Together they got Steve off and laid him on the floor and took his helmet off. They pulled off his suit. There was blood scabbed on a wound on his left shoulder where he had been hit.

"Will you two stop fussing," he groaned.

"Let's get you to one of the rooms and have a look at this," Max said with concern in his voice as he looked at Ben. They had completely forgotten about the trooper who just stood there, silently watching them.

Max went to relieve Hope on the bridge.

"Where are we?" he asked her.

"We have moved about ten kilometers away. Where is the prisoner?" she asked.

"Oh no, I forgot about him. You go and look after Steve; I'll go and lock him up in the other room. Then I will get us out of here."

Chapter Eleven

The Plan

Tolet was happy to escape the planet unscathed. Two of his crew were injured and being treated and would make a full recovery.

He had also been ordered back to Mour's home planet Knapp to explain in person what he had been up to on the Kalinian planet. His superiors were not happy with him, as his actions could have caused a diplomatic incident between the two races. He was leaning on two of his hands, while eating and drinking with the other two. His communications officer, Oyb, came over with another signal from his superiors requesting a time of arrival. He had ignored all the previous communiqués to give him time to think. They had tried to chase the pirate named Black, but there were just too many ships that had left the planet and the system at the same time for them to have a chance of chasing him. Tolet had made plans to return home but had then heard that an injured Cyclops trooper had been captured. He decided that he would hide out in the system to see if the pirates would return and rescue their comrade.

After a long wait they eventually spotted a ship slow down from light speed and enter the system. He did not recognize it, and it did not resemble anything that they had on their ship's computer banks. It flew near to where they were hidden; fortunately he had activated the ship's masking device that would hide them from any radars. He watched with interest as the ship made its way through the planet's defenses and headed through a storm to the planet's surface. Strangely, it was moving away from the main trading cities, but possibly towards the prison where the Cyclops was being held. His hunch had paid off, now he sat there and waited.

....

After leaving the surface Huntsman encountered a few drones that had shot them up a bit, but thankfully no damage had been done other than a few cannon marks on the hull, the shields had held. The trooper was locked in a room and was just sitting there saying nothing. Once away from the system they would question him as to where he had come from and what he knew of the pirate attacks on his parent's ship and the Sagaris. Ben was with Max monitoring the communications station.

"Huntsman, keep an eye out to make sure we are not being followed and also if there are any other ships in the vicinity," Max said. He looked at Ben and himself. They were both still covered in the yellow dust from the planet. He was looking forward to a sonic shower and a change of clothes.

"I cannot detect anything following us, however I think we need to get as far away from here as possible, where would you like to go?" came Huntsman's reply.

"I don't know. You know space better than I do. Find somewhere where we can hide while we come up with a plan," Max said getting up, then resting a hand on Ben's shoulder, "I'm going for a shower and change, can you hold the fort till then?"

"No problem. I want to pop down and see Steve once we clear the Kalinian system."

.....

Huntsman had picked up speed and was nearing a small moon which had a deep green sheen reflecting from its atmosphere. Looking out of the window Ben thought he saw a ship in orbit. He checked the instruments and asked Huntsman if he had detected anything, to which he replied in the negative. Looking back out again Ben could not see anything. He rubbed his eyes, perhaps he was just tired. The ship accelerated away from the system and hit light speed plus. With that Ben left the bridge and went to check on Steve.

Steve was sitting up in bed and Hope was feeding him some soup. When he saw Ben come in, a broad smile appeared across his face from ear to ear.

"Nice to see you have recovered," Ben said sitting on the end of the bed.

"Yeah, I'll have to get shot more often. It still feels sore but that medical machine is good. Anyway, I have a good nurse," Steve said as he tried to avoid a friendly punch from Hope.

"If you don't behave, I'll lock you up with the prisoner," she replied.

"Speaking of which, has anyone spoken to him yet?" Steve asked.

"No, Max is cleaning up then he said he'll speak to him afterwards," Ben said.

"Well we can't leave him locked up all the time. Perhaps I'll take him some food," Hope said as she got up from the bed and started heading towards the door, which slid open to reveal Max, who had got changed into a black jumpsuit with a yellow T shirt underneath.

"That's better," he said as he stepped aside to let Hope out. "Where is she going?"

"To feed our guest," came the reply as Ben pushed past to follow her.

"Max, help me into my chair!" Steve shouted.

…..

Max and Steve arrived in time to see Hope handing the trooper a tray of food and drink. He didn't say anything but took it from

122

her. A small visor lowered in his helmet and he started to eat and drink noisily. The friends just stood there and stared, watching, until he had finished. Putting the tray down he stood up.

"Thank you for that. Now that you have captured me, what do you want from me?" he asked. His voice had no accent and was dead pan, if a little metallic. Max stepped forward and raising himself to his full height, although he still felt short compared to the giant in front of him, asked, "You were with a band of pirates on Kalinian?"

"Perhaps."

"Because we rescued you, we need you to help us in return," Max said defiantly.

"Why do you assume that you rescued me?" came the reply. "If I wanted to, I could overpower you and take your ship. You are no match for me."

Hope piped up. "Stop being silly. You know we rescued you, and that even if you overpowered us you would not be able to fly our ship," she said, sounding like a school teacher. Huntsman joined in, "I wouldn't let you!"

The Cyclops stood there silent for a minute looking down, then raising his head, and looking at each of them in turn said, "That is a good point I have to agree."

"So, answer our questions!" Steve said moving his chair within a few feet of him.

He stood still and lowered his head again, as if in thought. "If I help you, I will become alienated from my people. If they know I have helped you they will surely terminate me as I will be of no use to them."

Max walked around in a circle in the room. Everyone was watching him in silence wondering what he was thinking. He paused by the window looking out as stars, elongated passing by the window.

"Tell me, if they found out that you were rescued from the planet by unknown people what would they, your superiors, think?"

"That is a good question. I think that they would no longer want me and terminate me."

"If I could guarantee your safety, would you help us?" Max asked.

"I think that I have no choice. I admire the fact that you risked your lives to save me. What do you want to know?"

"Were you with a group of pirates who attacked and captured my parent's star freighter and attacked the Sagaris? And if so where are they?" Max asked with a little excitement in his voice.

Everyone was now shifting around in anticipation of the response. Everything was silent other than the slight hum from the engines as they raced through space.

"I was involved in that operation. I remember seeing you as I came out of the lift. You were fast," replied the Cyclops. He then sat back down on the bed and continued. "We were after some cargo that you were transporting. As we couldn't get it off the ship we took the vessel. For your information no one has been harmed. We were then informed that another cargo was on the other ship you mentioned so we attacked that as well. After leaving we hid out in a system called the Carweg and came here to find out what was happening as we had made errors."

"Huntsman where is the Carweg?" Steve asked.

After a moment's pause the reply came. "It's about one light year from here. As far as we know, it is a new planetary system. It would be ideal to hide in and hard to detect anything in there."

"Change course and take us there," Max replied. Then turning to the others, he said. "What are your thoughts?"

Hope was the first to pipe up. "It sounds dangerous. Why don't we go to the nearest Treaty base and tell them everything, then they could go and rescue your parents?"

"I don't think they would believe us," Steve said doing a little circle in his chair. "For a start they think we had something to do with the attack on the Sagaris. Secondly, even if we do persuade them what we are up to and they dispatch a fleet it may be too late and the pirates might have left. We have to go there ourselves before it's too late." He had excitement in his voice and a smile across his face at the thought of more adventure.

"Ben what do you think?" Hope asked turning to look at him.

He stood there deep in thought for a moment, running his fingers through his hair. "I think Max and Steve are right. We have to find them ourselves before it is too late."

"That's that then," Max said. He turned to the trooper who was still sitting on the bed. It was hard to see what he was thinking because of the helmet covering his face. Bizarrely Max noticed that the body armor had come clean again and was now back to its bright red and black as though he were brand new again. "What do you have to say? Will you help us when we get there?" Max asked him. "And can you take off your helmet so we can who we are talking to?"

"As I said earlier, I will help you, but I don't know where exactly they are. I am a soldier so I don't get involved in these things, but I will do my best." He stood up from the bed and everyone took a step back as they looked up at him; Steve went higher in his chair to remain at the same height as him. He continued. "Although you may think I am, as you put it, flesh and blood, I am not. We were specially created by the Carpathians. We are organic robots that have been formed around this armor. I am alive but not as you know it. I do not breathe but can think. I don't need to eat but if I want to I can. All the energy from the food can be stored in my power pack. My armor is also alive and can repair itself when damaged. We were created as fighting machines for the Carpathians. Although a devious race they have no compunction for a fight themselves so we do all their dirty work. There are others like me, for instance some of our attack ships are built along the same lines. They have no crew, but are like me, they can think and react. We are controlled by a central commander who reports to a Carpathian leader. If we disobey an order they can terminate us with a device buried inside us. So no, I can't take off my helmet."

They all looked at each other in silence. Then Ben asked, "How come they haven't terminated you?"

"At the moment I am not a threat. Also, I am too far away. Once they detect me on your ship and find out I am no longer on the planet they will do so."

"Can we remove it?" Ben added. Max could see Ben thinking hard, because one area of school Ben liked was the robotic labs.

"They say not."

Hope went and stood beside him and looked at the others. Brushing her curly hair out of her eyes, she said, "We have to help him." Then looking up at him, she asked, "Do you have a name?"

"I go by the name Squala."

"Can you show Ben where this device is, perhaps we can disable it?" Max asked him.

"I can show you, but I don't know what you can do."

Just then Huntsman joined in. "There are some scanners and laser tools on board stored down below, they may be of assistance to you."

"Good we'll leave Ben with you here." Then turning to the others he added. "Let's leave them in peace. We'll all go and see what we can come up with once we get to Carweg."

......

Tolet and his crew watched the ship leave the surface. After exchanging fire with some drones, it accelerated and passed near to where they had been hiding, so close in fact that they had to move around the other side of the moon in case they were spotted. As they came around again to his horror the ship had disappeared. His radar officer quickly informed him that they had jumped to light speed.

Tolet's ship was a big battleship that had been designed primarily as an attack ship. The Mours had many enemies due to the fact that they were a race of pirates. They took what they wanted and either kept their plunder or traded it on planets like Kalin, whose inhabitants were just as bad as them. The ship was not only designed for attack but was easily able to capture other ships. It had a central hull with a big orb shaped plasma engine at the rear. On eight pylons around the center of the hull were eight smaller ships that had two wings housing engines. In time of attack these could detach themselves to give Tolet nine ships including his. These were heavily shielded and armored. To him this little ship that had rescued the Cyclops would be no match for his firepower. He ordered his chief pilot Pictu to go to light speed and follow them. He hoped they would lead him to Black. If he could capture that cargo he hoped he would get a good reception back home, and maybe even a promotion.

He stood there looking out of the view screen at the kaleidoscope of light, a grizzly smile showing off his fearsome sharp blue teeth, as they gave chase and hunted their quarry.

.....

It took Ben no more than two hours to remove the device from Squala, which they then jettisoned into outer space. They joined the others in the observation room. Getting the device out of Squala had made their plans a lot easier, as Max had decided that if they were unable to remove it, they would be unable to get near the pirates without harming their new companion. He felt that they were getting near to finding his parents. Everyone's mood had changed and there was now excitement among them. They had been chatting and joking about all their friends finding out about their exploits during the holidays. They were also happy to have learnt that no one was harmed on the ship.

Max's one worry was his promise to Squala to protect him after the mission. If he handed him over to the Treaty they would surely pull him apart to find out about him. This horrified him and the others. However Max thought he had an answer, but he would not know for sure if it would be accepted; time would tell.

They were all now resting. He was lying there looking up through the window above at the elongated stars streaking past, Ben and Steve left to go and freshen up, while Hope was with Squala in his room.

Just then Huntsman's voice came over. "We have company. There is a ship closing in on us."

Max jumped to his feet and ran to the bridge. Just as he got there Hope and Squala arrived closely followed by Steve and Ben. Everyone was now wearing black overalls, and utility belts around their waists which had holsters for laser pistols, and also contained a multi-purpose laser tool.

"What have we got Huntsman?" Max asked taking the seat at the helm.

"There is a ship closing in on us and fast, it must have come from the Kalinian system."

Just then on the rear-view screen they could make out a large white vessel bearing down on them. On pylons around the hull were what they all thought were eight engines.

Then Squala said, "We are in trouble. That is a Mour battle ship. Those are not engines; they are eight smaller attack ships. From what I can see we will be no match for them."

"Who are the Mours?" Hope asked.

"They are a race of pirates in effect. They prowl the trade routes looking for ships to highjack and steal their cargo which they can then trade to other, how would you say it, less honorable races. They will launch those ships to surround us and disable our ship before taking us aboard their parent ship."

Everyone sat there in shock looking at the ship which was a lot closer now. It was gaining on them quickly.

"Huntsman, can we outrun them?" Max asked.

"No, I have scanned them, they are a lot faster than us and also they are heavily armed."

Max looked at Ben who was also looking at the scanners.

"No way," he replied shaking his head.

"They are trying to communicate with us," Huntsman said.

"Let's hear what they want then," Max answered, looking at everyone.

A heavy gruff voice boomed out through the bridge's speakers.

"My name is Tolet, from the planet Mours. You are to surrender your vessel to me, or I will destroy you. Please power down."

Max looked at everyone, his face was stern. "Well, what should we do? We can't outrun them."

"I think we should surrender for now. Maybe when we have spoken to them they might let us go. We don't have any cargo," Steve said.

"I agree with Steve," Ben said.

"Squala, what do you think?" Hope asked.

"I think he is right. I can hide here on the ship, and along with Huntsman's help we can devise a plan. They won't let you stay onboard. However we need to come up with something and fast!" he said pointing at the view screen.

Everyone looked round to see the eight ships detached from their pylons and with their engines glowing blue, speed up towards them.

"How do you plan to hide from them? If they search the ship they will surely find you, you are not exactly small," Max said with a hint of sarcasm in his voice.

With that Squala's legs slowly started to disappear into his huge body, his head receded into the top part, and his arms seemed to mold to his sides. He now stood about four feet high and just looked like a red and black box. Just as quickly everything came back to normal, and he stood there looking down at them. "That is my transport mode. When they want to move lots of us around we transform so we don't take up too much room."

"Brilliant!" Steve said.

"I've got to say that is cool," Max said with a little nervous laugh. Then he asked Huntsman to open a channel to the Mours ship.

"My name is Max. What do you want with us?"

"You may have something that I want on your ship. You are now surrounded. If you do not power down I will order my ships to open fire."

Max looked at everyone then replied. "We will do as you ask. We have nothing to hide. Once you have seen that will you let us go?"

There was no response. Max ordered Huntsman to come to a stop.

Hope had gone with Squala to help him to find a hiding place.

The others sat on the bridge and watched as massive doors underneath the Mours ship opened and then they were sucked up through them into a huge hanger. Looking out of their window they could see another couple of ships parked up and various boxes and containers stored around the outside. Huntsman lowered the landing gear and they came to rest. Some doors at the far end slid open and about two dozen

Mours came through. They were quite tall and very stocky and to everyone's surprise they had four arms. They were wearing some sort of uniform which was hard to see because it was blue, virtually the same shade as their skin.

"Come on, let's go," Max said to the others, and then to Huntsman. "Track us and keep getting data on this ship because we will need it later if we need to escape."

"Don't worry Squala and I will rescue you."

"That's what I am worried about," came his reply and with that they went down and lowered the doors.

Chapter Twelve

The Mours

All four of the friends were at the bottom of the ramp dressed in their black overalls. They had their utility belts on but left off the pistols and laser tools, not wanting to lose them. The hanger was very bright and they had to squint. There were now at least two dozen heavily armed Mour soldiers facing them. A huge soldier came towards them. He had four enormous arms hanging on his sides, and beckoned them with one of them to follow him, grunting that his leader Tolet wanted to speak with them. With that they were encircled by the guards and led through many corridors which were very brightly lit but drab looking. They passed hundreds of soldiers who just stopped and looked at them muttering to each other and pointing. Steve had a guard standing on the rear of his chair as they moved deeper into the ship. They eventually came to a lift that just about managed to squeeze them all in.

Max took the time to look at his guards. They were a little taller than him, but because they had big shoulders and four stocky arms they looked bigger than they were. Their skin was a deep blue and they had razor-sharp blue teeth; their eyes were also blue verging on black. Each one wore a heavy blue uniform with big black boots. The leader had two gold stripes down the left side of his uniform, which probably indicated his rank. Their skin looked sort of scaly, although he had to look closely to see this. But the most overpowering thing about them was that they stank like an old forest. Max tried to grab the attention of his friends but was hit in the back by a guard behind him with his gun. The lift eventually stopped and they were roughly pushed out and led along another corridor until they eventually arrived at a room. The doors opened and they were pushed in.

"Wait here," came the gruff order from the lead guard. With that two guards were left outside and the doors closed. Looking around the room there were no windows. The room was bright but Max could not see where the light came from. It was fairly small and there was a built-in bench on one wall. Like everything else he had seen it was a light blue. He guessed that they liked blue. Ben had gone over to the walls and was feeling along them looking for anything that may be hidden.

"Well folks, I don't know about you, but I have no idea where we are in relation to the shuttle bay," Steve said doing a little circle in his chair.

"Me neither. However, I am intrigued to find out who this Tolet character is," Ben said looking at his friends, and added, "well there is no obvious way out other than the way we came in. The walls are made of some smooth material that is warm to touch," he remarked, walking over to stand by Max.

"I'm scared. I don't know how we are going to get out of this," Hope added nervously.

"Well we will have to rely on Squala and Huntsman to come up with a plan. Maybe they are just going to ask us questions, and finding out we are no use to them will let us go. I think we will just have to follow along for now," Max said.

Little did the others know he had spoken with Huntsman and Squala and come up with some sort of plan that would hopefully get them back to the ship. He was however reliant on them to come up with an escape plan after that. Once they had he would get the signal. He had not told the others about it in case they got interrogated and revealed the plan under duress. Although he was also worried, he felt that they needed to see who these people actually were, and why they were so intent on capturing them.

"Well, Max, I have got to say that you don't mind stating the obvious now and then," Steve said with a little anger in his voice. He continued, "We are in a right fine mess. I hope that you have a plan because I for one can't think of anything."

"I think we should get some rest and await the next chapter in this little adventure of ours," Ben said stretching out on the bench.

. . . . .

Huntsman scanned the shuttle bay. There were ten guards encircling the ship. They stood motionless but were facing away. There were no other life signs there. He called out to Squala giving him the all clear to come out of hiding. The Mours had searched the ship for some time, but after obviously finding nothing of interest, had left. They had tried to lift the Cyclops trooper but finding him too heavy had left him. They obviously did not know what it was, which was a relief. Although Huntsman was only a ship he was able to think, and after being dormant for so long had been enjoying the mission to which he had been assigned. He also felt that these youngsters were in a way his responsibility and would do anything to help them. He could also detect that the machine called Squala felt the same, was in some way loyal to them for rescuing him from the clutches of the Kalinians.

Squala appeared on the bridge and leaned over the control panel to look out at the shuttle bay.

"There are ten guards down there. I have scanned the Mours ship and located them. They are about twenty decks above us at present. No harm has come to our friends," Huntsman said.

"Good. Have you come up with any ideas as to how we can get off this ship?"

"From what I can see they are heavily armed against attack but are ill-equipped against escape. They seem a very confident race, and once they have something it never leaves their clutches. There are however several weaknesses, one of them being that their primary computer system is located directly below us."

Squala stood motionless for a time, staring out at the guards down below, before asking, "If we can get to that and take it off line would it shut down the ship?"

"Probably for about ten minutes. I would say that they wouldn't suspect sabotage. Once they realized that there was a problem they would get the systems back on quickly. There are also backup systems throughout the ship but they are on standby and would have to be activated to run all systems."

"Let's come up with a plan to do that. Once we know we can do that we'll put Max's plan into operation," Squala said.

"There is one problem though," replied Huntsman.

"What's that?"

"We are headed towards the Mour's home world. We will arrive in their system in twelve hours."

.....

They had all been dozing when the doors opened and a detail of guards poured in and dragged them to their feet. One shook Steve and then jumped on the back of his chair. Just then the guard leader came in and told them they were to meet Tolet. With that they were marched off along the corridor. Again people stared at them until they arrived at a large office type room with huge windows. Looking out they could see at least three of the attack ships moored on their pylons. Standing looking out of the windows, with his back to them, was obviously this character Tolet. They stood in silence for a while before he turned round. He was dressed in a grander uniform than any of the others. Looking at the guard he ordered them to leave his office.

"Now I have some questions for you," he said looking at them.

It was hard to read his expression, but the ruthless looking smile on his face was enough to send a shiver down all of their spines. Max involuntarily shook and replied, "I don't know what you want with us. We are no danger to you or your people."

"Rubbish!" he shouted at them, spitting a bit of saliva onto the floor. "You went back to Kalin to rescue someone that you left behind. He is not here or on your ship, what have you done with him?"

"We never rescued anybody," Steve replied.

Tolet walked over to Steve, and leaning into his face with all four hands holding onto his chair, spat, "So you are saying to me that you went to all that trouble to get to the surface and returned empty handed?"

"Yes. We came under attack and had to leave."

He pushed Steve away and leaned down and looked at Hope, who took a step back. He then moved onto Ben and gripping him in two hands lifted him up. Max went to intervene but was pushed back with another hand and sent sprawling on the floor.

"So, what are you little ones doing out here in deep space on your own then? Don't tell me you wanted to go to Kalin on holiday!" he said with venom in his voice, shaking Ben.

Ben looked scared, he had saliva all over his face from Tolet's spittle and looked at Max who had just got up. Hope went and stood next to Tolet and said, "Leave him alone you bully!" She punched him. He looked at her and laughed, a deep guttural noise coming from deep within him. He threw Ben down and picked her up with her legs kicking him to no effect.

"Aar, a brave one, you have courage, little one. Now what are you doing out here?" he said pulling her face close to his. She could smell the stench of his breath in her face.

"We are on holiday and got lost," she replied with a little shake in her voice.

"You expect me to believe that your elders gave you a ship, and told you to go and explore space? Rubbish! Earthlings are weak and protect their young. I don't think so!"

With that he put Hope down, almost gently, and then walked over to Max.

"Now the truth! You are obviously the leader of this little band. Why did Black send you back to Kalin? Is he afraid to do his own dirty work?"

All four friends looked at each other quizzically. Why had he asked them about the Pirate? Max's mind went into overdrive, why had he mentioned him? He thought about his next question and looking Tolet in the eye responded.

"We don't know what you are talking about. Who is this Black person you are talking about? We don't do any dirty work, as Hope has told you we are lost on our summer holidays." He tried to keep his voice calm. His heart was racing, this was the first time that the Pirate's name had been mentioned. What was Tolet's interest in him? Max felt that he had a card up his sleeve.

"I don't believe you. I had a fight with Black on Kalin. He left behind one of his soldiers. I knew someone would come back, so I waited, and you lot turned up to make a rescue." Tolet was now pacing up and down and he looked agitated. This worried Max. For the short time that they had known him he figured that this was a person not to mess with.

"So, I'll ask again, why did Black send you back?"

They all looked at each other. None of them dared say a word in case they gave anything away. He then walked up to Tolet and asked him. "Who is this Black, and what is he to you?"

"Black has stolen a cargo, and I want it. You are to tell me where it is, or I will kill you. I will give you ten minutes alone to discuss your response. If I get the right answer, you leave, if not you die!" With that he turned and left the room.

There was now total silence. Stars were streaking by the window and a distant spiral galaxy came into view. Even at that distance due to their speed it slowly disappeared.

Max put a finger to his lips telling everyone to keep quiet while he had time to think what their next plan of action should be. He felt that the Mours leader was telling the truth and that their lives were very much in danger. He hoped that Huntsman and Squala would come up with a plan and soon. He beckoned everyone into a huddle.

"As we know from Squala, and from what we have learnt ourselves, this Black is responsible for Steve's Dad and my parents' capture. Also he is responsible for the attack on the Sagaris. This Tolet is obviously an enemy of Black's, or he wouldn't have gone to such great lengths to find him. My guess is that whatever was on the Sagaris and my Dad's ship is connected and, that being the case, they want the cargo for themselves," he whispered. Everyone nodded in agreement. "So how far do we go? If we tell him the truth about our mission it could work to our advantage, what are your thoughts?"

As usual, Steve was the first to speak. "I think that if we give him too much information, he might just kill us anyway. Why don't we tell him that we were attacked by pirates and that we were cast adrift? I don't think he needs to know that we are searching for Black. If he finds that out he might think we want the cargo for ourselves."

"I think he has a point," Ben replied, then continued, "these people are after all nothing worse than pirates themselves."

Steve was making a noise on his hover chair. It was not only hard for them to hear anything but Tolet in the next room was having trouble and getting frustrated. He hit his communications officer around the head.

"Get out of the chair and let me have a go!" Tolet yelled.

He tried working the panel in front of him, trying to listen in to what they were talking about. But no matter how hard he tried he could not hear their conversation. Getting even angrier he banged his four fists against the consul, breaking it and sending sparks flying everywhere. His radar officer came over the speakers next.

"We have company, Sir. We have picked up two Kalinian ships chasing us."

Now he got even angrier. "What do they want?" he yelled. His anger was starting to get the better of him, and he was going an even deeper shade of blue.

"Don't know. We have tried contacting them but they won't communicate."

"What ships are they?"

"They are Kalig class destroyers," came the reply.

"Detach the ships and go to high alert. See which other of our ships are in the area and get us some back up."

Kalig class ships were well-armed and would cause him serious damage. Tolet needed information and fast. Hitting the communications button, he asked Oyb to contact the home world to send reinforcements to their location. He did not like the situation and his superiors would punish him severely unless he had something to appease them with. He needed that cargo.

.....

Meanwhile onboard the Huntsman, both of them had heard the communication that had been going on internally, and the calls for assistance to the Mours home world. If they could have smiled they would have, as they had been desperate for a better plan than the one they had come up with. Now they both felt chance had landed in their lap.

.....

Unseen to the guards a small hatch opened up high on the hull of Huntsman, and four small combat saucers flew out and took station in the hold.

These saucers were not only armed but were able to link into Huntsman's shields and create a protective cover to form a passage way. Max's plan.

When they were in place Huntsman started to pulsate the hull of the ship. It started to glow a deep green sending the guards scurrying for cover. In alarm one of them fired his laser at the ship, which sent a ripple through the shields. The guard hit the intercom and asked for orders.

.....

They were all huddled around Steve, talking in low voices. Max was telling them of the plan he had worked out with Squala and Huntsman.

They listened intently. The plan would only work when they felt they had an opportunity to escape the Mours ship. They had been worried that had they got to the Mours home world, escape would be virtually impossible. Max had instructed them to look for a weakness within the ship, which would buy them enough time to escape. They had spotted an area of space called dead space that they would be passing near soon. If they could escape and enter this expanse they would have a good chance of disappearing from the instruments of the Mours' ship. These areas of space were uncharted, and most instruments did not function in these isolated pockets. Moreover, many ships had disappeared when entering, so most ships' captains stayed well away. Once a plan had been formed they would create a distraction, hoping that the guards would take the friends to the Huntsman. This was the tricky part of the plan.

.....

Oyb had gone to the cargo bay where the strange ship was. He had been ordered there by Tolet. He was not happy with this order as the two Kalinian ships worried him more. They were known to chase their quarry no matter where they were. He could only surmise that they held them responsible not only for the first incident in the bar, but also any further attack on the surface, and that they were now looking for answers. Tolet, he felt, was now letting his anger shadow his better judgment

146

and this could endanger the crew and the ship. He had served Tolet loyally for many a year and although he doubted his judgment he had to remain loyal.

When he got to the cargo bay what he saw frightened him, it was as if this ship was alive. It was pulsating in different shades of green, and moving from side to side, and backwards and forwards. He had personally led the search of the ship and they could find nothing of value on it. He had never seen a ship like it. Standing there looking at it, with his guards stationed along the walls with their weapons raised he wondered if it was indeed alive.

"What do we do? Every time we fire at it seems to get angrier," one of his guards asked nervously.

"Don't be silly, it is only a ship, send a boarding party on and find out how to switch it off before it does too much damage. Now hurry!" he commanded.

With that, four guards rushed towards the rear of the ship, where the ramp was still lowered. As they got near, the ship started to turn, one of the guards had dived for the rear ramp, only to hit the shielding and get thrown across the hold and hit the far wall. In panic some of them opened fire with their lasers, which just sent ripples through the shielding. The ship now started to spin gaining speed and getting so fast that it became a blur. The remaining guards panicked and fled into the safety of the corridors, followed by Oyb who also did not want to hang about. Calling Tolet on his communicator, he relayed to him the events unfolding in the cargo bay.

·····

Tolet was back on the bridge monitoring the two Kalinian ships that were approaching them. They had now slowed down and were following them at a distance of twenty thousand kilometers. Between them and his ship were four of his attack ships keeping rear guard as they continued towards the home world. He had heard from central command that a ship was on its way to help him, under the command of a man called Toof. This had calmed him down a little as he and Toof were old comrades. Tolet ordered Oyb to get the prisoners down to the cargo bay. He did not want any more damage to be done to his ship. If they did not sort out their ship he would kill them, and then go and find Black alone. After leaving his orders, he made his way down to the cargo bay.

·····

The door burst open, and Max turned round to see a dozen guards enter the room, led by the slightly smaller figure of the character he learned was called Oyb.

"What do you want now?" Max asked.

"You are to come with me. Your ship is behaving strangely. You're ordered to stop it or we will kill you."

"Don't be stupid, how can a ship act strangely?" Hope replied, only to be grabbed roughly by a guard and shoved towards the door. She looked back and gave them all a wink.

They were led down corridor after corridor back to the cargo bay where Huntsman was kept. Max noticed that the Mours ship seemed to be on a high state of alert. Everywhere they went armed Mours were rushing around not even giving them a second glance. Max was walking by Steve and asked him, "Something seems to be happening. Huntsman can't have caused this, what do you think?"

"Don't know, everyone seems to be nervous. It looks to me as though they might be under attack. There are just too many of them running around armed," was Steve's reply.

Max got a shove in his back and was told to stop talking. Oyb signaled for everyone to halt and came up to him.

"I want you to go in there and stop your ship from wrecking my cargo bay."

"Unless we all go in there, I don't know what to expect. You will have to come in with us," Max replied.

"That ship is crazy; it has nearly killed four of my men. You and you alone will go in there, the rest of your friends will remain here, now go!"

With that the doors opened and he was shoved inside. However, nobody noticed the two small discs entered the corridor passing him as he went into the cargo bay.

Max stood there and looked at the ship, which was now hovering in the cargo bay. He looked around and noticed two guards stationed on the far wall with their weapons aimed nervously at him. The cargo bay was a mess with containers lying all over the place, some broken, spilling their contents out on the floor. One of the other ships that was in the hold had been slammed up against the far wall on its side. Its hull was dented and its black paintwork scratched. Max had hoped that they would all come into the bay together, simplifying their escape but now things were a bit more complicated. He approached the rear ramp of Huntsman. As he did he noticed that Huntsman started to glow and move around erratically. More than once he had to dive for cover as cargo was sent flying around. Eventually he managed to get a grip on the ramp and haul himself inside. Just as he did this one of the guards followed him and they both stood up facing each other. The guard had his weapon raised at him.

"Take me to the bridge, one false move and I will kill you."

He said that with such menace in his voice that Max had no option but to obey. Leading the way, they entered the bridge. He felt the weapon being prodded in his back.

"Now turn this ship off," the Mour guard snapped.

"I don't know how. As I said to your commander we found this ship and don't really know how it works," he said turning towards his guard.

"Well, I suggest you start to learn, and quickly!"

Max saw Squala enter the room behind the guard and without hesitation hit him on the back of the head, and the guard collapsed on the floor.

"Huntsman, what is going on? You nearly killed me out there?" Max shouted angrily as he headed towards the bridge.

"Well thank you too," came the reply, in what could be perceived as a sarcastic tone.

Before Max could reply Squala answered the question.

"We had to make it look real to get you on board. Our plans have somewhat changed." Squala had now walked round to face him.

"We have been monitoring their signals and communication. There is another one of their ships heading this way. Behind us there are two Kalinian ships on an intercept course that is worrying them after the Mours attacks on their planet. We had to do something fast to get you here before it is too late. We think that they will be under attack any moment now and this is going to be our only chance of escape."

Max stood there in silence as he let the information sink in. He looked out of the window to see the other guard cautiously making his way towards the rear ramp, he was talking to someone through his communicator, obviously to the Oyb creep outside. Huntsman powered up again and started to spin sending the guard running for cover.

Max looked at Squala. "What plan do you have in mind? For a start we need to get the others into the cargo bay to stand any chance of rescuing them."

"As you said earlier in your plan, we have sent some combat discs out into the cargo bay, there are now two in the corridor waiting for their next command, look." With that he looked at the view screen to see an image of his friends and the guards waiting in the corridor. Their weapons were no longer pointing at the friends and he could see Oyb talking in an animated manner to someone.

"Brilliant, I knew they would come in handy. Anyway, what is the plan now?" Max asked.

"I have managed to access the ship's systems and we should be able to open the cargo bay door. We will only have one chance at this. Once they know we are in their systems, we will be shut out. The discs will then cover Steve, Ben and Hope in a protective shield and open fire on the guards. We will be able to maintain the shield from here. I have modified the disks for this task. Once on board we will escape. We think that with the Kalinians hot on their tail they will be more focused on them than us."

"Wow, I've got to say that is ambitious. Have you not thought that the Kalinians might also attack us?" Max replied with a hint of fear in his voice.

It was now Squala's turn to reply. "We have no choice. If the Kalinians attacked they could destroy not only the Mours ship, but us as well. Or if the other Mour ship arrives in time we will be taken to their home world. Once there, escape will be virtually impossible. This is our only chance."

After a pause, Max answered, "I get your point, let's get started then."

.....

Steve was sitting there watching all the commotion going on around him. The guards were getting more nervous, and their leader Oyb was communicating with Tolet about some Kalinain ships that were approaching. He looked at Ben and Hope and mouthed "are you ok?" to them. They nodded and smiled in reply. Just then the doors slid open to the cargo bay, catching everyone by surprise, and cutting short Oyb's conversation. "Who opened the doors?" he shouted at his men. They all shrunk back and shrugged their shoulders. Ben pointed excitedly towards where Huntsman was. Standing on the rear ramp was Max shouting at them and waving for them to run towards him. Steve looked up to see the two discs appear above them and emit a translucent shield around them and then the discs started to fire lasers at the guards. Panic set in as they were caught completely off guard. Some of them opened fire at them but the shields just absorbed their shots. Oyb was hit by one of the lasers and got thrown against the wall. He slumped down on the floor shaking his head as another guard got hit and was sent skidding on his back down the corridor. Before they could get their bearings the three friends headed towards Max as fast as they could with the discs following them. The doors slid shut, just as one of the guards gave chase trapping him. The remaining guard in the hanger opened fire at Max hitting the side of Huntsman. Squala appeared and levelling his pistol fired at him knocking him over a crate.

"Come on, you lot, we don't have much time, quick!" yelled Max.

The noise in the cargo bay was getting deafening as Huntsman powered up the engines. Everyone made it on board, and Squala dumped the unconscious guard on the cargo bay floor before raising the ramp.

They all made it to the bridge and Max took his seat at the helm while Ben sat at the communications station.

"What's the plan now?" Hope asked.

"We are going to blow a hole in the side of the Mours ship and escape, we did get into their systems to open the door for you but they have blocked us again, so blasting a hole is the only thing we can do," Max said as he concentrated on the controls. "Ready when you are."

With that Huntsman began to turn on himself as Max worked the controls, a targeting pattern appeared above the command consul, which was the sights for the forward laser cannon. Max looked round to Steve. "Get ready to fire on my command."

"Will do," came the hesitant reply.

"Everyone hang on and buckle up!" Max ordered.

Just then the Mours ship shuddered violently which in turn threw Huntsman around.

"What happened?" Max asked.

"They have just come under fire from the Kalinian ships."

They all looked at each other, and Squala said, "It's now or never, time is running out."

Bringing Huntsman back under control Max ordered Steve to fire the cannons. Huntsman shuddered as the cannons were on full power. A huge explosion appeared in front of them, he fired again, and a huge hole appeared in the wall. All the debris got sucked out into space along with all the cargo in the hold, Max powered up and they shot forward through the hole; they cleared the Mours ship, and there was debris floating everywhere. Max turned Huntsman around and they followed the side of the Mours ship while they got their bearings. They could see the Kalinian ships in the distance firing on the Mours ship. In turn the smaller Mours attack vessels were weaving in and out firing back. Huntsman shuddered as they too were fired upon.

"Where's that come from?" Steve yelled.

"From the Mour's mother ship," Ben replied, adding. "Our shields are holding for now."

"Huntsman, is there anything else around to surprise us?"

"We need to get past the Kalinian ships, and head back the way they came. We won't be able to take too many more direct hits from their cannon." As Huntsman finished talking they were hit again, sending them in a spin, Max powered up, and started to zigzag away from the Mours ship. As soon as they cleared it he headed towards the fire fight that was going on between the Mours and the Kalinians.

Ben shouted a warning that they had picked up a Mours battle ship on their tail and it was closing fast. It opened fire and they saw a streak of laser cannon go past them as Max swerved. They were closing in on the first of the Kalinian ships when they were hit again. Sparks flew from the consul and smoke started to fill the bridge.

"Huntsman, divert more power to the shields!" Max yelled waving an arm in front of him to get the smoke away from his eyes.

Steve meanwhile had started firing the rear cannon at their pursuers. They could all see in the viewer as he hit the battle ship. It slowed it down enough for them to get some more distance. But not for long, the battleship started to speed up again firing at them even more rapidly. Huntsman was taking even more hits now, all the lights on the control panel were beginning to flicker as they took hit after hit. Steve kept up, firing at the ship, but their shields were too strong for their weakening cannons.

Max looked around at everyone, he could barely make out Hope through the smoke. She was sitting on Squala's lap who held on to her tightly.

He then turned around just in time to see the Kalinin ship open fire. At first he thought they had missed them until he realized that they were aiming not at them, but at their pursuers. An audible sigh of relief and tension seemed to float around Huntsman as they saw their attackers take a direct hit. The Kalinian ship flew straight over the top of them towards its target.

With that Max opened up the engines and they headed out into deep space leaving them to their battle.

Chapter Thirteen

Battle in the Carweg System

The Ajax had slowed down from light speed and was cruising slowly towards the outer edges of the Carweg system. The system itself was relatively small and was in its infancy. In the center was a small sun shining brightly, while circling it was a huge asteroid belt that looked a bit like the rings around Saturn. It would be many millions of years before any planets finished forming around it.

It was a spectacle that Captain Bainbridge would never tire of looking at. The sun was about one hundred million kilometers from their position and they were now coming to a stop on the edge of the outer belt.

His tactical and radar officers were working at ways of trying to detect if there were any ships hiding in the system. His tactics officer, a small slight man from Titan with olive skin, had made ready a recon drone which he wanted to launch to see what information they could gather without jeopardizing the safety of the Ajax.

"Sir, I think I can pick up a ship following us. It is at the extremities of our sensors," his radar officer called out.

"What do you think it is?" he asked, swiveling around in his seat.

"Don't know for sure. I thought I recognized the signature, although I don't know where it was from. It is too far away from us at the moment. I'll keep an eye on it in case it's a threat."

"Good work," he replied, then he got up and went over to the tactics station. "Is the drone ready yet, Tug?"

"Ready when you are," came the reply.

"Fire."

Everyone on the bridge watched as the drone sped up to the edge of the rocky belt. It stopped for a minute while it looked and scanned for a route, then sped off and disappeared from view.

"Keep me up to date with its progress," Bainbridge added.

He sat down next to Jim who was monitoring the scanners looking at the ship that was closing in on their position.

"What do you think?"

"Can't make it out, it's still too far away. I think it is heading this way but not on an intercept course with us. Wait a minute,"

Jim suddenly shouted with alarm, he called over to the radar and sensor officer. "Can you see that?"

"Yes Sir I can. It looks like another ship has appeared and taken the other ship on board somehow. It is now changing course and moving away from us. I don't think we need to worry about it anymore. I'll carry on scanning that region in case they return," came the reply.

"Must have been a transport ship or something," Jim said to Captain Bainbridge.

"I guess so. Anyway, I thought it was an odd thing to be happening this far out in space, well keep an eye on it for now just in case they return. Helm move us forward slowly let's start tracking the drone and see if we can find ourselves something to get our teeth into."

.....

Further inside the system Black was having trouble of his own navigating through the inner asteroid belts. His fleet had moved deeper inside while he had been away. He eventually caught sight of the captured star freighter illuminated on one side from the glow of the sun. Shadows were moving constantly as floating chunks of rock moved around on their orbit. He could now make out his other marauders and Mu's menacing looking ship, with its small winglets heavily laden with weaponry.

He had ordered the fleet to move further in after his scanners had picked up what they thought might be a ship following them. To his horror they identified it as the ship that came to the rescue of the Sagaris. What the hell was that doing this far out in space, and how had it managed to track them? He reasoned that perhaps they were just following anything at random, otherwise why had it not tried to catch them, or maybe their sensors did not have the range to pick them up. He felt that that was highly unlikely though, considering it was a long-range state of the art space cruiser.

He stood there watching as his pilot navigated the ship through the asteroids, the glare from the distant sun dancing off their surfaces. They had lost sight of the fleet as they had gone behind a large asteroid that was still glowing red with larva. As they passed close by he could see the surface bubbling away. Just as they passed it, he could see Mu's ship directly in front of them. His pilot took them on a path underneath the ship, as they slowed and docked with another one of his marauders.

He had called a meeting on board his ship to discuss their strategy, and now with a Treaty ship near to their location they needed a plan, and fast, if they were to stay ahead. He was also getting annoyed that Nino Bassi had not made contact with them now that they had his prized cargo.

All he wanted to do was get rid of it, collect his gold, and get back to base.

Although the reward was good for this mission the risk was far too great.

.....

Nino Bassi had been approaching the system at the same time as Black. He had been following him at a distance waiting for him to rejoin his ships. His Cyclops leader Mu had told him that they now had all the cargo and gave him the coordinates of the pirate fleet in the Carweg system. Mu had also brought him up to date about all the problems that they had encountered on Kalin. Nino thought to himself how uncouth these people were and was glad he did not have to deal with them on a daily basis.

He would catch them unawares, transfer the cargo and leave them to their own devices. He had great plans for this cargo he had captured. It would make him a hero in his home world. He sat back and closed his eyes, picturing the crowds welcoming him back, his superiors showering him with wealth.

An alarm sounded on his consul, disturbing Nino's thoughts. Sitting up he knew instantly that his sensors had picked up another vessel in the area. Fiddling with his controls he located the vessel and magnified his view screen to see the image of a Treaty ship some distance out also heading towards the system. Very interesting, he thought to himself. He quickly slowed his vessel down as he decided what to do next. They must be following that idiot Black after his escapades on Kalin. Judging by their speed they seemed more curious than anything, otherwise they would have attacked the pirates by now had they any idea who they were, and more to the point, where they were. A small evil smile crossed his face as a plan started to form, maybe this situation might play out to his advantage after all. He now came to a halt. He could now see the whole disc of the system in front of him, stretching away as far as the eye could see. In the middle of the disc was the new forming sun. Again, his alarm sounded. Magnifying, he picked out a small chubby space craft being pursued by another bigger craft. Nino sat back and decided to watch this event unfold. It was hard to see too much because of the distance, they were still some million kilometers away. This area of space seemed to be quite busy at the moment. He hoped no one else would be popping by as this might completely mess up his plans.

To his astonishment the bigger ship seemed to eat the smaller one, it then turned around, hit light speed, and disappeared. He then turned his attention back to the Treaty ship. It was now stationary and had fired a probe into the system. They were obviously hesitant to enter and were being cautious about their next step. He recognized the actions of an experienced commander. Nino would have to be careful during his next moves.

.....

Captain Black stood in his office. With him were Rolfe, Klad, and Mu, plus two of his officers from the fleet, an Ovarian called Cro, who was a giant of a man with black scaly skin, and Vista who came from a mining colony on Neptune. He was a small person but was well-built and strong. They were hardy people and totally ruthless.

"Well gentleman, we seem to be getting nowhere fast. We seem to have a Treaty vessel following us everywhere. This mission is turning into a nightmare. Mu where is that leader of yours? I want rid of this cargo, and fast!" His voice was calm, but inside he was getting frustrated.

Everyone turned to look at Mu.

"I have spoken with him, and he is on his way to meet with you. I have told him where we are and he will be here soon."

"When did you speak with him?" Rolfe asked angrily with a glint in his coal black eyes.

"Earlier today," came the reply.

"Why didn't you tell me this sooner?" Black shouted at him and pounded his fist on the table.

"I didn't think I should until I knew when he would arrive. He also told me not to tell you."

"Great," Black replied.

He stood there thinking for a minute then asked Cro if they could get the cargo from the Sagaris onto the captured freighter.

"I can have it there within the hour."

"Good, do it."

"Why do you want to move it there?" Mu asked.

"Because when your illustrious leader turns up, and we complete the business, he can take it away on that and relieve me of another problem."

"He won't agree to that," Mu said with menace in his voice.

"Tough. I don't like people sneaking up on me either," he replied with a smile on his face. Turning to Cro and Vista he asked them to start planning a safe route back home for them and then told everyone to leave.

.....

Ten minutes later, after it was confirmed that Mu had returned to his ship Rolfe, Cro and Vista returned.

"Now then, down to business. Hopefully Mu will report back to Bassi what our plans are. Now let's change them."

"What are you thinking?" Vista asked.

"I don't trust him as far as I can throw him. He will be planning to trick us that's for sure. I want to split up the fleet. Cro, I want that cargo moved to your ship. Get a team of people to make a dummy cargo so we can fool them with that. I know that the cargo on the freighter is heavy, and I don't care how you do it but I want it moved. Once on board you are to depart with vista and his ship, and five others and work your way through the system and head towards the Rowse Nebula and hide out there. If he has anything devious up his sleeve I want insurance."

"We are on to it," came the joint reply. With that they left on their mission.

"Don't you think we are treading on dangerous ground? If he thinks we are deceiving him, we might end up with more than we bargained for?" Rolfe asked as he marched up and down the office.

"Maybe, but I don't trust him. He knows what's been going on but he hasn't contacted us till now, and only because we asked Mu. I don't like it."

.....

Captain Bainbridge was at the radar station. They were looking at the data coming back from the probe. Although distorted here and there with static they could not find anything. He did not like it; the only way was to take Ajax in deeper. He was convinced they were on to something and his curiosity was getting the better of him.

"Jim put us on high alert, we are going to take a look deeper into this system."

"Are you sure, Sir?"

"We aren't getting much from the probe, so it's time to take a closer look."

"Helm, take us in, set our speed at 250,000 kilometers an hour," Jim commanded.

"Tug, keep all weapon systems ready."

"Yes Sir."

Bainbridge watched as they started to gather speed and head deeper into the system. Lumps of molten rock and small asteroids started to whizz by them, some smaller ones hitting their shields that sent a shimmering blue ripple through them as they glanced off. There was tension on the bridge as everyone went about their duties. They were flying into the unknown, but at the same time they were all now keen to make the mission a success and retrieve the stolen cargo and hopefully capture those involved.

Jim was at the radar station watching the scanners with the stations officer, a female called Diam, when they noticed a small ship coming up behind them and fast. It was instantly recognizable as a Carpathian cruiser. It was going dangerously fast for this area and risked collision. However, Jim could see that it was being flown expertly as it weaved in and out of floating debris.

"Sir, for some reason there is a Carpathian ship closing in on us and fast," Jim called out to his captain.

"What on earth is that doing out here? Tug, track it, and keep your cannons locked on just in case," the captain ordered. He then walked over to Jim and whispered in his ear. "I wonder if they are behind the hijacked cargo. It would be the sort of thing they would get up to. They would certainly get someone to do their dirty work. Put it on the screen."

With that, the fast-approaching ship appeared. It was long and slim with four laser cannons in its nose. To the rear were two engines emitting a red glow as it sped towards them. The ship was no match for the Ajax in terms of fire power, but it was a lot more agile because of its size. It did not take long to overtake them. As quickly as it came it disappeared into the system, the glow of its engines disappearing in to the distance.

"Pilot follow that ship and stay on its tail," came the command as the captain took his seat.

.....

Nino Bassi was impressed at the size of the Treaty ship. He knew it carried formidable weaponry, and that it also had a squadron of attack tanks on board. In fact, he was counting on that. Mu had contacted him to say that the pirates were getting restless, and that they were planning on moving the cargo from the Sagaris to the captured freighter. He also had noticed that some of the pirate fleet had now departed the system, although he did not know where they were going. Nino had ordered him to place more guards on the freighter to protect the cargo. He must not lose that at any cost. He was also losing his patience with Black; he was obviously up to no good.

Eventually he saw the huge delta winged cargo ship loom in to view. Encircling it were seven of Black's marauders and a little distance away was Mu's ship. He slowed down and without request went to dock on Black's ship.

.....

Black's scanners had picked up Bassi's ship some way out and he watched it as it slowed down and docked with his. They had also picked up the Treaty ship and were surprised to see Bassi fly so close to it, as if leading them on. Then it dawned on him and Rolfe that was exactly what he was up to. His instinct had paid off. However how long he could last he did not know, only that he was now treading dangerous ground. He was aware that Mu had sent more guards to the freighter, and hoped his decoys would hold up for now. Mu was sitting with him in his office when the doors opened and Nino Bassi walked in with Rolfe close on his tail.

"Ah, Captain, good to see you again. I gather from Mu that you have had an adventurous time retrieving the cargo I am paying you for?" Nino said with a little smirk on his face. He walked over to the table and fixed himself a fruit drink, sipping it, his face screwed up, it was far too sweet for him, but after his long journey it was refreshing enough.

"Adventurous isn't the word I would use. This whole mission has been nothing but a nightmare, as you well know I am sure," he replied with venom in his voice, looking at Mu. "Apart from the fact that I attacked a cruise ship, had a close call on Kalin, and now I have a Treaty ship closing in on my position, no thanks to you, leading them towards me. Why the hell did you do that unless you have an ulterior motive?!" he finished by slamming his fists on his desk.

"If I had an ulterior motive, Mu and his troopers would have killed you by now. I am not happy about the way you have acquired this cargo. What should have been a simple task has now turned into a farce."

"No thanks to your trigger-happy friends. How on earth can it be a simple task when we have to attack a cruise ship? I have put the cargo on the freighter. When you have handed over my payment you can have the freighter and we will go home. I never want to do business with you again. My debt is now cleared."

"I will decide when your debt is clear, not you, now where are my cargo?"

"I told you on the freighter, where is my payment?"

An alarm interrupted them, Black looked at Rolfe, who ran over to the consul on the desk.

"I think you need to look at this," he said to Black, who rushed over to have a look. Alarm spread over his face, as he hit the communicator. "How far away is it?"

After a moment, the reply came. "It's about 100,000 kilometers away. It has spotted us and is closing fast. They will arrive in about thirty minutes."

Black cut the call and turned on Bassi, Mu had stood up and had drawn a laser pistol.

"Why did you lead them to our location?" then turning to Rolfe, "Get the fleet ready to depart, and put them on battle stations, we might have to fight our way out!"

Rolfe went to leave but Mu covered him and told him to stay where he was.

Black then hit an alarm button and instantly the doors opened and five of his crew entered the room, heavily armed. Outside they could hear fighting and then three Cyclops troopers also entered the room, they were now at an impasse.

"As you see I also have back up. Now I am going to leave with my cargo. If you try and stop me, Mu's ship will open fire on your fleet."

"That would be suicidal. His ship, although powerful, is no match for my marauders. You have double crossed me and I will not let you leave till I have my payment."

Without warning and capturing Black and his crew completely by surprise the Cyclops guard opened fire, hitting one of his guards and sending them all diving for cover. At the same time his ship shuddered as it came under fire from Mu's ship. Alarms started sounding throughout the ship, his guards had started returning fire, but they were pinned down, Black contacted the bridge and ordered them and the fleet to start returning fire and get ready to leave before the Treaty ship arrived, he did not want too many battle fronts opening up.

Bassi, Mu and the guards had now made it to the doorway. Black looked up to see laser fire ripping through his room smashing everything they came into contact with. Bits of furniture were flying around, smoke had started to also fill the room from a fire that had been sparked, another one of his men was hit and he fell to the floor groaning. He looked out of the window behind him and saw one of his marauders engage Mu's ship with laser cannon, but it just bounced off the shielding; it then banked steeply to miss the return fire.

Bassi had now made it to the corridor and with him were his troopers running towards the docking port and his shuttle. Black with Rolfe and the remainder of the guard gave chase, firing at the fleeing Carpathian, but it was too late, they made it. The doors slid shut and they heard the whoosh of the ship departing.

Black made it in time to the bridge to see the departing ship, along with Mu's and the freighter. Thankfully they had got all of their own crewman off in time. To his surprise they were heading straight for the Treaty ship. They then opened fire on it and turning around headed straight back towards his fleet's location. The Ajax, in response returned fire, and started to pick up speed in pursuit of the Carpathian ships and the freighter.

His crew was now doing what they did best in a crisis, they were at battle stations and were turning away from the immediate threat. He could see his remaining fleet of twelve ships doing the same. However, they were not fast enough and Ajax was catching up fast. It had now launched eight of its attack tanks and they had joined in the battle. With no choice Black ordered half his fleet to turn about and attack.

.....

Bainbridge and his crew were not only surprised to see the Carpathian ship, but they were also dismayed to see it rendezvous with what they thought must be the pirate fleet. He was concerned that they were being led in to a trap.

Why would they fly so close to the Ajax and then lead them directly to the pirate fleet? He had seen the Carpathian ship dock with a large ship and they could make out another thirteen ships including a delta winged cargo freighter. Bainbridge felt excited, this must be the ship that was seen by the Sagaris crew and the one chartered by the Treaty to transport the military cargo.

"Jim, how long before we can intercept?"

"About twenty minutes at our current speed. It is difficult navigating because of the debris."

"Can we get a better view of this fleet?"

"It's quite hard due to the volume of debris around."

"Use our cannons to start blasting our way through."

With that Ajax picked up speed. It was weaving around large asteroids while at the same time blasting smaller ones in its path. They were now the hunters closing in on their quarry.

After fifteen minutes they could now clearly see the ships in front of them.

"Sir, look!" came a voice from the bridge.

All eyes looked as they saw another Carpathian ship starting to open fire on the ship which the other Carpathian ship had docked. Immediately a smaller vessel moved away from the fleet and attacked it, swerving just in time to miss the return fire.

The Carpathian ship then undocked from the pirate ship and along with the other ship and the freighter headed towards them at speed.

"Signal battle stations!" Bainbridge shouted as they headed towards them and started to open fire. The Ajax rocked slightly as their shields took the fire. In the distance the pirate fleet started to power up and move away from their approach.

"One troop launch," Jim commanded. And with that they saw on their screen eight of their battle tanks come into view. Immediately the Carpathian ship and its other ships turned and headed back. The tanks opened fire at them. With that ten of the pirate ships turned round and started opening fire, both at them and the other ships.

"Sir, our ships are taking heavy incoming fire, their shields are holding for now."

On the screen Bainbridge and his crew saw a pirate ship weave through the tanks and head straight for them, firing its laser cannons. The Ajax shuddered under the onslaught.

"Weapons stations target that ship, before it does us damage."

Blue bolts of light shot towards the enemy. It started swerving sideways as the cannon fire passed it by harmlessly and it was still firing at them. Some of the shots from the Ajax's cannon were now hitting it but were being absorbed by its shields.

"Damage report?" Jim shouted.

"Our shields are holding but if it gets too close it could cause us damage," came the reply.

An attack tank had seen the pirate ship firing on the Ajax and had turned round to give chase firing its cannon in reply, hit the target's rear engines and an explosion followed. With no power but with its speed intact it headed straight for them. Ajax started to try and move away from it but it was too late. It hit the front of the Ajax and exploded. The force of the impact rocked Ajax and anyone standing got flung to the floor. The collision warning alarm had started going off.

"What's the situation?" the captain called out to the officer in charge of the ops station.

"It has hit our forward section, damaging our sensors and radar. From what I can see we only have light casualties. Medical and fire teams are on their way. Our forward shields are also down."

Looking out they could see a full battle going on. The attack tanks were fighting with the pirates, who in turn were trying to destroy the Carpathian ships and the freighter. These were trying to leave the battle and head in to open space.

"Jim, contact the lead tank and see if he can disable the freighter, or at least get a locator beacon on it so we can track where it goes to. Pilot, move us closer into the battle, I want to try and destroy that lead pirate ship," Bainbridge ordered.

Through the viewer he could see the fire on the front of the Ajax as the oxygen escaping fueled it. Suddenly the fires started to die down as the emergency bulk head doors closed.

They were now heading into the fray, occasionally getting hit as pirate ships managed to get the odd shot in. One of their attack tanks took a direct hit to its engines and came to a stop. Its cannon turret however carried on firing and turning, tracking the ship that hit it. Eventually the pirate ship exploded in a big ball of fire.

Their laser cannons had now locked on to the lead pirate ship and opened fire. Its shields rippled and the ship turned nearly hitting a stray asteroid, which then exploded from another shot from the Ajax. The pirate ship returned fire, aiming for the weak front of the ship causing even more damage.

"Sir the lead attack tank has reported that they hit the freighter, although the damage is light, however they didn't manage to get a tracking device locked on."

"Never mind. Good work though."

They then saw the three ships accelerate away directly upwards and hit light speed.

With a final flourish the pirate ships re- grouped up and fired off a load of space mines, before departing the scene with six of the remaining attack tanks giving pursuit. One of them hit a mine and spiraled away.

"Call back the tanks and get a rescue vessel out there to tow in the damaged ones."

"Yes Sir," replied the ops officer.

.....

Captain Black was sitting in his chair looking out of the viewer as the Ajax and its ships receded and they went deeper into the system. He ordered they set a course to meet up with the rest of the fleet at the Nebula. He was cursing to himself. He had never lost a ship before, let alone two with good, experienced crew. They would be hard to replace. He knew the Carpathian would double cross him, and was pleased he had planned for that. He knew that once the Carpathian realized that he did not have the cargo he would come back for it. This time the fight would be where he wanted it on his terms, and he would get revenge for the loss of his ships and crew.

Chapter Fourteen

The Repair

Huntsman was badly damaged after their escape from the Mour's ship, and the following battle that ensued. Most of the ship's power had been taken up by keeping the shields at maximum. They had been chased for a while by one of the Mour's attack ships, but that soon turned back to help out against the Kalinian ships, which had given the Mours a battering. To add to their problems, they were also losing power, as one of the fuel cells had been damaged in the fight. They were limping along at sub-light speed while Huntsman, with help from Ben, was trying to patch up the damage as best they could.

"Well, we need to get ourselves fixed up and fast, we have enough power for at least four days. If we can make it to the Treaty base called Nero we might be able to get repairs and get fuel for our power cells there," Max said talking to his friends. They were sitting up in the rest room, leaving Ben to work on repairing the ship. He looked around at everyone, and with the exception of Squala, they all looked shattered and a little dirty.

Hope sort of coughed a little, as if trying to attract everyone's attention.

"Well?" Steve said rather testily.

"If we go to the Treaty base, and ask for repairs to our ship, it won't take them long to figure out we were involved with the Sagaris." She said looking at everyone in turn. "However, I think I have a plan. A galactic ferry regularly leaves there for the solar system. If we could book a trip on this, we could get to Titan and see if Sarana's Dad would help us repair the Huntsman," she finished with excitement in her voice.

"That sounds like a good plan; however, how do we book our ship on without alerting them as to who we are, and secondly, what if Sarana's Dad won't help us, and hands us over to the authorities?" Max replied with a frown on his face as he looked out at the stars.

Steve was moving around in his chair scratching his head; he was deep in thought and nearly bumped into Squala who held out a hand to stop him.

"Oh, sorry."

"That's ok."

"Anyway, I was thinking, getting on these ferries is easier than you think. Before Dad joined your ship, we used to use them a lot as we traveled throughout the galaxy. He was a relief captain." Steve said as if for effect, and then continued. "Anyway, sometimes we used to get to them quite late, and rather than lose the fare they would let you straight on. Once on board you would sort out the fare then, however, because they let you on board they didn't bother doing any checks."

"Are you sure?" Max asked with a little skepticism.

"Positive. We were sometimes on such hard deadlines for him to get from one assignment to another. We more than once nearly missed them," he replied.

"Once on board it shouldn't be too hard for me to access their system. If I can do that I can take us off the manifest, and no one would know we are on board," Squala added.

"Ok. Hope can you contact Sarana and see if she can help us out. Tell her we need repairs and fuel. Get the details of what we need from Ben and Huntsman." Turning to Steve and Squala he continued, "Can you investigate what ships will be at the station and look at what the layout there is? If you can come up with a plan, that would be great. I'll go and see what Ben is up to, and we'll plot a course there. Let's catch up later on the bridge."

…..

After talking with Ben, they discovered that the Huntsman was seriously low on fuel, and the damage inflicted had been more severe than at first thought. They shut down all unnecessary systems and left life support and navigation running on low power. They had calculated that if they made it to one of the ferries, and then after being dropped off at the space port near Pluto they might just make it to Titan before running completely dry.

Hope had contacted Sarana, and after a lot of explaining, and convincing her that she had not gone mad, had managed to get her to help them. They had agreed to contact her again once they had made it to Pluto and were on their way to Titan.

Meanwhile Steve and Squala had managed to log onto Nero's systems and had discovered that a ferry called the Star Racer was due to leave for the solar system in three hours' time. They would make it.

.....

They were now all on the bridge and they had slowed down to two hundred kilometers an hour. They could see Nero in the distance. She was the latest design in space stations. At her center was a huge ball-shaped structure, with four smaller ones coming off arms from the center. These were docking stations for large ships to dock, or hangers for smaller ones which would come by to refuel or get repairs. In an orbital ring around it, very much like the rings of Saturn where other ships, of varying shapes and sizes were parked up, and standing out from the crowd was the Star Racer. She was at least two kilometers in length and sitting high above the hull at the rear was the command center. All along her sides running down the middle of the hull the loading bay doors were open and smaller ships were entering the decks ready for departure. On her side in red was a large letter Z, for the Zeuss Corporation which ran the ferry.

"Ok are we ready?" Max asked.

"As ready as we can be," Steve said.

"Squala are you sure you can do this? If they find out who we are, we are dead in the water."

"Just get us on board, and I'll do the rest," was his steely reply.

"Ben when you are ready."

Ben set up a comms link to the Star Racer.

"This is the pleasure ship Huntsman, we are running late and would like to book a passage to the solar system, can we board direct?"

They heard no response and Ben repeated the request. There was a nervous tension on the bridge as they waited for a reply, then finally, "We read you, Huntsman, you need to book your passage through Nero's command center."

"If we do that, we will delay your departure. As you know they will hold you up while they process our documentation. This will cost you money and time. We are happy to pay double the fare for your inconvenience."

"Wait while I speak with the ship's commander."

"What do you think, Steve?" Max asked.

"They won't want to be delayed, as they run a tight schedule. They will agree to it I am sure."

As if reading Steve's mind, the reply came. "You are cleared to load, please go to loading bay twenty where you will be guided to your parking bay. Once there, report to the load masters office and he will deal with your ticket."

Everyone yelled in excitement and with that Max piloted the Huntsman towards their loading bay, sitting behind a small Kapon freighter that was in the queue of other ships moving slowly forward. As they moved along the queue, a small silver ball appeared in front of them, a neon sign flashing on it saying simply "Follow Me" as it shot off ahead. Max powered up and followed it into the loading bay.

The loading bay was vast, there must be at least three hundred ships parked up. Once they had landed, the rear doors opened and Squala leapt out and disappeared. After what seemed like ages he returned and informed them that he had been successful and had erased them from the ship's logs.

Looking out they saw the huge doors slide shut as the ship prepared to leave. They had all agreed to stay onboard the Huntsman to avoid any problems they might encounter.

.....

Huntsman had alerted them to the fact that they had arrived at the space port near Pluto. Max got to the bridge just in time to see other ships powering up and leaving the hangar. Just as he brought the power systems on line the others joined him.

"Ok here goes," he said. With the others strapped in and Steve's chair secured, they left the large hangar and angling upwards they shot off into space. They calculated a route and changed direction and headed off towards a small star in the distance, Saturn.

The journey was uneventful. Everyone grabbed some rest except for Squala who just sat there silently on the bridge. Eventually Saturn came into view growing larger and larger. The different colors of the planet were mesmerizing and the rings captured the imagination.

"Hope, make contact with Sarana, we need to know where to go once we arrive."

"I am on it," came the reply. Hope sat at the comms station and called her.

"Sarana, can you hear me?"

"Loud and clear, I have arranged for you to go to the repair facility called orbit two five. I have sent you the coordinates and a password. The facility is totally automatic and will provide us with everything you need for repair. It isn't used much so we shouldn't attract too much unwanted attention. I'll meet you there." With that she cut off transmission.

The huge planet was now over-shadowing them, it was like a wall of whites and greys, reds and blues swirling around. They were flying over the rings of the planet as they made their way round the other side and on towards Titan. As they neared, it was as if the entire Treaty fleet was stationed here. There were at least fifty battle cruisers in orbit, some in various stages of build or repair, with loads of robotic drones flying around them. There were also huge ship-building structures in orbit, some had ships in, others were empty. Weaving slowly through all of this, they eventually saw their repair facility, which looked like a piece of space junk. Max guided the Huntsman in and docked. They had literally used the last of their power.

"Let's go," Max said and led them to the air lock. As the door opened they were greeted by Sarana and to everyone's surprise, her father, who looked them all over and spoke, "Welcome aboard."

.....

He led them through a bright corridor to the facilities' command center. This was filled with banks of computers, and looking through the huge windows they could see the Huntsman which was now clamped in place.

It looked in a sorry state of affairs, most of the color had now been replaced by scorch marks all over, and in places there were huge dents on the hull.

"Well, you lot seem to be having some adventure. Sarana has told me your story," he said as he sat down at one of the consuls and swiveled in his chair to look at them in turn. "Now before I decide what to do, I want you to tell me exactly what has happened, how you acquired that ship and your friend here?" he said in a stern voice pointing at Squala.

So for the next fifteen minutes Max, with interruptions from everyone, told him everything from the moment of the attack until now.

"Well," he finished, "that's everything. We need to get our ship repaired. We need to find them." He sounded exhausted. He slumped down into one of the chairs and looked at her father finally saying, "Will you help us?"

Sarana's Dad's name was Cross, and he lived up to everything Max imagined a scientist would look like, tall, thin with unkempt grey hair, and intelligent green eyes.

The room had become quiet as everyone waited for his response. Sarana walked over to him and pleaded, in a way that children do when they want something.

"Ok, I agree to help. I have met your parents before and they seem like nice people. I fear that if you went to the authorities you probably wouldn't get any sympathy from them. Bizarrely, if you look at that repair facility over there," he said pointing out of the window.

Everyone gathered round. They could see in the distance a huge structure that was engulfing a ship. It was hard to see from here but they could see loads of repair craft moving around it, until their view was obscured by a huge triple hull cargo freighter that was navigating its way through this busy area.

"That is the Sagaris. It arrived here five days ago for repairs. Anyway, I digress. My scanners are already analyzing the material your ship is made of, and how its fuel cells work. It is of no design I have seen before, but with luck we should be able to replicate most, if not all of it. I suggest you all get some rest and clean up while I go about getting you on your way again. Sarana, show them to some quarters."

Max and the others looked at each other, they were exhausted and didn't need telling twice.

…..

The repairs took five days. In that time, they were allowed nowhere near the command center, so they did not know what to expect. In the meantime, they had rested and tried to come up with a plan. It was only on the last day when they heard the news about the battle Ajax had been in that they had a glimmer of a plan starting to form.

They were called up to the command center, and as they filed in they saw a very happy and beaming Cross. In fact, he looked downright proud of himself. They had barely seen him for the duration, he had been locked up there busy working.

"Ta da!" he said pointing out of the window.

Everyone rushed over, including Squala, and in unison everyone went, "WOW!"

The Huntsman was now not only totally repaired, but also had been painted a new deep green color, and on its nose in gold letters was the name Huntsman. On the rear engines, encircling them were two more gold bands. Hope ran over to him to give him a hug as did Ben, which made him go red.

"Now now, it was nothing," he stammered, but Max could see he was enjoying the moment. Steve had started going in circles in his chair with Sarana standing on the back and Squala even let out a yelp, if you could call it that.

"That looks brilliant, I don't know how we can thank you enough!" Max said excitedly running his fingers through his now long hair.

"All you have to do for me is rescue your parents," Cross replied. "Now, I have modified your engines for you so you can go even faster. The power packs have been replaced with a more up to date Tyrillion power source. This should last you years now. Also, I have put a Treaty recognition program into your computer. This will fool anyone unless they delve too deeply. Finally, I've left the best for last, follow me."

He led them to the airlock and once onboard the Huntsman, who greeted them, led them down to the lower deck. Sitting next to their two hoppers, which had also been repaired and painted in the same green, were two oval space cars, with big clear domes on them, which opened to the side. In the nose of each was a laser cannon.

"These, as you may know, are space cars. There is room for three passengers in each. I have modified each of them with a laser cannon. They can reach speeds of five hundred thousand kph. They are easy to use, but don't try and go near any atmosphere as they are unable to re-enter, they are only good for space. They have a force field that can be activated for defense, but hopefully their agility will be enough should you need it."

Max had climbed into one of them and sat there playing with the controls.

"Won't you get in to trouble for stealing them?" Steve asked with concern in his voice.

"They won't notice them gone," came the reply with a smile.

Squala had squeezed in the back behind Max. "A little tight, but comfortable enough," he said.

Hope laughed and gave his head a hug, saying that he looked funny in it.

"Now you had all better get going. I know you want to go too," her Dad said to Sarana giving her a hug. "As promised I'll speak with your parents too," he added, looking at Ben and Hope, "to let them know what's going on. Now make me proud."

With that he turned and left them with one final wave.

Chapter Fifteen

Earth

They had left the ship repair facility and headed towards Earth. Sarana was now on board with them. They had heard about the battle that the Ajax had been in with the pirates and the involvement of the Carpathians had been all over the Galactic news. Even better news was that the freighter of Max's parents had yet again escaped, meaning there was still hope for them. They had heard that the Ajax had returned to the military base in orbit around Earth, probably to get repaired and top up supplies. They had all agreed that they should go to Earth and its orbital cities to see if they could arrange a meeting with the captain of the Ajax, to see if they could get any information and help from him as to where he thought Max's parent's ship might have gone. They realized this could be a dangerous move, but the information they might gain far outweighed the risks.

"Isn't that a wonderful sight?" Max said as he looked out to see planet Earth and its giant orbital cities. These were great discs and there were three hundred of them orbiting. Each one was named after the great cities of Earth, London, New

York, Kyiv, etc. Earth itself was still populated but not to the levels it once had been. It had been virtually destroyed through overpopulation and stripped of its resources, which forced humanity to spread its wings, first to the moon then through the solar system to seek more resources. Now after a thousand years it was slowly repairing itself and its oceans and continents were teeming with life again.

"It's beautiful, have you been there before?" Sarana asked everyone.

"Only once when I went with Mum and Dad to the deserts of central Europe on holiday," Max replied.

"I went to a place called Phoenix in America with my Dad; he had some business there. It's amazing, they have these huge skyscrapers that tower high up to the clouds. I'd like to go to London one day as they have preserved the center. Apparently, it's still the same as it was in the twenty first century," Steve added.

"I have never been," Ben and Hope said in unison.

"Me neither, have you?" Sarana asked Squala.

Everyone laughed at this, and Squala just looked at them all and spoke, "Perhaps I'll invade it one day."

This brought out more laughs.

"While you all have fun, where are we going to start our search for this Captain Bainbridge?" Huntsman chipped in.

Ben had been scanning all the cities in orbit, until he had singled a smaller cylindrical structure that was in orbit above the north pole. Zooming in on it, they could see one end completely open with light coming from the inside, this was the entrance to the vast internal hanger where the Treaty fleet for the Earth system was based. Coming off the sides of it were at least a dozen pylons. Most of them were empty but on one was what looked like a re- supply ship and on another was the Ajax. Its gleaming white hull was covered in black patches where it had taken hits, and the front of the ship was completely damaged from the collision with the pirate ship.

Flying around the outside of it were dozens of small drone ships slowly repairing the damage, with the small figures of repair men walking along the hull guiding the repairs. They were in heavy space suits and had jet packs on their backs.

"Well, there's our ship," Ben replied. "Now how do we get in contact with this captain?"

"Huntsman, can you figure out a way for us to get on board without being detected? Max asked.

"I have scanned their defences. It would be impossible to get on board the station. I suggest we go to the nearest city, which is London One, and see if there are any ships that go there or see if any of the crew are taking leave and see if you can question them."

"Well I can't think of anything else, what do you all think?" Max asked.

Everyone agreed that it was their best shot, so they headed off towards the huge city and joined in the stream of traffic heading along the space highway towards one of the terminals.

.....

The terminal was huge, and they were automatically led to a parking bay where they landed. They had all decided to stick together for now, and that included Squala.

Hope and Sarana had done some creative dressing, and he was now wearing a black turban and a long black cape to best hide who he was. He now looked even bigger than before, but didn't look like a soldier, which was better than nothing.

They descended the rear ramp and followed the walkway out of the terminal into the main reception area. Here there was a tram station that would take them into the bowels of the city. They decided that the best place to start looking was on the main recreation deck, where all the shops and restaurants were. Climbing into the open carriage they headed off to this deck called Soho.

On arriving there, the place was absolutely teeming with people. Up to a million plus people lived and worked in the city and it felt as though every one of them were here. The whole deck was surrounded by floor to ceiling windows, at least one hundred feet high. From one side you could see Earth, and going round you could see some of the other cities, some near some far, with thousands of ships of all sizes zipping along the invisible highways to and from their destinations. They all just stood there in silence soaking in the noise of talk, music, advertising cubes floating by telling everyone about what to buy, where to buy, even updating you on Galactic news.

Steve was looking around, stunned by the scene in front of him. "Well, where do we start; this place is huge?"

"I think we need to look at the bars first. As they have been away, like most good crew they will be enjoying themselves," Sarana chipped in, adding, "I think we should split into two teams: Hope, Squala and me on one and you boys on the other. If anyone sees anything, call on the communicators and we'll meet up."

"Ok let's do that, if we have no luck let's meet up at that café over there," Max said pointing at a café called the Boulevard. "We'll go right, you go left."

.....

Max, Ben, and Steve had been searching every bar and restaurant for nearly two hours, they had been in contact with the others, and had nearly given up when they spotted a group of people sitting outside a bar called Rogues. They wore the unmissable blue uniforms of treaty crewman and were sitting there getting quite drunk. On their sleeves was a badge with the name Ajax in red letters. Bingo.

Steve whispered to his friends, "How shall we approach this; they look a bit boisterous to me."

"Ben, any ideas?" Max asked.

"Let's just go up and play off their egos. Let's act like schoolboys and ask them about the battle they were in. Don't forget it was all over the news. I think that with the drink and our hero worship they will soon start talking."

"Ok let's go, I'll let the others know where we are."

As they approached the table the crewman spotted them and one of them, a blond-haired man with white skin yelled at them and waved them over.

"Hello boys what are you doing here?" he inquired with a little slur in his voice, this bought a laugh from the others.

Steve went up to him and hovered there between him and another crewman who had a smooth skin with a gold complexion, he was a Venusian.

"We have read all about your great battle and wanted to hear about from you," Steve said excitedly, looking around the table, Ben and Max nodded enthusiastically.

So for the next half an hour they had an animated, and at times heated, run-down of the battle from everyone. As they continued, the story seemed to get even more flamboyant as the excitement grew. Finally, the others turned up, and not wanting them to miss out, they told the whole story again, although this time round it sounded different from the first telling. Eventually patting each other on the back they finished. The friends looked at each other smiling, and this seemed to cheer up the crewman even more. They ordered more beer and fruit juice all round for their audience. People on the other tables who had been listening started to clap.

Before anyone could say anything else the crew stood up to attention. Looking round Max and the others saw why... standing there was a small figure of a man with grey hair and a small beard.

"As you were. What's going on here then?" he enquired.

"Nothing Sir, we were just talking to the kids," replied Blondie.

"He was telling us about the battle!" Hope said.

"Aar," he said with a smile on his face. "I guess they gave you the full heroes' version," he said looking at the crew, who all looked sheepishly at the floor.

"Who are you Sir?" Max asked knowing the answer. He felt butterflies in his stomach. He looked around to his friends who were just looking at him.

"My name is Captain Bainbridge," came the reply.

…..

Everybody had now left, along with their captain. The six of them just stood there in silence, none of them could think of anything to say. All around them people were busy going about their business, some were coming into the bar chatting excitedly about the day they had been having. Max took a seat and appeared to be in deep thought, when Squala came over and put a hand on his shoulder.

"What do you want to do?" he asked him.

Max looked up at him and smiled, Squala looked funny wearing the turban and having the scarf wrapped around his face.

"Do you think you could follow him and find out where he is staying?"

"Yes." He looked over the heads of the crowd and could still see Bainbridge and his crew in the distance. "I'll leave now. Once I have found this out I'll contact you on the communicator." With that he melted into the throng of people and set off on his mission.

"Come on let's go to the café we saw earlier and get something to eat and drink," Sarana said.

.....

The Boulevard café appeared to be a popular place and they had to wait for a table. Once seated an automated waitress glided over to their table. A 3-D menu was in the middle, and after taking their order for fruit drinks and sandwiches, left them. "When Squala has found out where he is staying what do you intend to do?" Steve asked.

Max had a determined expression written across his face and his brown eyes had a glint in them.

"I think we should tell him the truth right from the start and ask him if he will help us."

"Don't you think that would be dangerous? What if he doesn't believe us?" Sarana replied with alarm in her voice. Ben then chipped in, "He could have us arrested and have Squala taken away!"

Just then the waitress arrived with their order. They then sat there quietly while they ravenously tucked into the food and drink. Once finished Max continued, "He could but I doubt it. Everything that happened on the Huntsman has been recorded in the ships log, and I still have the recording from Dad's ship. After that, and what happened to the Sagaris and his ship I think he will be all ears," he finished, sounding confidant.

"I hope for our sakes that you are right," Hope said.

"If not, we'll have to leave here, and fast. And go and find these pirates for ourselves."

"The captain was the last person to see your Dad's ship, and where it was headed, we have to convince him," Ben countered.

Max banged his fist on the table in frustration, some of the other diners looked round to see what was going on, then seeing it was a table of kids carried on with their meals.

"Well I think Max is right, we have nothing to lose. The trail is all but cold now, I don't know where we would start looking," Ben said.

"Are we all agreed?" Max asked. Everyone nodded their head in agreement.

"Good. Steve and Hope, I want you to go back to the Huntsman and get the ship ready for a quick departure. If anything goes wrong we will need to get away quickly. If you receive a signal from any of us that just says Ajax, that means we have been captured. You will need to escape, after that it's up to you two what to do."

Everyone sat there quietly with grim faces until Steve said with a smile on his face, "Cheer up, that won't happen." With that and a wave he and Hope set off back to the ship.

.....

Squala had been able to follow Bainbridge and his crew as they left the recreation deck and board an open tram which spiraled up through the city. He could hear their conversation as he sat at the back. His hearing was stronger than the humans which helped him blend in with the crowds. The crew were being told off for talking to strangers about their mission.

The tram eventually made it to level fifty-two. This was the business hub of the city. On exiting the tram, Squala could see a central avenue with a park down the middle. On either side of this were office blocks and hotels which reached up to the ceiling some one hundred metres above. The park area was busy with people strolling or sitting around in groups enjoying a break. However, it wasn't as packed as the recreation level, so he hung back a bit and watched the crew as they walked towards a hotel called the Yellow Flower. They stopped at the entrance and had a quick conversation, then bidding everyone farewell, Bainbridge set off again and entered a hotel called the Roxy. Squala followed him in and saw him enter an elevator. He, even at this distance, heard the captain command the computer to take him to level five. He then headed through the lobby, which was quiet and entered another elevator to take him to level five. The elevator doors opened and Squala was greeted by the captain holding a blaster aimed at his head. With the blaster he waived for him to exit and stand in the corridor.

"Who are you, and why are you following me?" he asked in a quiet but menacing tone.

Squala looked around him, the corridor was empty, and with lightning speed he grabbed the blaster and wrenched it out of the captain's hand, and with his other hand he pulled out his own weapon and aimed it at Bainbridge. The captain recoiled in shock as he realized the tables had been turned on him.

"No sudden moves, now lead me to your room and I will explain."

The captain looked alarmed, and his face had gone a dark red with rage at being so easily disarmed. He had few options available to him, so he followed the orders and led the way to his room.

It was a spacious room with a big bed and a sofa and chairs arranged around a table with a 3D holographic vision system in the middle. As soon as they entered, scenes of Earth came on 3D monitors on the walls to give the impression of windows. Squala waved at one of the chairs and told him to take a seat. Bainbridge went over and sat down then asked, "Who are you, and what do you want?"

Squala removed his head gear and saw the startled look on Bainbridge's face.

"I am a Carpathian Cyclops trooper. As you can see, I am an android of sorts, I am not here to harm you, my friends just want to talk with you."

Bainbridge had got some of his composure back.

"I remember now, I saw you with those kids earlier. How on earth did you end up with them? You are light years away from your system."

"They rescued me," came the reply and he contacted Max.

.....

Max listened to what Squala had to say. The others saw him go as white as a sheet and could see concern etched across his face. When he finished he stood and started to run towards the tram stop yelling to the others to follow him. Ben and Sarana looked at each other, shrugged their shoulders and set off after him. Catching him up as he got to one of the trams, Ben asked as they sat down. "What's happened?"

He relayed to them the conversation he had had with Squala.

"Blimey," was all he could say in return.

.....

They entered the room to see Bainbridge sitting there with Squala standing aiming his blaster at him.

"Squala put that thing away!" Max ordered, which he duly did.

"Well, you kids have got some explaining to do, kidnapping is a grave offence."

"We mean you know harm. Sorry about the way we sort of introduced ourselves, Squala can get a bit passionate at times. All we want to do is tell you our story and ask for your help," Max replied taking a seat opposite him.

"I have better things to do than listen to stories. However, I would like to know how you managed to befriend this android?" the captain asked with anger in his voice.

So for the next hour the four of them told the story from the very beginning, leaving nothing out, other than the fact that Sarana's Dad had helped them repair the Huntsman. The room was deathly quiet, and Bainbridge got up and paced up and down.

"Well, that is some story you have, it certainly ties in with some of the events that have happened recently," he paused, with his right hand on his chin, thinking quietly to himself, then continued, "I hope you have proof of this. What I don't understand is why you didn't come to the Treaty in the first place?" he said in a very calm voice.

"If we had done so, would they have believed us? I doubt it. Secondly events moved so fast that before we knew it we were fugitives ourselves. We were so close, but after the battle with the Kalinians and the Mours the trail went cold. We heard about the battle you had with the pirates and knew you would know what had happened to my parent's ship. So we guessed you would head back here for repairs. We also guessed that you might want to get even with them," Max finished and took a sip of water from the glass in front of him.

"Will you help us?" Sarana asked almost pleading.

"It not as easy as that young lady. The pirates are terrorists, and as they also have the help of the Carpathians the situation is out of my hands."

He came over and sat down again looking at all of them in turn and continued. "Also, if it ever gets out that I sent you off chasing them across the universe, I would be stripped of my rank, and worse if anything happened to you. I can't risk that happening."

"If you don't help us, we will go and look for them anyway. We can't just let Max's Dad be held by these people and do nothing," Ben said, with a hint of frustration in his voice.

After thinking for a while Bainbridge finally said, "As you know the battle was in the Carweg system. If the Carpathians have them, they will take the ship to their own system." He paused letting that last sentence sink in. "That is the only help I can give you; I have no other information. You know as much as I do. I will have to report this incident though. I sympathise with you, and to that end I will give you two hours before I report it. This should give you a good head start. And be careful out there. My repairs will be completed by tomorrow and we will be joining another ship to hunt down the pirates, so don't go and cause me any more trouble. Good luck." He said this with understanding in his voice, and winked at Max.

Thanking him they all left and headed for Huntsman at speed.

Chapter Sixteen

LA Service Station

They got to the ship as fast as they could, Max had called ahead and told them to get ready for departure ASAP. Although he knew Bainbridge would keep his word, he didn't want to risk it, as failure at this stage was not an option.

After leaving Earth's orbit, Max had decided to go and see the Tagons on the Los Angeles space service station. They were all unhappy with the way the final meeting had gone with Captain Bainbridge. Although he couldn't or, more to the point, wouldn't help them, they all understood the reasons why and respected them. But he had given them a vital clue as to where they were headed, and they intended to follow no matter what.

They were now on their own once again. The only small lead they had was the Tagons and the clarification from Bainbridge regarding the Carpathians. It felt more than a lifetime ago, watching the Tagons speaking with the hooded man and his friend. Max felt more and more as the events unfolded, and pieces started to link together, that he had seen the pirate leader that day. They must have been given information about his Dad's cargo prior to attacking. It seemed strange that the hooded man and his friends had not only followed them on the Jupiter station, but also that they appeared on the Los Angeles station.

After discussing it between themselves they decided that their search should start from there. They had to be careful because the captain would have put out an alert to report any sightings of them to the Treaty. They were now, in effect, fugitives again.

….

They were all on the bridge looking out ahead. They were now slowing down on the approach to the service station and could clearly see it in the distance. There were a few ships on the docking arms, and a few bigger ones in stationary orbit. They slowly crept past a huge triangular shaped cargo ship that had slowed down and was heading towards where the other larger ships were orbiting. Max spotted a free docking port and maneuvered Huntsman in gently. Once docked he kept all systems running.

"Ok, as agreed I'll go with Steve and Squala down to see the Tagons. You all need to keep an eye out, scan everything, we don't want anyone sneaking up on us." Max looked at everyone. Although they were tired, they all had a determined look about them.

"Good luck," Sarana said patting Max on the shoulder.

"Thanks," he replied. "Let's go."

.....

They stood there absorbing the atmosphere, with Steve hovering and Squala just looking up at the stars through the clear roof. They looked a motley crew. Max could again see darts of light as ships continued their journey on the space highway. A huge cargo ship flew slowly over the top of the station, it had four hulls all linked together side by side and was headed towards the parking area. He couldn't identify where it was from. Looking around the central plaza, the station was busy with a lot of aliens who had obviously stopped to resupply or just rest after long galactic journeys. Max knew where to go and led the way to the elevators. Once inside they descended to the lower level and on exiting, headed off towards the office of the Gilbert's new and used spaceships.

The place was still a mess with about fifty tatty old small ships of various sizes parked up in no particular order. The office where Max had heard them talking was dark, with no noise coming from within, and with the overhead lighting turned up brightly it gave the area a sinister feel. They decided to have a look further around the deck and see what else there was but most of the space was empty, except for in the far corner where there was another occupied space. Obviously as this was a lower retail deck no one wanted to hire the space, so it remained virtually empty except for the Tagons and this other shop that, on closer inspection sold old junk and scrap. The area was very bright from the overhead lighting, and you could hear the constant hum from the station's engines.

The junk was piled high, and had it not been for the neon sign that was flashing with the name Koob ships supplies, anyone passing would have thought that it was discarded scrap. Steve hovered high up and pointed over to a door in the corner. Max started making his way gingerly through the bits and pieces, some being metal, and others being synthetic, all different shapes and sizes. Some he thought might be from engines, but he couldn't be sure. He looked up to see Steve ahead moving towards the door. As he did that he slipped, but before he landed painfully Squala grabbed hold of him.

"Easy, Max," he said, then he effortlessly lifted him high and put him on his shoulders.

"Thanks Squala," Max replied patting him on his helmet.

They eventually made it to the door. Steve was already there. "What kept you?" he asked with a smile on his face.

"See anything?" Max asked.

"No, the window is filthy, but it appears dark in there," came his reply.

Max approached the door, it tried to open automatically, but was so dilapidated it just slid open a bit then shut again. He called over Squala to get his fingers round the door, and with all his strength managed to pull it open. There was a loud bang, then it stopped opening altogether. A puff of smoke came from where the motor was above the door.

"Guess that's broken then," Steve said sarcastically.

"It's dark in here I can't see a thing," Max said squinting through the door.

Squala moved past them, they looked up to see an invisible hatch slide open on Squala's helmet which revealed a high intensity light that bathed the room in light.

"Didn't know you had that!" Max exclaimed.

"You didn't ask me," came the reply.

Steve also went alongside and turned his lights on to add to Squala's. The room was dusty and stacked floor to ceiling with even more junk. Max heard a coughing noise coming from a corner of the room. Followed by the others he made his way over. It was obvious a shelving unit had collapsed and buried someone. With the help of Squala he started moving the junk until they uncovered a very small round purple-skinned man. His clothes were filthy, and he had a little tuft of black hair on the top of his even rounder head, Max went to give him a hand, but he brushed it aside.

"What are you doing in my shop and get your hands off me!" he shouted.

"Woah, we are only trying to help you. If we hadn't come in, you could have died."

"Rubbish. I would have got out eventually," he replied in a squeaky voice.

He was now standing up and just about came up to Max's waist. He was from a race of people called the Spantal. Max had never seen one before, mainly because their home planet was so far away. They were known as peaceful race who liked to trade, inasmuch as they would buy anything.

Obviously the problem with that was, as in this case, they ended up with junk more often than not.

He looked at Steve. "Do you want to sell that?" he asked pointing at Steve's chair, licking his lips.

"No way," Steve replied reversing up.

"Pity, I could offer you good money for that," the little foigure said with a huff, patting the dust off his ragged, filthy clothes. "So now you are here what is it that you want to buy, engine parts perhaps, or food processing units? All my equipment is of the highest quality."

Max and Steve looked at each other in disbelief, it didn't look as if anything had served a purpose for years.

"Actually, it was your neighbors, the Tagons we had come to see. There doesn't seem to anyone in, so we wondered if you knew where they were?" Max asked.

"Ah, those people. What do you want with them? They are nothing but slimy. You wouldn't want to buy anything from them. Dishonest that's what they are," came the reply, which was almost spat out.

"I take it you don't trust them then?" Squala asked.

He looked round and up at him; Max could see that he was looking at Squala with a glimmer of recognition on his face.

"You are a Carpathian trooper!" he blurted out suddenly, trying to retreat further back into his shop, but Steve cut him off.

"He is at that, but he won't harm you," Max said hurriedly as he could see fear in the Spantal's face. On hearing that he seemed to relax again and continued. "No one trusts the Tagons, they have no honor, they will trade with everyone, unlike my people who are fussy who we deal with." He said this trying to puff out his already round chest with the buttons straining on his shirt.

Not wanting to upset him Max said, "I can see you are an honorable person. We need to speak with the Tagons about some people I saw them with sometime ago, do you know where I can find them?"

He eyed Max suspiciously and considered the question. "Who was it you saw them with?"

"There was a man with a hood—" Max got cut short before he could continue.

"Aar, that man, he is very dangerous. He is always here meeting with them. They buy a lot of things from him. However, you are best not getting involved with him."

"Who is he?" Max asked eagerly.

"I don't want to get involved. If they find out I gave you any information, it could be very dangerous for me," the Spantal replied with fear in his voice.

"We could pay you for the information," Steve said.

"I don't want to get involved. It would be bad for my health. No amount of money will make me talk about this." He was now very fidgety and nervous.

Max was getting annoyed with this little man, although he wouldn't help them, he was now convinced more than ever that the hooded man was the infamous Captain Black. He looked at Steve who just shrugged his shoulders.

"Ok if you don't want to tell us about the *Pirate*..." Max emphasized the word and let it hang. Steve looked at him and smiled, liking the tactic he was employing.

"I didn't say anything about pirates," the little purple man retorted, getting even more nervous.

"I know you didn't, but I did. Now is he the man known as Captain Black?" Max said forcibly, leaning down with his face inches away from his.

The Spantal tried to back away, but he was stuck against Steve's chair.

"C-c-could be," he stammered. "Now leave me alone before you get me into more trouble."

"One final question, where can we find the Tagons? Answer this and we will go."

"They will be in the bar on the top deck. Now get out of my shop! And don't come back!"

With that they left.

.....

Once back on the main promenade they took a seat in a quiet corner.

"If we go up to the Tagons and question them they will go and warn off the pirates," Steve said.

"What do you think, Squala?" Max asked quietly, as a group of people walked by.

"I agree with Steve. If we alert them now, we will throw in our hand that we know that the Tagons deal with the pirates. I think we should keep this to ourselves for now, it might be more useful to us later."

Max sat there thinking and then called Huntsman and asked if those little saucers could relay live images to the ship.

"Yes, they can relay not only live images but sound too," was the reply.

"What are you thinking?" asked Steve.

"If we could hide one of them, it could relay video of anything that goes on in their shop. If we don't have any luck and Black returns to them we might have a chance to follow him," replied Max.

"It's a good idea, but if we are all the way across the galaxy we will never get back in time," countered Steve.

"Agreed, but if we left someone here, Ben for example with one of the space cars, he could try and plant a transmitter on the pirate ship and follow them at a distance until we return," said Max.

"But what if he got caught?"

"He doesn't have to approach them on the station, if he can remain hidden, we can notify him when they arrive at the Tagons."

Max contacted Ben to tell him to bring two discs to the service station and to inform him of his plan.

…..

Once they had hidden and activated the devices they went back to the ship and got one of the space cars moved to an internal hanger on the station. Max and Ben flew it there and had a little practice around the huge space station just to help Ben get familiar with it. Then everyone met on the promenade deck at one of the cafes for a farewell to Ben, before they then left for the Carpathian system to continue the hunt for his parents and Steve's Dad. Max kept a close eye out for the Tagons but didn't see them. The mood was sombre, because the friends didn't like leaving Ben on his own, but to his credit he was lapping up the thought of his task.

Chapter Seventeen

The Carpathian System

After getting themselves settled, Max laid in a course for the gateway. Getting clearance from the station, they joined the Space Highway and sat back to watch as they sped past slower vessels. The highway was busy with a lot of transport ships heading out to far flung destinations with their cargos. Max didn't know what to expect when they got to the Carpathian system, or in fact what plan of action he could come up with. They would have to play it by ear and remain alert. Just then Squala came on to the bridge and stood there looking at him.

"What are you planning to do when we get to the Carpathian home world?" he asked.

"I don't know to be honest. I am hoping that you can help me with that," Max replied leaning back in his chair and putting his feet up on the control panel.

"The system itself is well protected. They have thousands of remote defense systems that are not only heavily shielded and armed, but are linked to the various command centers they have. If any ships approach the system from any direction, they will detect it long before those ships can become a threat." Squala leaned forward onto the control center, and with his fingers gliding effortlessly over the panel brought up a 3D holographic image of the system. There were five main habitable planets, the main planet in the system was the largest, and the one closest to its sun. It had three moons in orbit and was blue in color. The other four planets had two moons each and were a greenish brown in color. The system was small in area compared to the solar system as all the planets were close, but they were also huge, two of them were bigger than Jupiter.

"All the planets are habited, including about half the moons." Squala pointed to a white moon orbiting the second planet called Nuth. "This one here is a hydrogen moon that is so cold it is impossible for anyone to even land on its surface. If we can get to this moon their sensors don't work there. We could hide there while we study what's going on in orbit around Carpathia. They will more than likely have your father's ship docked at one of their military's secure docking stations. These are heavily guarded and are virtually impossible for any captured ships that are held there to escape."

Max leaned over and revolved the image of the system through three hundred and sixty degrees as he studied it. Although it didn't show any defences it helped him think. He noticed a small planet even nearer to the sun than the home world.

"What's that planet?" he asked.

"It's nothing but a small asteroid. It got caught in this orbit about three hundred years ago. It's called Dexan, or in translation 'the lost one'. It is so close to the sun that it constantly glows," Squala replied.

"Huntsman would we be able to get near to this?" Max asked.

"Yes, our shielding is strong enough for this, although it would get quite hot on board, but our life support system should cope. I would say we could stay there for ten hours at most."

"Thanks."

Just then, Steve arrived. "What are you two planning?" he asked with an inquisitive smile on his face.

"Hi, we are looking at the Carpathian system, and looking for ways to get close to the home world. The problem is the whole system has thousands of remote defense systems patrolling. As soon as we get anywhere near they will detect us."

"Hmm, I see," Steve said as he sat there looking at the display. The three of them were just looking at it in deep thought, when Huntsman announced they had arrived at the station guarding the entrance to the gateway.

…..

They were now almost stationary, in a queue of at least a dozen ships as they cleared their passage out of the solar system. They declared their destination as the Rier's system which was the closest place they could go without raising any alarms that they were headed to the Carpathian system. Once cleared they entered the gateway and with a kaleidoscope of light, accelerated, and got transported towards Rier's. On exiting they headed off towards Carpathia at high light speed.

"Huntsman, are there any ships out there? Max asked.

"Nothing, we are now alone. There was a few waiting around the Rier's gateway, but nothing else," came the reply.

. . . . .

The Treaty attack fighter Nimbus was a small, three-man, high-speed ship. She was designed to fly at light speed plus, was heavily armored, and had a lethal array of weaponry. These craft were designed to fly combat missions in space and could, with their winglets, enter any atmosphere and carry out any surface-based missions they so desired. Their fuselage was long and sleek, and right at the front were the cockpit windows. When the armored shielding was lowered you could see the three crewmen sitting side by side.

The Nimbus was piloted by a young officer called Falick, from the Rier's system, as was his crew. They were humanoid in appearance, had a dark green skin under their treaty uniform, and had four ears around their heads. Falick pressed a button on his control panel and opened a comms link through the Treaty's military system.

"Ajax, this is the Nimbus."

"Hello Falick, how are you?" came Bainbridge's reply.

"Fine, Captain, thank you. Just to let you know that ship you put an alert out on has now come through the gateway and has headed off at light speed towards the Carpathian system. What would you like us to do?"

"Follow it, but keep them at arm's length, at the limit of your sensors. I don't know anything about their ship as it is, as you know, unfamiliar. So I don't want them to know that they are being followed if I can help it. Keep me updated on any developments. The heavy cruiser Badger should be in the Rier's system within the next twenty-four hours should you need any support, which I hope you won't. But it has been sent as insurance just in case."

"Will do Captain, I hope we won't be needing any back up, but thanks for the thought."

With that he turned round to his crew and smiled. "Let's go and follow our target. As you heard we need to be vigilant so keep your ears and eyes open."

With that they moved out from behind the huge cargo ship they had used to hide behind and set off in pursuit of their quarry.

…..

Nino Bassi had just come out of a meeting with the military special command council. After having a hard time trying to explain how he had been tricked by the pirate Black, who had run off with his cargo and left him with that piece of junk freighter. The council had told him that he had to recover the cargo from the pirates and eliminate them before any more damage could be done. They weren't worried about what the Treaty would think as they were old enemies anyway, but at the same time they weren't prepared to go to war with them. If he failed, this time he would be stripped of his rank and property and sent to a mining colony. In other words, he must not fail. They had agreed that he could take a fleet of six ships and fifty Cyclops troopers to recover the cargo.

He sat in his office looking out over the city, the sky was bright blue, and the tall buildings shimmered in the heat of the day. There were thousands of transports buzzing around as people went about their business, behind him Mu stood patiently waiting for orders from his master.

"What do you think?" Nino asked his trusted aid, as he sat there staring out at the view.

"After the battle at Carweg the Treaty are going to be on high alert. It will be hard for us to sneak so far into their Solar system and attack this Pirate. Even if we succeed it will be even harder for us to escape."

"I agree with you. However, we have that piece of junk out there. If we hide our ships on that, rename it and calibrate its systems to be recognised under a new name we should be able to slip in to get our cargo, and slip out before anyone knows what has happened. Once safe we will destroy it and its crew, so there will be no evidence to lead back to us." Nino's voice was shaking not only because he had been made to look foolish by this Pirate, but also he was still smarting from his dressing down by the council.

"Get everything ready. I want to leave in three hours from now," he finalised.

With that Mu left. Nino got up and walked over to a door hidden in his office wall. Behind this was a room where he kept his battle armor. He got changed into the heavy traditional suit. It was no longer made of traditional material and had to be replicated because the animal that provided the shell was now extinct. The material still looked the same with a purple hue to the deep black. He strapped on his laser pistols and left his office with a determined gait and headed to his personal transport to take him to his ship which was in orbit.

.....

Captain Black had made it safely back to his lair in the asteroid belt, after linking up with the rest of his fleet in the Rowse nebula. Some of his ships were in a bad shape after the battle with the Treaty ship. Although annoyed at the loss of his ships, he was pleased that they had inflicted damage on the Ajax. They had a repair facility on the asteroid, and his repair teams were working around the clock to bring the fleet back up to be battle ready. He wasn't expecting any trouble from the Treaty, but he knew that once the Carpathians had found out that the dummy cargo had replaced the real one, they would be hot footing back here.

Rolfe had placed some small single-man fighters around the asteroid belt on guard to report back any movement. Also on closer asteroids they had remote laser cannons stationed. These had now been activated and could be operated from his command center. If anyone wanted to attack him this time, he would be ready.

Rolfe came into his office and stood by him, looking out over the asteroid belt. "What do you plan to do with the cargo?" he asked.

"I think we need to go and see our friends the Tagons and see if they would like to buy it. The sooner we get rid of it the better."

"I agree, but it would be dangerous for us to be seen anywhere at the moment," he replied nervously shuffling his feet as he watched a small fighter fly past.

"I don't think so. For a start no one knows who we are on that station other than the Tagons. I think we should go in that old transport that we have so as not to arouse suspicion, if it makes you happy," Black replied with a hint of friendship in his voice, and patting Rolfe on the back, continued, "if you go and get it ready with a small crew we should depart as soon as possible."

Rolfe looked at him and smiled and turning on his heel left the room.

…..

Bainbridge was happy with the way his plan was working. They had followed Max's strange ship at a distance. He knew that to try and stop them would be futile, so the next best thing was to follow them and see what they would uncover. His superiors had been against the plan to start with, but also admired how the kids had gotten this far. They had agreed with him in the end that the only chance of recovering their prototype weaponry was to see which road the kids led them down. He was surprised to see that they left someone on the service station, and even smiled when he saw that somehow they had acquired a space car and parked it there. They obviously felt something might happen on the station, so he placed a young officer by the name of Kardo there to keep an eye on young Ben.

After asking Falick to keep an eye out for Max and dispatching the Badger to back them up, Captain Bainbridge decided that the best place for him to wait was in the solar system, as he felt all roads would eventually lead back here. His ship hadn't been fully repaired but it was battle ready and remained on high alert. He didn't think they would have long to wait. He had also got the cruiser Dreadnaught captained by his old friend Sino on standby. Nothing was going to defeat him this time round.

.....

The journey to the Carpathian system had been uneventful, and they had now slowed down to a virtual halt as they scanned, looking out for any of the defense drones that Squala had warned them about. Everyone was on the bridge and the atmosphere was tense as they all discussed a plan of how to get near the home world. They had detected at least five thousand drones which were flying around on a set pattern, more were undoubtedly out there out of sensor range. This system was so well guarded that they would be destroyed as soon as they went any closer. Just then Huntsman said that he had detected a ship coming up behind them on a parallel course.

"On screen," Max said.

A large cargo ship filled it. It was a Carpathian vessel. The front of it was a huge hole and the ship was semi-circular in shape behind this. Mounted at the back were huge engines above the structure. It was huge.

"Squala, what is that thing?" Steve asked.

"It's a mining vessel, they basically swallow up space debris from small asteroids to comets and mine the minerals on board. Once full they return with their cargo. It will be on its way to the processing stations in orbit around Carpathia."

"That's our ticket to ride!" Sarana said excitedly. Everyone looked at her.

"What do you mean, our ticket to ride?" Hope said, confused.

"Well if we can get underneath and attach ourselves to its belly no one could detect us, and we could hitch a ride right to their front door."

Everyone looked at her as the idea began to sink in. "Brilliant, Huntsman can we do that?" Steve asked eagerly.

"Well in theory yes, they haven't noticed we are here. Or if they have, they are paying us no attention. We could send out a false signal to hide us while we carry out the maneuver, however for it to be successful we would need to be directly underneath as it passes us by."

"Do it!" Max said.

With that the ship slowly moved until it was in position, just in time as the vessel started to fly over them. It literally blacked out space itself, it was nearly five kilometers long and was the largest ship any of them had ever seen. Max switched on the outside lights as they scanned the belly. It was made up of a network of huge pipes, some hundreds of feet in diameter, and it was between two of these that they chose to hide as it would be virtually impossible for anyone to see them. It took Max some time to find the right spot, as he had to match the speed of the mining vessel. Once, he had clanged against the hull sending a loud bang and vibration through the Huntsman. Everyone was holding their breath, but eventually they managed to lock on. The sensors showed that they hadn't been detected, and so silently they entered the Carpathian system undetected.

Squala then told them that the system had an outer defense ring and dispersed through the system were entry and exit corridors. Once cleared they had virtual freedom from the defense drones. Now and then military vessels would perhaps stop ships for identification, but with the volume of ships entering and exiting this was few and far between.

They had turned off all internal lighting and only the glow from the instrument panels illuminated the bridge in dim glow. Everyone was now busy at the various stations monitoring speed and sensors for detection. Squala stood silently watching. Suddenly the massive ship started to slow down. The external cameras picked up a ship below them with high intensity lights scanning the belly of the vessel.

"Don't be alarmed, they are just looking over the ship. It is part of the security checks at the gates into the system. Routine," Squala said matter-of-factly.

Everyone let out a sigh of relief as they saw the ship slip out of view.

"Any more surprises?" Sarana asked him with a quizzical look.

"No, I don't think so, once cleared we will be fine," Squala replied patting her on the shoulder.

No sooner had he said that, than the ship picked up speed and accelerated to continue its course. The atmosphere was tense as everyone watched the view below them. Now and then a ship or satellite passed below them as they headed deeper into Carpathian territory.

After sixteen hours they again felt the ship slow down and come to a stop.

"I think we are at the processing station," Max said as he worked on the controls to bring up a holographic image of where they were.

"What do we do now?" Steve asked.

"I don't know, any suggestions?" Max replied, swiveling around in his chair.

"If we leave this hiding place, won't we be detected?" Hope chimed in.

"Huntsman, can we detect any other ships beyond our position, in other words the freighter?" Steve asked.

"Our sensors are not too effective due to our proximity to this ship. Also, its electrical pulse is interfering with our other systems. We can send out some probes, but they could be detected."

"What about if we used the space car?" Sarana added.

"That sounds like a good idea. Squala, what would they detect and treat as a threat? If we launched the car and maneuvered it slowly, would they detect us?" Max asked him. On the screen they could see another huge mining vessel below them moving slowly towards the processing station, with several other smaller ships whizzing around. Leaning forward Squala pointed at the small ships. "They are maintenance ships checking the hull for damage. They are automated. If you launch you could be mistaken for one of those, but it could be dangerous. They fly on a pre-planned course. If you can learn this, you should be able to fly and hide when needed. But if you go beyond the ship, you will be detected as an alien body and destroyed, so you need to be careful, and precise."

"Will it be enough for us to scan and see if we can detect the freighter?"

"Hopefully," came the reply.

"Ok we need a plan," Max asked everyone in general.

"Well I suggest you stay here, and Hope and I will take the car and see what we can see," Sarana replied with a determined voice. Hope looked at her and nodded her head in reply.

"I think I should go." Max said.

"No, you should stay here. If we need help you and Steve are better equipped to rescue us as you know how to pilot Huntsman better than we do."

"I agree with Sarana," Steve replied and continued. "If there is any complication, they don't know how Huntsman handles, and that could be dangerous."

"It is a better plan," Squala said in defense.

Max had a resigned look on his face. He wanted to go on this mission, because he wanted to see firsthand if his father's ship was indeed there. But he could see that they were right. "Ok," he said with resignation in his voice. "Go and get yourselves ready, but please be careful."

.....

They all met by the space car. Hope and Sarana had put on the deep blue space suits that her father had provided, the canopy was open, and the power systems had come online. All the instruments were glowing a deep purple.

"Ok, we have scanned the bottom section of the vessel. There are some huge antennae dotted along the underbelly, plus huge vents that are used to get rid of any waste debris from the mining process. Obviously nothing should be coming out of them but be careful. We haven't detected any drones yet so keep an eye out," Max said, looking at each of them in turn, and continued, "also don't go any further than the front of the ship or you will expose yourself. Any sign of danger call immediately and we will come running, any questions?"

"You sound just like my Dad," Hope said with a smile.

"This is dangerous territory, if you are spotted, we are all in serious danger." Squala added.

After that sombre warning the girls climbed in and checked systems, while the others left and went to the bridge to watch on the monitors. All lights were turned off in the bay and a force field activated as the rear doors opened. All they could see was the glow of the cockpit with their heads silhouetted.

The rear engine glowed and they moved slowly out of Huntsman and disappeared.

.....

Once they left Sarana stopped to take in the view ahead. The front of the canopy was now a heads-up display and had adapted to the darkness; their view out was now crystal clear. The belly of the ship stretched off into the distance and they could see huge pylons, and antennae hanging there like stalactites. Above them they could just make out Huntsman wedged in between two massive pipes. If they didn't know what to look for, they wouldn't have seen it.

"Are you ok back there?" Sarana asked a bit nervously.

"Fine, it's amazing though," came the reply. Hope had two screens in front of her, one was showing the view ahead, the other was displaying all the car's systems.

"Ok let's go."

And with that they moved forward keeping as close to the belly as possible. Sarana, who was piloting the car, weaved around a huge pylon and then flew between two huge pipes. They were now going at twenty kilometers per hour. Behind Hope was looking at the monitor which was now scanning for anything that might pose a danger to them.

"I think one of those vents is coming up, you need to change course now to miss it."

"I can see it, changing course now." With that she pitched the car into a tight left-hand turn. There was a heat shimmer coming from the vent which distorted the view on the monitors only fractionally as they headed further along the ship.

"I think I can see one of those drones ahead," Hope said in alarm. "Quick hide behind that box- shaped thing to our left."

"Ok."

They got to the box and Sarana cut all power. The car was now stationary on its side, as a drone came into view. It had two powerful lights on the front and looked like a crab with two long arms out in front with clamps on the end. It was moving slowly looking at the ship for damage. It came close to the car, its lights picking them out, moving closer it looked at them, and losing interest moved on again, the light disappearing into the inky blackness.

"Blimey that was close," Sarana said in a shaky voice.

"You could say that again, lucky you turned off the power."

After waiting for ten minutes, they continued their journey, seeing only one more drone away in the distance. Eventually their view began to open and they could see Carpathia in the distance and the processing stations. The stations themselves were huge and made up of a framework, with large funnels coming out from the center. Attached to one of these was another mining vessel, probably the one they had seen earlier. These things were obviously how they got the cargo off. They came to a halt and sat there looking at the scene in front of them. Apart from the processing stations, the area of space was busy with ships of varying sizes moving around on their missions around the planet. They magnified the view and started to look for Max's ship.

It took them almost an hour before Sarana whispered, "I think that's it over there."

She magnified again and the image now appeared on Hope's screen.

"It certainly fits the description. The cargo bays are open by the looks of it, what do you think they are doing?"

After a moment Sarana replied, "It looks as though they are loading space craft into it, I wonder why?"

"Seems strange," Hope said, as she watched a ship enter, then the loading bay doors closed.

"Should we let the others know what's going on?"

"No, if we open a link to the Huntsman we will be discovered. Let's record it and wait and see what they are up to."

They didn't have too long to wait, no sooner were the doors shut, the huge delta winged ship powered up and began to move away from orbit. It made a sharp turn and headed towards them, its hull was blackened in places where it had obviously been hit by laser cannon, but apart from that it appeared in reasonable shape. It picked up speed and got bigger as it neared, then disappeared as it flew over the mining vessel.

Without hanging around, Sarana turned round the ship and headed back as fast as possible.

They were moving as quickly as they dared back along the belly of the ship. Behind them a drone was following. Its sensors had picked up the movement, and it came out of its dormant state. Sarana was busy at the controls looking out for danger, when suddenly she felt something hit the car. With alarm in her voice, she called out to Hope.

"What on earth was that?"

"Don't know, it happened behind me, I'm checking now."

As she was looking at her sensors the car seemed to go completely on its tale, then move from side to side. Hope went pale as she saw what the problem was. They were being shaken around like a baby's rattle.

"We have a probe that has grabbed hold of the car in its pincers. It is trying to pull us backwards, put more power on forward thrusters."

"I'm trying but it is no use, if we put too much power on, we could crash."

With that they were swung around all over the place. Both girls were beginning to feel sick and dizzy as they fought the controls. Another drone had now joined the first one and had a grip on the car. They were being pulled backwards and being banged against the bottom of the ship.

"Hope can you get a call out to Huntsman?"

"I'm trying but the comms is down, these things are jamming our systems," she yelled back as they hit a huge pipe.

"Look!" yelled Sarana.

Just coming into view was Huntsman. One minute it was there, the next gone again as they got swung around against a huge pipe. All of a sudden the shaking wasn't so bad, and they looked out to see one of the drones leave, then and head towards Huntsman. It didn't get far as it got blasted to pieces. Huntsman then fired on the one holding the car. The car felt as though it was dropping as Sarana fought to get control of it and head for the safety of the Huntsman.

Back on board they all sat round, and Max relayed the story that they had detected several drones moving around. Worried they had tried to contact them but having no luck, they set off to look for them, and just as well.

Both the girls still looked a little shaken, but the color was returning to their face with a warm fruit tea. They all sat and watched the images that Sarana and Hope had captured. Both Steve and Max sat there silently for a time letting the information sink in, then Max gave Steve a hug and they were both grinning from ear to ear.

"Well at least the ship is here which means our parents will be too. We need to move fast and follow them and see where they are going before it's too late."

"You two did a good job there," Steve said with respect.

"Sorry," Max said apologetically. "I forgot to say well done you two."

"Max, we need to travel slowly out of the system. If we go too fast, we will arouse suspicion. Although all ships leaving are left alone, they will be on alert, especially if what happened here gets reported," Squala added cautiously.

"Understood." Max replied. "Hang on everyone, let's get out of here."

Huntsman sped along the underbelly and exited at the rear. In the distance they could make out the glow of engines, on magnification it was clearly his Dad's freighter making its way out of the system. Slowly Huntsman built up speed and kept a distance of a hundred thousand kilometers.

After a while Steve asked, "Where do you think they are headed?"

"I don't know but they do seem to be in a hurry. It looked as though the ships they have stored were military. Perhaps that's the cargo," Max replied concentrating on the flight controls.

"I doubt it," Squala added in his usual unemotional voice.

"Why do you say that?" Hope countered with an inquisitive tone to her tired voice.

"They don't sell military equipment, only buy it. Also they are headed towards Treaty space, not towards any of their more friendly systems."

Everyone thought of Squala's comments for a few minutes, before Sarana interjected. "Perhaps they are using it to hide in. if they were to fly into Treaty space in their own ships they wouldn't get far, but having hidden them they could travel anywhere they wished."

"A Trojan horse," Max said as if to himself.

"What?" Steve replied.

"Don't you do Earth history on Mars? In ancient times they built a wooden horse and filled it with soldiers and offered it as a gift to an ancient city. When the city fell asleep the soldiers emerged and let their armies into the city, destroying it," Hope said triumphantly.

"Exactly. I think they have been double crossed by the pirates and they are using my Dad's ship to go after them. It can be the only explanation."

"Shouldn't we let the Treaty know, maybe try and contact that Captain?" asked Sarana.

"Not yet, it might endanger the crews' lives, besides we have no proof. Let's wait and see."

.....

The Nimbus had followed the ship as far as they dared towards the Carpathian system. They were now sitting motionless in the middle of space. In the distance they could see the system spread out across before them and most of its planets were twinkling away. Their sun was bright, and even at this distance, it bathed the bridge in its glow. They had positioned the Nimbus at a distance for them not to be detected, so they just sat there and waited. After what seemed like weeks their sensor alarm sounded.

"Sir, I have just picked up a ship heading our way," Tret the first officer said.

"Can you pick it up on screen yet?"

"No, it's still too far away."

"Ok, let's power up and be ready in case it is hostile."

With that all the ship's other systems including engines came back online.

"There is another smaller ship coming into range, about fifty thousand kilometers behind it. Judging by its power signature I think it's our friends we were following. I can now bring up images."

With that the display came alive and they could make out a delta winged freighter.

"That's an Earth ship."

"What is that doing out here, and why are they following it?"

Falick called up Captain Bainbridge and briefed him as to what they had seen.

"The plot thickens. Ok, do not intervene, follow them, and let me know where they are going. I am going to tell the Badger to move away too. I don't want to make them nervous, and Falick, be careful out there."

"Will do."

With that Falick moved the Nimbus to a safe distance away from scanner range of both ships and followed and watched.

.....

"Our detectors have picked up something at the space station," Huntsman announced.

With that an image appeared on screen of the Tagons' shop. They were having a conversation with two men. Although the image wasn't too clear Max could see instantly that it was the hooded man and his accomplice.

"That's them!" he shouted excitedly.

241

"Are you sure?" Steve asked.

"Positive. I'll let Ben know and he can go and investigate and report back."

.....

Ben had been sitting around the station now for ten days while his friends went after the Carpathian to try and rescue Max's and Steve's parents and the crew of the freighter. He had gone down to the lower deck where the Tagon's shop was on many occasions to see what they were up to, but apart from a few visitors no one matching Max's description ever appeared down there, or on any of the promenade decks. It was easy to keep an eye on the Tagons as they spent most of their time in the bars and the gaming center on the station.

Ben thought to himself that he wished he had gone with the others, although he didn't know how they were getting on as they had agreed to stick to communication silence just in case someone picked up their signal. The only thing of any significance that had happened was on his third day there, when he heard that the Treaty ship Ajax was due to dock at the station. This caused a bit of a buzz, as it was uncommon for a battle cruiser to stop at a station like this. Obviously everyone knew that it had been damaged in a fight with the pirates, and as rumor had it, that after its repairs it was going back out to fight them. He had wanted to let Max know of this but couldn't, however after their meeting with its captain, he had told them as much.

After having something to eat he made his way up to the observation deck high up in the station. You could sit there and look out across space and watch the ships speeding by on the space highway, watch ones slowing down to dock, or others speeding up to leave. It was fairly dark up here as the lighting was down to a minimum, not only for the people who came up here to relax and watch the goings on in space, but also for the people on the promenade decks who wanted to look up, and see the heavens.

As he sat there, he saw a small, battered freighter come into view. He could see movement through the bridge windows, but it was too far away to see any faces. Behind the bridge was an open hold which was empty and behind were four engines giving off a red glow. It had at one point in its life been painted silver, but it was just stained through being in space for all its life and never being looked after. As it slowed down it banked sharply and lined up with a docking arm. Once docked, its engines faded into a faint glow as they powered down. Not paying much more interest than that Ben went back to watching the streaks of light on the space highway and grabbed some sleep waiting for a signal from Max.

.....

The control room was full of monitors, and the young officer by the name of Kardo had sat there now for seven days watching every movement of the young man called Ben. His orders were to observe only and report back on a regular basis to his superior officer anything that Ben did, or anyone who he spoke to. Kardo was in his early twenties and at six-foot-five tall with no hair, and olive skin, he cut a forbidding figure. This was his first assignment since he left the Treaty's Space Academy. At first, he was excited that they would trust him not only with an assignment on his own, but according to his superiors it was high priority.

Well, he had sat there now for seven days in the security room of the station watching an eleven-year-old boy roaming. He thought it odd that there didn't seem to be any parents around, but this didn't worry him. So far this supposed high priority mission had been, if anything, nothing but a bore, however he would do the job to the best of his abilities. Little did he know this assignment would end up being far from boring.

.....

Ben had been in a deep sleep. A slight vibration started to lift him out of his slumber. Groggily, he rubbed his eyes, and realized that his communicator was ringing, looking at the panel he could see that it was Max.

"Max," he said sleepily, "What's going on?"

"I don't have time to explain, we are on our way back to the solar system. The cameras have picked up the suspected pirates down in the Tagons' shop."

"I have been there every day and not seen anyone of note," Ben retorted.

"Believe me they are there now. Do you think that you can get down there and observe, and see what they are up to?" Max countered.

"I am on my way. If they leave, what do you want me to do?"

"You have the space car, follow them and keep in touch, but don't do anything foolish until we get back to help you," Max answered, "and be careful that you are not spotted."

After a little silence Ben answered, "I'll do my best but get to me soon."

"We are on our way, stay safe till then."

.....

Ben cut communication and set off for the Tagons' shop. He was nervous, there were loads of people around on the main decks, but as he made his way down to the lower decks and towards the Tagons' shop he was shaking with fear. If they captured him, what would they do? However, he was also worried that he might let down his friends. This alone spurred him on. Again, it was a cold and uninviting place. When he got there, he hid and watched the Tagons talking with the pirates. The conversation was heated, and the Tagons were, for them, very nervous, something was going down.

The one with the hooded man was doing all the talking, waving his arms around. At one point his hood fell over his shoulders and Ben could see his deep brown weathered face. Even at this distance he looked a powerful man and not one to be crossed. His partner looked even more menacing, with grey skin and deep blue eyes, he was obviously keeping watch on their surroundings in case anything was to happen.

Ben kept getting snippets of the conversation, and it was to do with the fact that they wanted the Tagons to sell some goods for them, which in Ben's eyes meant the stolen cargo from Max's parent's ship. After a long debate they eventually shook hands on a deal and without wasting anytime the pirates left for the elevator.

Once out of sight Ben ran to some service stairs and, taking them three at a time, made it to the main deck to see them exit the elevator and head towards a bar, where they ordered a drink and sat at a table to carry on whatever they were talking about. Keeping an eye on them Ben called Max.

"Did you manage to see any of that?" he whispered.

"We saw it but couldn't pick up on the conversation. Did you manage to hear any of it?"

"From what I could gather they wanted the Tagons to sell something for them. I can only imagine it's the cargo from your Dad's ship."

"Maybe, but we are now following Dad's ship. It has left the Carpathian system and seems to be headed in your direction. We think the pirates have double crossed them and they are on their way to either meet with them or perhaps attack them. It all seems a bit strange. How are they acting?"

"Don't seem to have a care in the world. Now they are sitting in a bar chatting. If they had double crossed the Carpathians, then they seem to be rather confident about the matter." Ben paused for a moment thinking, then went on, "or they know that they wouldn't dare come into the solar system and attack them after the battle with the Ajax."

Sarana's voice then came through. "That's it then, they wouldn't expect them to come in their own ships, but they have hidden some ships in the space freighter; they could arrive unannounced and ambush them."

There was a long pause as everyone thought of this. This could be fatal for Max's parents' ship.

"Max, I'll call you back, someone has joined them, I'm going to try and get closer."

"Be careful."

Chapter Eighteen

The Plot Thickens

Kardo was watching all this on the monitors; he had tracked the boy from the observation deck, down to the Tagons' shop, and now was watching as he tried to creep into the bar where the group of people were who he seemed to be following. Things were now getting interesting. He decided he now needed to report back to the Ajax.

After a long discussion with his senior officer, he was under no illusion that he must not let the boy out of his sight. Not wanting to damage his career in any way he decided to take this literally, so changing out of his uniform into something less conspicuous and arming himself with a laser pistol he set off for the main level and the bar.

…..

Ben managed to follow a group of Rowse traders who were headed for the bar to quench their thirst after their long journey. As they took a table he managed to get a seat near to the pirates and their new guest. He was a Nerel, his pasty skin was bright blue and he came from a race known as 'people for hire'. They had no allegiance to anyone unless the price was right.

He could just make out the conversation. It was to do with the transport of a cargo, but as the Rowse got boisterous, he couldn't hear much more than that.

After a while he left and reported back to his friends. After filling them in on the developments, Max replied, "Squala says the Nerel are basically Galactic mercenaries. However, they remain loyal to their paymasters for the duration of the contract as it would be bad for them to break it. We think that the pirates are getting them to deliver the cargo on their behalf, thereby keeping them out of the loop. We are still some time away from you, if they move you need to try and follow them."

"The car is not too fast. If they go to light speed, I'll never keep up."

"Rumor has it that the pirates' base is in the asteroid belt so they are never going to go too fast, you should be able to keep up with them."

"I'll do my best, how far away are you?"

"We are coming up to the gateway in the Rier's system. So, we are not that long behind you if everything goes smoothly. However Squala has come up with a plan so listen to him carefully as this may help us in the long run."

Chapter Nineteen

Return to the Solar System

Captain Bainbridge had put the Ajax in orbit around the prison planet Pluto. Even from this distance the planet looked cold and uninviting. He felt a pang of sorrow for the poor devils holed up on this miserable planet, especially for the prison guards who had to spend six months at a time on duty there. Most prisoners spent their entire lives there as it was a high security facility, with no chance of escape.

He could make out the gateway in the distance, the Treaty station guarding it was cube shaped, and had a large outer ring around it. Also, it had a squadron of galactic class attack tanks stationed there. They were now on high alert should he need them. There were about a dozen ships nearby waiting for clearance to leave the solar system.

Through the intel he had received from Badger and the young officer Falick, the captured star freighter was heading his way, with the young guns in hot pursuit. From the messages they had managed to intercept from them there were some Carpathian ships hiding in the hold.

To him this meant that the pirates must have double crossed them and they were on their way here for revenge. This bought a smile to his face… as usual criminals couldn't trust each other. On top of that he hopefully had the chance to capture, or destroy the pirates, and their base and put an end once and for all to their antics. This would be a huge feather in his cap especially as he was looking to retire and reverse the embarrassment of their last meeting. This would be a good day for him and his crew, all they had to be was patient.

…..

Max and the others were watching the scene in front of them. They had detected a ship near to their location. It was a Treaty destroyer, and they had identified it as Badger. It was a long sleek ship with a command tower situated at the rear of the hull. At first they thought it was waiting for them as it cruised near to the Rier's gateway, but it eventually turned and with a flash of its engines disappeared into the distance. His Dad's ship was about twenty kilometers in front of them and it was stationary as it got ready to be cleared and enter the gateway to move onwards to its destination. Hopefully it was headed for the solar system, if it wasn't they were stuck and would lose it. After speaking with Ben, and Squala telling him of his plan, which everyone thought brilliant and clever, they were now in a waiting game to see if their hunch was right.

"There is another ship that has come out of deep space that has just stopped about one hundred kilometers behind." Steve said.

"Where did it come from?" Max asked anxiously.

"Looking at its path I would say it's been following us," he replied.

"It's probably nothing," Hope said, with not much conviction in her voice.

"I doubt it," Squala replied.

Everyone looked at him as he continued, "The simple truth is that the ship has probably been following us since we came here."

"Why do you say that?" Max asked tersely.

"Because as soon as we got here that other ship, Badger, turned around and disappeared. That is a classic move, watch but don't let your target feel threatened. My guess is that the officer in charge of the ship behind us has got a bit enthusiastic and shown his hand."

"You think we have been followed all along?" Hope asked him.

Everyone was now looking at Squala.

"I do. I think the captain Bainbridge has had us followed since we left Earth. He is probably waiting to see how this unfolds and thinks we are at the center of solving this problem for him."

Everyone sat silently thinking of what Squala had just said. The more Max thought of it the more it made sense. For had he been in he captain's shoes, he probably would have done the same, especially with the resources he had at his disposal.

"What do you think their next move is?" Max asked everyone.

"If I were in his shoes, I would notify the security forces to intercept and arrest us and the freighter," Steve said, swiveling around in his chair. Just then he looked out of the window and saw the freighter enter the gateway. Everyone watched as it sped up and disappeared.

"I guess that rules out that idea," he concluded with a smile as everyone else, bar Squala laughed.

"Looks like the opposite is true, I think they will let us through and see what everyone gets up to," Sarana said, as Max guided the ship to the entrance. They had already booked passage and once they had clearance from the control officer, they entered the gateway and began their quick journey back to the solar system.

.....

Bainbridge was sitting in his office when the intercom buzzed him.

"We have just had a report from Falick that the two ships have now entered the gateway," his first officer Jim reported.

"Excellent, when are they due to arrive here?" Bainbridge asked excitedly.

"They are due here within the next five hours, I have alerted the commander of the station that when they arrive, they are not to be hindered in any way. Although he didn't like the idea of that too much."

"Tough. Keep me posted Jim and send my thanks to that young officer Falick." he said, then before Jim could sign off, he continued, "also, how's that young officer Kardo doing?"

"He has just reported in. The one called Ben seems to have come to life and is following some people on the station. He can't get a fix on who they are, so he is going down to keep a closer eye on things."

"Good. Tell him under no circumstances is he to lose sight of the young lad."

"I've told him many times already."

"Well once more won't hurt. Keep me informed." With that Bainbridge cut the link, got up and went to his window and looked out over the surface of Pluto. He had a broad smile on his face. He felt the end game was drawing near.

…..

Ben sat there and watched his quarry. If Squala's idea worked, any moment now something should happen. The three of them were in a heated conversation, but as hard as he tried, he couldn't get close enough to hear them. While they had been sat there Ben had gone to a shop and bought a reusable VM pad. This was essentially a voicemail pad which you could put a message on, and it would then appear as readable words, or as a holographic image. They were cheap and people only ever bought them in case of emergency, or as in his case, if you didn't want the recipient to know where the message came from. He had recorded the message that Squala told him to and as he walked past their table dropped it on the floor behind the hooded man. He then went back to his chair and waited.

.....

Kardo had been watching him and saw him drop the device by the table. "What on earth is he up to?" he thought to himself. He could see that he was nervous. He decided that he needed to get closer to Ben, so spotting a table free near him, he took a seat and ordered a drink from the waitress and waited. The bar was filling up with people again, which helped his cover.

It wasn't long before one of the waitresses moved by and, spotting the device on the floor, notified the hooded man he had dropped something. He leaned back and picked it up, his table fell silent as they looked at him, he activated it and read what was on it. He immediately passed it to his partner, the grey-skinned one, who read it. He then started looking around the room nervously. Kardo looked away and took a sip of his drink and looked out of the window trying to seem relaxed, although adrenalin was now pumping through his body. As he looked back around again he could see that they had left their table in a hurry and were now scurrying towards the docking ports. In fact, they were virtually running. He caught sight of Ben who was also moving through the crowd and working his way towards the elevators that would take him to the station's internal hangars. He knew he had a ship here, although it was only a small space car.

He started to run as fast as he could, pushing people out of his way. Ben had already made it to the elevator, and the doors slid shut. He went to the next elevator and commanded it to go to the hangar deck. He was gulping in deep bursts of air trying to get his breath back under control and as the elevator stopped, he exited and looked around. Thankfully it wasn't too busy, and he quickly saw Ben who was running towards a green space car. It had its clear canopy open. He set off again as quickly as he could and started to gain on him. When Ben got to the car, he started to climb in. Thinking quickly, Kardo got out his pistol and yelled for Ben to stay still or he would open fire.

. . . . .

Once he'd seen the hooded man pick up and read the device, Ben was ready to move. He had to get to the car and launch it before the pirates had time to get themselves on their ship and underway. As they left, he set off as fast as he could. In fact, he was so focused on getting to the car that he didn't notice he was being followed till he heard the shout from behind him.

He was half in the cockpit as he looked round to see a tall man with no hair and olive skin levelling a pistol at him. He had seen him in the bar but had paid no attention to him. Now he was walking slowly towards him. He needed to leave and fast.

"What do you want?" was all he managed to say.

"I have been ordered to follow you, now don't move, you are under arrest."

Ben thought as quickly as he could, and slowly put two and two together.

"Let me guess, Bainbridge sent you?"

He could see a look of puzzlement cross his face and continued. "I have met him. We went to him for help in catching the pirates, but he refused to help us."

"No one told me about pirates," came the hesitant reply.

Ben looked at his communicator. He was running out of time.

"Those people in the bar were pirates and I need to follow them. Now time is running out. I know you won't have orders to shoot me, so I am going to get into this car and follow them."

Other people were now stopping what they were doing around their ships and watching what was going on. A small one-man space scooter shot overhead and exited the hangar. Ben watched this man as he slowly started to get in the car.

Kardo didn't know what to do. He had been ordered not to lose sight of Ben. If he shot him, he knew he would be in deep trouble. He didn't know anything about pirates but watching him in the bar told him something must be going on.

"What was that you dropped at the table of the man with the hood?"

"I haven't much time. Please let me go," Ben answered with near panic in his voice.

Kardo was thinking hard, if he let him go, he would have failed in his mission, but he had been told that Ben must come to no harm, so the best thing to do was go with him. His mind made up, he said, "Do you know how to fly that thing?"

Ben looked at him suspiciously, but before he could reply the man came over.

"My name is Kardo, I was top of my class in these, jump in the back, I'll pilot, and you tell me what all this is about."

Chapter Twenty

A quick exit

After reading the message Captain Black sat there frozen. Looking round he could see no one who he thought was responsible for dropping this message by him. All he knew was that either someone was trying to help him or lead him into a trap, either way he had to react. After passing it to Rolfe, who read it in silence, he thought that the Nerel by the name Dre was behind this.

"What do you think Rolfe?" he asked.

"A trap, why would anyone want to help us, and how does anyone know we are here?"

"Could be the Tagons?"

"No, too risky even for them. We should have destroyed that freighter when we had a chance. I suggest we head back to the ship and leave for base, just to be on the safe side. All our defenses are in place, so we should know if an attack is imminent," Rolfe replied.

"Agreed. What worries me is that our cover is blown, and someone knows what we have been up to."

"What are you two talking about?" Cre asked.

"Nothing to concern you, but we need to leave now, and you are coming with us," Black said menacingly.

"But what about my ship?"

"You will tell them to wait for you here for further orders, let's go."

With that they all got up and hurried towards the docking port. Rolfe called ahead and told them to be ready to leave as soon as they got onboard.

Once they had got to the bridge Black took his seat and watched out of the view screen as they reversed away from the docking module, which disappeared as they turned and slowly moved along the side of the station, weaving in and out of other ships in their path. A signal came from the control center telling them they weren't cleared to leave and to await a leaving slot, which Black ignored. Their progress was slow, and at one point they had to veer to the right as a small green space car appeared in front of them. This then disappeared under their belly, and with full power he ordered the helm to set a course for their base. With that the ship dived down the side of the space station, then took a course away from the space highway. In their haste, no one noticed the small green car follow them at a distance.

.....

Ben didn't know what to make of Kardo, he was obviously an officer and seemed to have an air of authority about him. Also, he wasn't too sure how to fly the car, and as Kardo seemed to know what he was on about, and the fact he didn't have much choice, he was grateful for the company. Although what the others would say he did not know, he would cross that bridge when he came to it. They had now exited the hangar and were speeding up the sides of the space station, looking to his left he could see figures at the windows walking around or in some cases looking out.

"So tell me what it is that we are meant to be following?"

"I thought you wanted me to tell you the story?" Ben replied feeling a little stupid at his reply.

"You can tell me that later. I thought you wanted to follow their ship. If we are to do that it would help if you told me what it looks like."

Ben described the ship he thought the pirates had arrived in, and no sooner had he done this that they nearly hit it head on. Kardo was right when he said that he knew how to fly the car, because as Ben closed his eyes thinking they were going to hit the pirate ship, Kardo put the car into a steep dive and at the last minute did a summersault and they were now on the ship's tail as they skirted along the side of the station, built up speed and disappeared.

"Blimey you can certainly fly. We need to follow them though."

"We will, now tell me why I am risking my career on this little adventure?"

So, with nothing else to do but look at the stars Ben told him everything he knew.

.....

Nino Bassi was happy with the way his plan was working. They had now entered the solar system and were in a stationary orbit high above Neptune. They were far enough away that the authorities wouldn't pay a freighter any attention, but it helped him take stock of the situation.

The captain and his first officer of this infernal ship were causing him nothing but problems, to the extent that he had threatened his crew with death if they didn't cooperate. They now sat sullenly at their positions.

He needed them to gain entrance to the gateway and get them here in case they were stopped and questioned. He thought that they had got here too easily, but needs must, and he would have done with them once they got to the asteroid belt. Once there he would disable the ship and leave them to the destiny of that dangerous area of space. He'd studied the space charts, he knew exactly where Black's lair was, however he also knew that Black would be waiting for him to come and take what was rightfully his, so he worked out a plan that would make them show their hand.

"Captain, you are going to take your ship into the asteroid belt, to this point here," he commanded, pointing on the holographic image of the area on the main screen.

"One of my officers, Im, will be with you on the bridge. If you do not obey him, he has orders to start killing your crew, do I make myself clear?" he said in an almost whispered threat.

Patriq looked at his boss.

"What do you think? If we help them, I have a feeling we are going to be dead in the water once we reach there."

"My thoughts exactly. However, after all we've been through, perhaps this is the end game. The one thing I don't think they know is about our third line of power which I had built in in case of such an emergency. We need to keep that close to our chests as that might save us. I think for now we go along with this idiot, dressed in his silly suit, until we have a chance, or an opportunity that comes our way."

"I agree, I have managed to organize the computers to cut off life support in certain areas of the ship without them knowing, including the bridge. I have also managed to hide two emergency oxygen sticks; they are both under the helm station."

Max's Dad looked at Patriq with respect and whispered, "Well done."

He then stood up and walked over to Nino and looked him square in the eyes.

"I'll get you there, but once there I want my ship back!"

"You are in no position to make demands of me. But if you do as I ask I will have no further use of you, or your infernal ship," Nino snarled back.

With that he left the bridge leaving the Cyclops Im and three of his henchmen to watch over them. There were also guards down below keeping an eye on the crew, although they didn't know how many.

They then took up position at the helm and headed for the asteroid belt.

They also noticed on the sensors that a small craft that had been hiding on the other side of Neptune settled in behind them and started following. As no one else had noticed this they quickly blocked it off from the ship's sensor log, it was now invisible. They didn't know what it was, but they had seen it before. It could be friendly, so it was best no one else knew for now, just in case it was that little bit of luck they needed.

.....

Max had hidden Huntsman on the other side of Neptune, and Squala and Steve had taken the space car out in low orbit to go and watch what his Dad's ship was up to. While Squala piloted around the giant blue Planet, Steve focused on the navigation. Twice they came across satellites in orbit and had to slightly alter their flight path. They also saw way below them a huge orbital space station for the system as it moved lazily around the planet. Eventually they came to a stop and saw the huge freighter just sitting there high up in the distance. They sat there and watched its magnified bulk on their systems and waited in silence. Eventually it started to move again. Letting everyone know, they waited for Huntsman to pick them up, then follow at a discreet distance.

…..

"What do you make of it Max?" Sarana asked.

"They are on their way to the Pirate's lair I would have thought. It is going to be hard to plan what happens next, but we need to be on our toes, Steve call Ben for an update as to what he is up to, timing could be crucial."

After a while they all heard Ben come across the speaker system. Everyone sat there in silence as he relayed his story and told them how a young officer called Kardo had now joined him in the pursuit of the pirate's ship.

Next Kardo's voice came over. "Hi, I guess I am talking to you all. I've got to say, I have found it hard to believe your story. It seems to tie in with what happened to us when we encountered the pirates, certainly with the freighter. Now my job was to look after him so in a way I am, although what the good Captain will say when I tell him who only knows."

The others looked at each other stunned; of all the turn of events no one could have thought this would happen.

"If you were asked to look after Ben, are you aware if anyone was sent after us?" Max asked.

"I didn't even know why I was asked to look after him. It was in theory my first mission on my own, and more than likely my last at this rate."

Although he sounded fed up, they could also detect a sense of excitement in his voice.

"I think we can count on it that he has tried to keep an eye on us. It was too easy for us to clear the gateway. We must assume he is with us somewhere out here, which I guess is not a bad thing," Steve chimed in

"I agree, all we can do is keep on the tail of Dad's ship and see where it leads us. Ben where are you now?" Max asked.

"It looks like they are headed for the asteroid belt as you guessed, they are about three thousand kilometers in front now, and going too fast for us to keep up."

"But if that is their destination, they will have to slow down at some point so we should still manage to track them," Kardo added.

"Good keep us informed, because if that is the case, we will probably be meeting up with you soon."

With that Max broke the connection and turned round to his friends.

"Well in a way I'm glad that Ben seems to have found a travelling companion. What are everyone's thoughts?"

"I am worried about what will happen next," Sarana said nervously.

"Me too. I think if they do start having a fight with the pirates again it could put our parents in terrible danger, and we don't have the resources to mount an attack and rescue them," Steve said with an edge to his voice.

"I agree with Steve. Perhaps we should try and contact the Ajax and tell them where we think they are going, perhaps they could rescue your ship before they get there," Hope suggested as she looked at the display screen showing the freighter magnified ahead of them.

Everyone sat silently deep in their own thoughts, before Squala gave something resembling a cough.

"What are you thinking?" Steve asked.

"I think that if you contact him at the moment he won't help, because if he wanted to, he would have done that by now. If he had Ben followed that means we would also have been followed as we know. He is hoping that all roads will lead to the pirates and their capture. And for the moment we are in the thick of it."

"How can you be sure of that?" Sarana asked testily.

"Because if it was me, I would be doing the same. However, I do have a plan, which I think will work."

They all replied in one to that comment, so he told them what he had been thinking at great length.

After everyone digested what he had to say, Max replied "Do you know I think it might just work. The only thing is I am worried about you, it is dangerous."

"Do you have a better plan?" came the reply.

Max looked at everyone in turn and they all shook their heads.

"No, I don't. Let's get to work, time is of the essence."

Chapter Twenty-One

The battle at the Pirates lair

They had pulled back a bit from the freighter, judging the distance so as they could remain out of the sensor's range. It wasn't too hard for Huntsman to follow them as they could follow the engines' emissions.

Steve, Sarana and Squala were down below modifying the car, while Max and Hope stayed on the bridge, and with the help of Huntsman, managed to modify the laser cannon to give off an electronic pulse.

Just as they had finished, an alarm went off. "What is it?" Max asked.

"I think it is our friends the Ajax. I have detected them on the outer reaches of our scanner's range. They are matching our speed," replied Huntsman.

"Interesting that they should show their hand now."

Steve's voice came over the intercom. "What was the alarm for?"

"The Ajax has just come into sensor range, it's still someway off and from what we can gather is just following us."

"Ok. We are finished with the mods on the car, where are we now?"

Max looked out of the window he could see Jupiter in the distance, although the freighter was heading that way it had changed course and was now heading towards the asteroid belt. It seemed a lifetime ago that this adventure had started there. They had been all over the galaxy, and now bizarrely like in his dream, he was headed towards a showdown in the asteroid belt.

"I can see Jupiter in the distance, we have changed course again and are headed for the asteroid belt. You had both better get ready because I think we will be putting the plan into operation soon."

With that he turned his attention back to the controls, while Hope powered up the laser cannon and put it on standby.

.....

Meanwhile Captain Black was pacing nervously up and down the bridge, their sensors had detected a small craft following them from the space station. It was too small to pose any threat to him in terms of fire power, but it must be following them for a reason. He and Rolfe had questioned Cre at length

271

about the warning they had had from the device that had been found under their table. The warning had been very explicit, the Carpathians were on their way, but it was apparent that he was none the wiser. He reminded them time after time that he was there at their request not his. He now sat sullenly in the corner.

"Rolfe how long till we reach base?"

"We will be there in twenty minutes. The scouts have confirmed that the freighter came through the gateway and is headed in our direction. Once it's in the belt we will be in a better position to see what the Carpathian is up to. Which, as we know, isn't going to be good. All marauders are on standby and other resources have been sent to hide away just in case."

"Good, hopefully our fleet will be able to monitor them, are the defenses on the other asteroids active still?"

"Yes vista has them already to go'.

"Good. Contact Cro, I want him to look at the ship that has been following us, in fact get him to destroy it, we don't have too much time and I don't want it wasted."

"Consider it done."

…..

Ben and kardo had been following the ship for some time now. The view out of the car was amazing, they could see the

Milky Way in such detail, millions of stars twinkling away, and you felt as if you could just reach out and touch them. Ben felt a little sorry for Kardo, but deep down he was glad of the company, especially an experienced officer like he was. However, when he had contacted his officer Jim of the Ajax, he was in no doubt that he would be in serious trouble. Kardo had said that once in deep there was no turning back and his responsibility was towards him.

They could now see the beginnings of the asteroid belt ahead and had slowed down as they passed the odd lump of rock that was on the outer rim. The pirate ship that they had been following had appeared briefly as they caught up but following it now through the belt was difficult. Ben was monitoring the sensors as Kardo concentrated on piloting the small craft.

Although the pirate ship had disappeared, now and then it came back into view. The pirates were flying through the area like it was their back yard, which it was. They, however, were novices, but Kardo was confidant at the controls of the car, and he was reliant on Ben being alert to any threats.

Just then Ben detected a ship heading their way.

"Ship heading 33320 degrees towards us and fast!"

"What is it?" Kardo replied slowing down the car.

"Unsure but it is travelling directly towards us. It has just passed the pirate ship. I would say it is not going to be too friendly."

"I have visual, hang on this could get rough."

No sooner had he said this than the ship, which had a round hull with six winglets, each holding laser cannons at the front and engines at the rear, opened fire.

Kardo had anticipated this, in an instant he spun the car to the left and the laser fire streaked passed them with the ship narrowly missing as it flew overhead.

Just then Max called them.

"Where are you?" came his relaxed voice over the comms.

Ben was being thrown all over the place as Kardo swung the car in every direction to throw off the pursuers. He replied, "Not now we are under attack, all I can say is we are in the belt, speak later.

"Kardo they are behind us!"

"I know, get ready with our lasers, they are not much but might buy us some time."

Suddenly, he threw the car into a summersault, Ben could then see the ship below him, trying to correct its course, then they were behind it.

"Fire."

He opened fire with the lasers. They didn't seem to cause any damage as Kardo headed off again towards a small asteroid. As he got round it, he braked hard throwing the pair of them forward in their seats. The ship overtook them as he opened fire again. They then accelerated behind their quarry, which ducked and dived in every direction. Ben opened fire again and saw their shielding glow blue. The ship then virtually stopped and started heading towards them. Kardo threw the car in to a steep dive and headed towards an asteroid, there were red flashes following them as the pirates opened fire with all they had.

"Told you I was top of my class on these," came a strained voice from Kardo as he fought the controls. Ben could see the surface of the rocky asteroid coming on them fast, but with steel resolve, Kardo kept on going. He could see small explosions on the surface as their enemy's cannons hit the surface time after time throwing up dust and debris.

"Hold on."

With that Kardo put the car in to reverse. They could hear the hull straining as it came to a dead halt. The nose of the car stopped literally feet from the surface, Ben could see the rocks of the surface illuminated in the light, before Kardo put it in full reverse and they shot back into space, passing the pirates who had a heavier ship, and were trying to slow down. With no hope of this, they just managed to turn and clip an outcrop of rock that ripped off two of the winglets. These went floating off and crashed into the wall of another outcrop. The ship was damaged and had come to a stop, just floating above the surface of the asteroid. Ben fired their lasers and managed to hit another two of its engines. It was now disabled, and floating about under very little power, they could see holes in the hull and bits of debris floating out of them. With no time to waste, Kardo opened the engines, and they headed off back into the belt looking for their quarry.

…..

Nino Bassi was ready, his crew had got his ship ready, and he was now on board, he had ordered Im to slow down the freighter and open the hanger doors while the crews of the attack ships got ready to depart. He knew that the traitor Black would be expecting him, but he hopefully would surprise them with his ships hidden in the freighter and the speed in which he managed to get here. He looked out across the vast hangar at the other five ships; they were now powered up and were just hovering there waiting for the word to leave and head towards their target. He could see them checking out the cannon turrets on top and below, and on small winglets were rocket pods ready to unleash their devastating power.

…..

Bainbridge was sitting in his office and Jim was pacing up and down venting his anger that Kardo had informed him that he was on a ship with his charge, and that moments ago they had been in a fire fight with a pirate vessel in the asteroid belt.

Bainbridge got up and put a hand on his shoulder.

"Well," he said smiling at his first officer, "he has done what we asked of him, if not a little too literally. But we did task him to keep an eye on the young rascal, and he seems to have done that. If we were younger, I guess we would have done the same."

Jim went and looked out of the window at the stars beyond, they were now passing Jupiter's system and he could see Ganymede in the distance.

"I suppose so. I must hand it to him, he came through well, although I dread to think what would have happened if they got blown up. The kid's parents would have gone ballistic with us, especially as he is a high-ranking diplomat."

"I'm sure, this bunch of kids is proving to very resourceful in their quest. They are managing to achieve what the Treaty has wanted to in little more than a few months. I am still wondering where they managed to get that ship from though."

"Yes, it is a strange one, its design is like nothing I have seen before, a little brutal and ugly. Our scans of its materials is a mishmash of some we know and a lot that we don't, if that makes sense."

"Let's go to the bridge and see what they are up to now."

As they got there the crew were busy at their stations. On the view screen they could see both the ship that the children were on, and the freighter at high magnification. Bainbridge stood at his station and could see the cargo bay doors opening on the freighter.

"Can anyone tell me what's going on?" he asked urgently.

"We don't know for sure Sir; the cargo bay doors are opening, and the ship has slowed down to about two thousand kph. It is now on the outer edge of the asteroid belt."

In front of the freighter, they could now clearly see hundreds of asteroids appearing, all different shapes and sizes. On the split screen they could also see the children's ship slowing down.

"How far away are they from the ship?" Bainbridge asked as he sat down.

"They are slowing down but are still at least five hundred kilometers behind," the sensor officer on duty replied.

"Jim. I don't understand how they are managing to get so close, although what they are going to do I have no idea."

"Well let's get closer ourselves, they know we are here now."

With that the Ajax picked up speed and slowly closed the distance between the two ships.

"Sir something is happening on the freighter."

All eyes were now glued to the screen as six ships exited the freighter and gathered speed and headed towards the belt.

"Battle stations!" Jim shouted, and the alarm sounded.

"What are those?" Bainbridge shouted.

After a while he got a response, Carpathian battle ships.

Just then the rear cargo bay on the other ship opened and a small space car appeared, pulled up, and then flew towards the freighter.

"Well, I'll be," said Bainbridge almost to himself. "It looks like they are going to rescue the freighter. Jim, follow those attack ships and get a squadron of tanks on standby, and fast, I think we are going to need them."

.....

The tension on the bridge could be cut with a knife, Max, Hope and Sarana were watching as the Carpathian ships left the ship and immediately accelerated into the belt.

"Squala, Steve, now is your chance, good luck." With that they heard the rear door open, and after a few seconds the space car came in to view and headed towards the parent's ship, as fast as they could, just managing to disappear as the cargo bay doors slid shut. They had made it.

"Ship approaching," Huntsman said. Just then the huge bulk of the Ajax shot overhead and followed the Carpathians into the belt.

"Blimey they're in a hurry, I didn't expect that!" Max shouted.

"Huntsman keep an eye on them. Steve, can you hear me?"

"Yes, we are in the hold, no one is around, what's going on your end?"

Max filled him in on the Ajax chasing the Carpathian fleet.

"Well you follow them, we will deal with this. You need to find Ben before he gets into any more trouble."

"We'll hang around just to make sure that you don't need any further help. We have the cannon and lasers ready should you need it."

"I don't think we will be needing that. There is nothing more you can do for the moment. Squala reckons there will be only a skeleton crew on board, waiting for them to return. Go and find Ben then come back for us."

…..

Max didn't like the idea of leaving them alone in tackling the Carpathians on the freighter, but the hope was that Squala could deceive them enough to get them near to his parents and help them escape and overwhelm any Carpathian guards.

Now that the Ajax had shot past them on the way to the way to the belt, they had to get going and come up with a plan of their own. Huntsman had been tracking both the Ajax and the Carpathians, and their ships were on a split screen in front of them. Looking out ahead of them the asteroids were growing in size as they neared the edge. It stretched out into the darkness of space, and the sun's faint glow glanced off the surfaces of the hundreds of asteroids both big and small. They were now catching up with the Ajax and could see the glow of its engines ahead.

"Sarana, try and contact Ben and find out where they are and what they are up to?" Max asked as he concentrated on piloting the ship.

He was busy at the controls, while Hope, with the help of Huntsman had reconfigured the lasers.

"Ben, this is Sarana can you hear me?" There was a lot of static but eventually she made contact.

"Hi, we can hear you, where are you?"

We have just entered the belt, I'll send across our coordinates,"

A moment went by as she sent the information.

"Cool, thanks."

After a while Sarana got a signal back and entered it into their computer.

"How far away are they?"

"They are further in than us and are about five thousand kilometers away. I have put all their details on the screen in front of you."

Sarana looked at the three-D image in front of her, it showed all the asteroids, plus the Carpathian fleet and the Ajax, also it showed some other ships dotted about, and now Ben's space car was tagged.

"Well done, Huntsman," she said.

"Ben there is a ship moving slowly behind you."

"Ah that must be the pirate ship we had a run in with, is there anything in front of us?"

Max chipped in, concern on his voice. "Are you sure that is the one you had a run in with earlier?"

Kardo joined in and told them about how they were following a ship when another appeared. Through a bit of teamwork they managed to defeat the ship and badly damage it. They both sounded proud of their endeavors.

"Well done you two!" Hope shouted excitedly.

"Well, I guess that's one less ship to worry about," Max said with a smile on his face. "Sarana is there anything in front of them that they maybe can't see?"

"There are two ships about two hundred kilometers in front of you, can you see them?"

"No, our sensors aren't strong enough with all these lumps of rock around us. We are slowing down and going to take it slowly. Can you get to us?"

"Not now, we have the Ajax in front of us and beyond that the Carpathians. They are on a mission, and I'm worried that if we get too close to them, they will open fire. Stay on your current course, we will keep an eye open for you with the sensors and let you know of any dangers."

Just then Huntsman reported laser fire ahead and magnified the screens further. What they saw was the six ships passing a nearby asteroid. They had come under fire from a laser cannon that was on the surface. They could see red flashes hitting one of the ships. There was a ripple of its shields as it turned sharply and opened fire with its own cannons. Another ship also fired back as streaks of light from the cannons went back and forth as each tried to destroy the other. Eventually some rockets were fired at the asteroid and a huge explosion engulfed it. The ships got back in formation and carried on their journey.

"I can see some major activity around a large asteroid on the flight path of the Carpathians. There are at least fifteen ships heading towards them, I think we are going to see a bit of a fight," Sarana said excitedly.

"Hope how's our weapon system coming on?"

"They are now ready and fully charged."

"Good we might need them. while they are busy fighting, let's see if we can go and get Ben, then get back to Steve and see if he needs any help."

.....

Steve and Squala had managed to get into the cargo hold just as the doors slid shut. After landing they quickly got out and headed towards the exit. There was no one around and it was deathly quiet. Squala had his two laser pistols at the ready while Steve moved off in front of him, in case they bumped into anyone, and he could play the prisoner.

They left the hold and entered a stair well. Stopping and listening, they couldn't hear anything, other than the faint hum of the engines. The stairwell was bright, just as Steve remembered it.

"Let's go up," he said to Squala.

"You lead the way but go slowly just in case. Where do you think they will hold the crew?"

"I would think in the crew lounge, where everyone meets off duty. It would be the only logical place as it can hold everyone and only has one entrance."

"Well let's head there then and use it as a starting point."

They eventually made it to deck 3 where the lounge was. The corridors were deserted, they hadn't seen or heard a soul and the progress had been slow. They had checked every corridor and room along the way just in case. They turned a corner and Steve stopped in his tracks and reversed quickly, bumping into Squala.

"What is it?" he asked.

"There are two Cyclops guards ahead outside the crew lounge. I don't think they saw me."

"Ok leave it to me, stay here."

"What are you going to do?"

"See what's going on'.

With that Squala holstered his pistols and headed off boldly towards the guards. Steve flipped his chair sideways down so he could just see round the corner as Squala headed towards the guards.

As soon as he approached, they became cautious and raised their weapons at him, they were wearing the same black and red armor as Squala. Steve had attached a noise amplifier to his ear so he could hear what they were saying. They were suspicious of what he was doing down there as no one had informed them of his arrival.

Without warning one of them went to grab him, but Squala was waiting for this and turned on the guard catching them both off guard. Suddenly he had one of his blasters in his hand and shot one of the guards in the chest disabling him in a puff of smoke. The other one got off a shot that hit the wall and Squala smashed him against the wall, while holding the arm with the gun as another blast hit the floor, they tussled and fell to the floor. Squala eventually got hold of him and twisted his blaster and fired, the guard fell, still with smoke rising from his chest plate.

Steve flipped over and made his way over.

"Are you ok?" he asked.

"Fine. I don't know if there are any guards inside, so we need to move quickly in case anyone tries to contact those two, are you ready?"

"Yep let's go."

With that they opened the doors and they both shot through them. There were another two guards inside, but with lightning reflexes Squala quickly dispatched them.

Everyone in the room looked at them in stunned silence. There were at least twenty people here. He spotted Sandy and was just about to say something when Max's mum pushed her way to the front. Although slight she cut a formidable figure.

"Hello, Marni, hi," he said, embarrassed, not knowing how to call her.

She gave him a hug. "We thought we had lost you, where's Max, is he ok?" she asked, her voice filled with worry.

"He's fine, and not too far from here. Where's my Dad?"

"They have him on the bridge with Max's Dad. There was a horrible little man up there with them dressed in some sort of outfit."

No one else had moved, and they were all looking at Squala, Steve looked at him and he had to say he looked quite menacing with his two pistols held down at his side.

"He's with me. So, you can relax a bit. His name is Squala, Squala give them a wave." This Squala did, still holding the gun.

"Do you know how many are on the bridge with them?"

"No," Marni replied. "But I'm going to find out," she said as she headed for the door and looking back at Steve and Squala, said, "Well, are you two coming? The rest of you stay here for now, Sandy, I might need you on the bridge."

"Coming," he replied, his bright red hair was all over the place and like everyone else in the room looked a bit filthy, but you could see their spirits rising as they all started to talk amongst themselves.

Marni was running off down the corridor, and everyone else had to run just to catch up, Steve pulled up beside her. "Take it easy, there might be others ahead, Squala can you take the lead?"

They encountered no one on the route up to the bridge, the ship felt deserted. Eventually they got to the bridge, and everyone stood still not knowing what to do next.

"Squala it's down to you, what's the plan?"

"Again, we need to be fast, I don't know how many are on the bridge. If you go in first as fast as you can I'll follow, hopefully this will distract them enough, let's go."

Steve opened the door and shot through; his Dad and Max's Dad were at the helm piloting the ship, there were three other troopers standing guard, one of them was all black and must have beeen the leader. His Dad looked round with shock written all over his face, Max's Dad did a double take, regained his composer quickly and hit the panel in front of him with his fingers moving fast, looking out of the view screen Steve could see all the asteroids come to a halt as he stopped the ship.

Two of the guards immediately fell to the floor as Squala shot them. The lead one, seeing what had happened, opened fire at Squala hitting him in the arm and sending one of his pistol skating across the floor. He took a shot at Steve, and it hit his chair sending him spinning in a flash of sparks against the wall. Squala was crawling along the floor trying to get to his pistol, and firing but missing with his other one sending sparks flying, but he got hit again in the leg. There were flashes of laser fire all over the bridge as the black-clad trooper hunted out other targets. Marni had now entered the room and was shouting at him to stop. He fired at her sending her diving for cover right where the pistol was. Without thinking she stood up holding the pistol in both hands and started firing at the Cyclops. Although way off mark and sending flashes and sparks all over the place, it was enough for him to also dive for cover. Max's Dad had crawled over to her and took the pistol off her and gave her a big hug.

They were now lying there behind the sensor station. Squala was crawling along the floor towards the place where the other Cyclops was hidden.

"Drop your weapon Im, the game is up!" Max's Dad shouted, only to be answered with a flash from the pistol. "Pat, Steve are you ok?" Marni shouted. They both replied that they were.

Sandy meanwhile had made it to the helm and working by touch alone had put the ship into motion again, and very quickly, he turned it on its side, and started to accelerate. This caught the cyclops called Im completely off guard. He came round to try and see who was at the helm when, with all his energy, Squala dived at him. He hit him square in the chest and they started to swap punches. Steve got his chair upright, and as fast as he could flew at the guard knocking him off balance. This was all Max's Dad needed, he aimed and opened fire at the Cyclops, sending him to the ground smoking.

Everyone got up except Squala who had leaned himself against the wall.

"Well, where the hell did you come from son?" his Dad asked giving him a big hug.

"Long story Dad."

"Sandy well done, that was a good move. Are there any more of them on board?" he asked Steve.

"I don't think so, Squala," he said pointing at his friend, "killed the others. You have your ship back; however, we need to find out where Max and the others are."

"He's, ok?" came the reply as he hugged his wife. "And what do you mean the others?"

"I'll tell you later, can we get Squala looked at?"

"Sure. Sandy sound the all clear and get the doc up here ASAP." He leaned down to Squala. "Thank you for what you have done, how are you feeling?"

"I'll be ok. Someone had to look after him," Squala replied, pointing at Steve who hovered there with a sheepish grin on his face.

"Ok let's get this mess cleaned up and go and find my boy," Marni said. As always, everything had to be tidy, even in times of a crisis. They all laughed as the tension of the moment evaporated, other crew members turned up and the doc arrived with an automated medical suite.

With help, he loaded Squala up and took him to sick bay.

"Look after him doc," Max's Dad said.

"No problem, he is in good hands," the doc nodded.

They all then turned-to Steve, and his Dad who had a hand on his shoulder told him to tell them the story from the beginning.

.....

Nino Bassi was caught out with the attack from the asteroid. His sensors had not detected anything around them. One of his ships was damaged, but it was still able to carry on. They were now moving cautiously through the belt, checking out each asteroid in turn in case there were any more surprises. He was also aware that a pirate ship had had a run in with a space car and had come off worse. This made him smile, they were obviously not that good pilots to let a little poorly armed ship like that get the better of them.

They were now nearing Black's lair, and he was determined to finish him off this time.

"Your eminence," his navigation and sensor officer said.

"Get on with it, what's wrong?" he replied curtly.

"There are ships approaching us from the pirate's location, and coming up behind us fast is a Treaty ship. It is logged as the Ajax, the one you saw in the Carweg system."

"How did that get here? Put all ships to battle stations, they are to engage the pirates and create a diversion. Then we can go and attack their base. Keep a lookout on that Treaty ship I don't want that ruining this for me. I need that cargo recovered!" he shouted out getting even angrier. He was so close to this cargo that he couldn't let them get in his way at any cost.

"Weapons, release some robot mines into the path of the Treaty ship, this might slow them down."

He sat in his chair looking out at the belt. Coming into view were the pirate ships, and he could see his five other ships turn and engage them. A huge fire fight erupted as the ships engaged each other. They entangled and were weaving around all over the place. Two pirate ships exploded, and another crashed on a small asteroid... the battle was fierce. Nino's pilot navigated his way through, and the weapons station shot at anything in their path as they skimmed the surface of a lump of rock. As they rounded this a cannon opened fire on them from the surface and the ship shuddered violently, sending some crew members to the floor. Nino held on to his seat as tightly as he could, as his weapons officer sent a rocket off to destroy it. Their shielding held and as the clouds of smoke and debris cleared, he could see Black's lair ahead.

.....

Captain Black and Rolfe were not having a good time. Reports back from his fleet weren't good. Apart from Cro, he now had four ships lost to these powerful Carpathian ships and five damaged floating uselessly in space. To add to his problems there was that Treaty ship the Ajax on the scene, and the Nerel was as nervous as a Martian dog.

Looking out of his window he could see in the distant flashes of the battle; he also saw an explosion on one of the defensive asteroids which meant it had been taken out.

"Come on we need to leave and fast," Rolfe said in a calm voice.

"Is the crew ready?"

"Yes, but we need to leave before that Carpathian arrives."

"Cre come with us we are evacuating the base!" Black shouted angrily.

He had been here for years and it felt as if his empire was disappearing in front of him.

Just then there was a loud explosion as a ship flew directly at his office firing away with its cannon. The building shuddered and the lights fluttered as dust came down from the ceiling; coughing, they all ran. There was a guard of twenty people to escort him to his ship, the Cutlass. The cargo had been loaded onto their old freighter and that had been sent ahead to hide, with an escort. At least they would have some chance of success of getting the highly prized cargo away.

They ran down the corridor, most people were on the marauders fighting the threat, or had headed off to their other base, or were escorting the small freighter.

He was in no doubt that no one knew where this was, however, the journey there was dangerous as it was even deeper in the belt.

The base was now taking a lot of damage from the ship that he saw in his office. Black knew that Bassi was on board, he could sense it, and just hoped that he could get to his ship in time.

As they got to the hangar, the Cutlass was ready to go. She was hovering there with the side doors open ready for them to board. As they got near the Carpathian ship entered the hangar, its lasers firing. Two of his guards got hit, and there was a shimmer over the Cutlass as its shielding deflected incoming fire, which bounced off the walls. As the Carpathian ship slid to a halt, a forward ramp appeared and ten troopers exited and opened fire. Black and his guard fired back as they tried to make their way to their ship. They hit several of the troopers. Black stood there firing and then he saw Bassi come down the ramp in some sort of ceremonial body suit. He looked at Rolfe who had a smile on his face. The hangar was filling up with smoke, and there were small fires where the lasers had hit equipment and stores. The Cutlass sat there ready to go, and this evil man had appeared as though he was in a play.

All fire had been suspended on both sides as Bassi stood surrounded by his guards.

"Can you hear me Black?" he called out across the hangar.

"What do you want?" Black replied, knowing full well what the reply would be.

"Well you seem to have a short memory," hissed Bassi. "You were hired to collect something for me. You obviously have no honor as you then double crossed me and took it, with the intention of trying to obtain a higher price no doubt. Now, I want it back, so where is it?"

"There is one thing you missed out. If we handed it over, you would have tried to destroy me. And after your performance in the Carweg system I was left in no doubt about that, so please don't stand there in your pantomime suit and tell me any different," Black shot back.

"Well give it to me and I will leave you alone."

Black looked at Rolfe, rolling his eyes, then turned back to face Bassi.

"I wish it was that easy, but again, that Treaty ship is behind you. I don't know what your plan is, but you will not get that cargo."

With that he fired his pistol, just missing Bassi who had hidden behind one of his troopers, then all hell broke loose as both parties started firing again.

Rolfe made it to the doorway with three of the guards who put down covering fire, and one of the side laser cupolas of the Cutlass also now opened fire on Bassi and his group. They had to retreat into their ship or risk getting killed.

Eventually they all made it on board with the ones who had been hurt taken to the medical room. Rolfe had been hit on the shoulder but not badly, so he went to the bridge with Black. The scene out of the bridge window was a mess, the hangar was strewn with containers that had been blasted and supplies were littering the floor. Smoke was hanging in the air from the fire fight and from small fires, and in front of them was the Carpathians ship hovering there, with pylons brimming with rockets and laser cannons in its ugly snout. They could see the crew on the bridge through their windows.

"What shall we do Captain?" Scottex his chief pilot asked.

"I think we need to show them what we are made of. Rolfe can you disable the shields to the hangar?"

"I think we should be able to link into the station's systems, what are you thinking?"

All the crew were looking at Black, but Scottex answered the question for him. "Brilliant idea. Shut down the force field and all the air and debris will get blown out in to space including us, and them," he concluded, pointing at the Carpathians.

"Exactly, also we'll shut down all the safety systems, so everything that isn't bolted down will come this way.

Also, we'll kill the lights to add to the surprise, this will buy us enough time. Scottex have the crew ready, we will need to move fast once we put the plan in to action. Ready when you are Rolfe."

The tension on the bridge could be cut with a knife. The ship was on red alert, and everyone was strapped in as this was going to be rough.

The lights in the hangar were doused, and the only thing they could see was the light emanating from the Carpathian's bridge. There were people looking at them one minute, the next their ship shot backwards at such high speed, that it looked as though they were on a huge run of elastic. Following them out was all the loose debris from the hanger and the base. It was being sucked out from deep within. They could hear it clattering along their hull as Scottex fought to keep the Cutlass steady in the hangar, with engines in reverse thrust.

As the Carpathian ship started to tumble out into space Captain Black yelled now at Rolfe, who then opened fire with their laser cannons hitting the ship constantly. Bright blue flashes appeared as the fire hit the shielding, weakening it through each shot.

"GO!" he then shouted at Scottex, who released power and they shot out of the hangar. There were all sorts of debris in front of them, their lights picking out chairs, beds, lockers, and cargo containers. These now bounced off their forward shielding as they took a sharp turn, narrowly missing the Carpathian ship as they headed away from danger.

"There are other ships approaching, two Carpathian ships and a squadron of tanks from the Ajax in pursuit. Our ships have now scattered from what I can see."

"What's the damage to our fleet?"

"Apart, from Cro, he's limping to the other base, we have lost four ships and six more have been damaged. They, along with the rest have headed for the safety of the belt and will stay hidden till the time is right. The freighter is stationary by asteroid twelve, awaiting instruction from us, as they don't want to lead anyone to the Base."

"What a mess Rolfe, how on earth did this happen? We will no longer deal with those Carpathians again."

"I agree, it's going to take all our cunning to stay one leap ahead of anyone till all this dies down."

As he finished his sentence, their ship took a direct hit, sending a shudder through it.

"What was that?" Black yelled.

"A Treaty tank has just appeared from behind an asteroid," came the reply.

.....

Ben and Kardo were moving slowly through the belt, apart from the glow of their instruments, it felt as though they were themselves physically lose in space, because their heads were in the clear canopy of the space car. It gave them a great view of the surrounding area. Although it was pitch black, the light from the Milky Way above them and the glow from the sun which they could see as a small ball of light high up, provided enough light to see any asteroids and smaller bits of rock ahead. Kardo had switched on the powerful lights, and they were picking out their route ahead, with the beams bouncing off the surface of passing asteroids. Further in the distance Kardo pointed out flashes of light that must have been the battle that the pirates were having with the Carpathians. The flashes were getting nearer. The static from the comms was getting noisier as the frequencies were being jammed, by either party, or as Kardo, suspected the Ajax.

As they rounded a small lump of rock a bigger asteroid came into view, the lights were dancing over its surface when something caught Ben's eye.

"Kardo pull back!" Ben yelled with alarm.

No sooner had he said that when a streak of light from a cannon shot over their heads. Luckily Kardo's reflexes were good, and he managed to pull the car back in the nick of time. Another shot hit the side of the rock and large chunks got blown off and floated off into space.

"Well spotted, that was close."

"You bet it was, we need to go around it."

"Will do." With that Kardo did a summersault and headed back the way they had come, then turned a sharp left to go round the back of the asteroid and continued on their way. After a while, zig-zagging in and out of asteroids, the scanners picked up a slow-moving ship ahead of them. Although they couldn't see it yet, Ben knew from its signature that it was the freighter. Two other ships appeared, which must have been escorting it. Ben told Kardo what he had seen, and they decided to turn off the lights and stop to see where they were headed.

"It's slowing down and heading towards a huge asteroid, the other ships are moving off and leaving it, what do you think?"

"I presume it is going to hide there and wait till the battle has subsided before it gets new orders. That cargo Max's Dad had on board and the one from the Sagaris, I bet it is on that ship."

"We need to tell Max," Ben said.

…..

Max had been following the Ajax, and in turn the Carpathians and after seeing the pirate fleet appear all hell broke loose as a huge battle ensued.

There were ships diving around all over the place, the Ajax had come to a stop, and a huge hangar door opened, and a squadron of attack tanks appeared, their turrets immediately spitting cannon fire at both fleets just to cause mayhem. Under cover of this, three of them disappeared into the belt on their respective missions. Just then they had an incoming signal from the Ajax, and Bainbridge's face filled the screen.

"I must advise you to stay away from here young man, you need to leave this to me now before you get hurt. Another Treaty ship is on its way, and I need you to give yourself up to them. They will also hold your Dad's ship until we can sort out this mess."

"I can't do that, Sir, I have another friend out there with your officer. It is my intention to go and help them."

"I order you to not do that!" came the sharp reply.

"As I am not in the Treaty, or a member of your crew I will not accept such an order."

Max and the others could see Bainbridge's face get redder, and it looked like he was going to explode. He leaned out of shot and spoke with someone, and then continued. "If you interfere with this operation, I will have you arrested, and your ship impounded, do I make myself clear?!"

"Perfectly."

They all sat and watched as the Ajax built up speed, and with laser cannon targeting any pirate or Carpathian ship in its way, pushed itself through the battle.

They could see four destroyed pirate ships with flashes of explosions coming from within, floating there. Another four more were limping away deeper into the belt. The four Carpathian ships that they could see were also damaged but were still able to function. However, as the Ajax and its tanks moved through the area, they had little intention of taking on the Treaty fleet as they would be destroyed. After a few of them had been targeted they just moved out the way; it was obvious that the giant ship was on a separate mission.

They followed it for a while, watching as it pushed itself deeper into the belt, then they turned the Huntsman around and went back towards his Dad's ship. They had also heard back from Steve to say that they had managed to free the crew and were now sitting in the bridge with his Dad and Max's parents. Squala had been hurt but was well on the mend in the medical bay. Max was looking forward to speaking with them.

.....

He had been busy talking to his parents, and for the second time telling them about their adventure, filling in the bits Steve had left out. He could tell that they were both proud and worried about his adventure to rescue them. He was pleased to hear Squala was recovering well and had now joined them on the bridge. Hope and Sarana asked Max's mum to tell their parents, including Ben's that they were ok and sent their love. Max's mum said she would be more than happy to do this.

.....

They sat there looking out at the huge ship, it still carried huge black marks and scars all over it from the various battles it had been caught up in, but apart from that it was in good shape.

After speaking with Bainbridge, they had decided it was best to stay away and let him continue his battle with the Carpathians and the pirates.

He had also informed them that the Treaty ship Dreadnaught was en route, and that they should wait for it to arrive.

His Dad had told him that it wasn't too far away. It was a smaller ship than the Ajax, but it was an attack class cruiser and heavily armed.

They had heard from Ben and Kardo and now had a positive fix on their position. Also, they knew where the small pirate transport was hidden. Max had confided with the others that he was worried as to where the other two pirate ships had gone.

They were sitting there talking about how they could capture the freighter when they got a call from Ben.

"Max we are under attack, those two ships must have spotted us and have come up behind," he said in a shaky voice.

Max looked at the others and heard the ship get hit over the communications. Sarana looked at the sensor display and could see him moving quickly around an asteroid, with two other blips on the screen chasing them, and informed the others.

303

"How long can you hang on for?" Max replied.

Kardo's voice came over. "I can keep dodging them for a bit, but I don't know for how long. Our fire power is no match for them. We are nimbler, but we could sure use some help."

"Leave it with us I'll get back to you."

Max broke the connection and asked Sarana to raise the Ajax. Without even questioning him she worked on that while Max asked the Huntsman to plot a course.

Bainbridge soon appeared on the screen.

"Young man if you hadn't noticed I am in the middle of a battle now. What do you want?" he almost yelled at them, his face rosy.

The picture looked a little shaky and they heard loud bangs like thunder as the Ajax got hit again.

"Ben and your officer are in trouble; they need some help can you send a ship to help them." Max asked almost pleadingly.

"If I could, but I have a pirate ship encircled and his comrades have launched a counter attack, so for the moment no. They'll have to manage on their own." And with that he cut the connection.

"Well." said Sarana. "How rude. What are we going to do?"

"Go and rescue them that's what!" Max said defiantly.

…..

"Dad, can you hear me?"

"Loud and clear. Are you going to get your ship into one of our loading bays?"

"I need your help; Ben is in trouble."

Sarana sent the coordinates through to them. And after a small pause he replied, "I can see them. They are in too deep for me to get there directly. We would need to go over the belt and come down on the other side. We'll leave now, you go through the belt, and we'll meet you there, and I don't have to say be careful."

With that they saw the huge ship virtually stand on its tail, and with a bright glow of its engines shoot up and out of sight.

"Huntsman, I need you to get us there, and quickly."

"Hang on," came the reply as they shot off into the belt, passing a crippled pirate ship still sparking away from the damage it had sustained.

…..

Nino Bassi was positively raging and his crew new better than to aggravate him anymore, so they kept their distance.

The ship was damaged after the trick Black had played on them to get out of his lair.

They had given chase as best as they could, but no sooner had they got under way, when a ship from the Ajax appeared and opened fire on them, its two turrets spitting laser cannon fire at them. Fortunately, their shields were holding, and they returned fire, which made them back off a bit.

Then another dozen ships passed them in formation, heading at high speed towards where Black had gone.

He had decided that the traitor probably didn't have the cargo on his ship, so retreated, and left him to the fate of the Treaty ships.

"Scan for other ships, I want to locate that cargo," he barked at his crew.

After a while he was informed that a small ship was under attack on the other side of the belt. This bought a small smile to his evil face. "It must be the cargo," he thought, and slamming his fist down on his chair, ordered them to set a course for those coordinates.

.....

Black's day was going from bad to worse. Not only was he surrounded by these infernal tanks, but his sensors had also picked up the Ajax closing in on their position, and fast.

306

Their communications had been blocked and he couldn't even call for help, so they just sat there surrounded, and waited for an opportunity, if any, should it arise.

"Rolfe what do you think?" he asked.

After a pause for thought Rolfe replied dryly, "Let's see what their intentions are, but I think we should fight to the death."

Black sat back in his chair and laughed, the crew all looked at him, and after a while everyone joined in, except Rolfe who looked around bemused.

"Well Rolfe, as much as your idea might appeal to some, we need a better plan than that," Black replied patting his friend on the shoulder.

They all sat or stood there looking out at the visible tanks, each one had its turrets aimed squarely at them.

"Helm reverse slowly let's see what they do," he commanded.

As they moved, one of the tanks opened fire, the blue light shooting past them, and again it fired, missing them, but closer this time.

"Well at least they don't want to destroy us just yet," he said ruefully before adding, "full stop."

Just then laser fire hit one of the tanks. Then all the tanks opened fire as a marauder appeared and flew directly in front of them before disappearing, all its lasers firing at once.

"The cavalry has arrived!" Black shouted triumphantly. The atmosphere on the bridge was one of excitement at this turn of events. "Helm fast forward, weapon stations target and fire at will."

With that they moved off. Another six marauders had arrived and had now engaged the stunned crews of the tanks, who were now regrouping and returning fire.

The Cutlass headed directly at one of them, and fired, disabling it. As they headed away from the scene, the Cutlass was starting to build up speed, firing at anything in its path as they tried to escape, but the tanks were like a swarm of bees chasing after them and they started to take heavy fire. The Cutlass was getting knocked about all over the place. Sparks were flying all over the bridge and smoke was filling the room; one of the weapons stations exploded, sending the two crew members flying across the bridge.

Black could see that three of his marauders were on fire as the Ajax entered the fray. Seeing this, another three of them turned and took on the Ajax, firing with everything they had. There were ships all over the place and the scene was flashing with the bolts of light from all the laser fire. Two attack tanks collided with each other as they gave chase after a marauder, which shot off underneath the Ajax firing its rear cannon at them. The two tanks went off spinning, one of them corrected itself and continued, while the other one floated away with a loss of power. Two of the marauders kept up their attack on the Ajax, with tanks hot on their heels. They were flying all around it, blasting away, the other remaining one was having a fire fight with three attack tanks. It had badly damaged two of them and was skillfully dodging their fire.

There were streaks of cannon fire zipping around all over the place.

"Weapons fire all our missiles at the Ajax!" Black yelled as they got hit again.

"They're launched," came the reply.

He saw the blue glow of their engines as they appeared in front of them heading directly towards the ship. The Ajax and the tanks were now not only targeting the marauders, but also were opening fire on the new threat. They destroyed six of them, but four made it through, and the resulting explosion briefly turned the whole area into daylight.

The Ajax was now badly damaged on its left side. There was a gaping hole where the missiles had struck, and they could see flashes from within, but it wasn't enough. The Ajax was now slowly turning towards them with the other marauders buzzing around it like flies, until they got too got disabled, one of them bouncing off the Ajax's hull, which then ended up spinning away.

The Cutlass was giving it all it had. Hit after hit shook it, but still they carried on firing till eventually a missile fired by a tank struck their engines and they lost momentum and slowly ground to a halt, floating dead in space. The bridge was now full of smoke, and flames were leaping up from instrument consuls. Half of his bridge crew were injured, while the others frantically fought to put out the fires.

The power was now slowly draining as she got hit again, sending Rolfe crashing to the floor. The lighting was now flickering as emergency power came on fitfully.

Black looked out to see the Ajax come above them. All he could see now was the belly of the huge ship. Suddenly there was a big thud as it docked with the Cutlass.

Black stood there and drew his pistol, as did the remainder of the crew who were left standing, and they waited for the boarding party to arrive. They could hear laser fire out in the corridor as the crew fought with the enemy, but then that died out and a hush descended on the bridge as they waited.

As the doors opened about thirty robotic spiders scurried in. These were able to attack and fire an electronic web at their target to disable them.

They immediately picked out their targets and headed towards them. Everyone opened fire with their pistols trying to defend themselves from this threat, but they just kept coming firing their webs. It seemed as soon as one was destroyed another took its place. One by one the crew were hit with the webs and overpowered.

Black managed to destroy two of them and had managed to dodge several webs fired at him, before he himself was hit. As the charge went through his body, the last thing he remembered was looking at Rolfe and seeing heavily armored Treaty troops enter the bridge before he fell unconscious himself.

.....

Bainbridge was shocked at the ferocity of the counterattack. The marauders had been hding behind an asteroid. He saw them appear from a distance as his tanks held the pirate ship at bay. He managed to get a warning off to them, but not quicklt enough as the pirates quickly engaged his ships and destroyed three of them, with another two taking heavy damage.

The Ajax itself was also badly damaged from the missile attack, but his fire crews had now got the damaged area under control.

However he was now over the moon that the pirate Black and his crew were now in the cells. One of the marauders had escaped. The remaining ships had been destroyed by his tanks before they returned to the hangars just to make sure that no one would salvage them.

.....

The captain of the Dreadnaught came on screen.

"Captain Bainbridge, I see you have had a busy time. Do you have everything under control?"

"Good to hear your voice Sino. Yes, everything is under control. What's the news on the freighter and the other ship?"

"When we got here, they were gone, I was hoping you had them?" was the reply.

Bainbridge called out to his sensor officer. "Do you have their coordinates?"

"Hang on Sir," the officer responded.

"I don't have time to hang on, where are they?" he yelled.

After a while, the officer, with Jim's help, finally called out, "The freighter is high above the belt and heading to where our last report of Kardo was, wait, I can see Kardo being pursued by two ships, he is flying well, by the looks of it. We can also see the other ship headed through the belt towards him. There is another ship headed in that direction, I think it is that Carpathian ship that left the scene of the pirates' lair."

Turning back to the screen where Sino's face was., Bainbridge asked, "Did you get that?"

"We have them all on our sensors. We'll leave you here and go and give them some assistance as I think they are going to need it."

"Thanks. Make sure nothing happens to them. I have an officer on board that space car who I would like to see again."

"No problem."

And with that the Dreadnaught powered up and disappeared.

.....

Ben and Kardo were having a rough time. They had been hit several times, but their shields were holding, just. Ben was also grateful to have Kardo flying the car, as he wouldn't have been able to do half the maneuvers Kardo was doing. He was running ribbons around them, somersaulting, stopping dead, and flying so close to the surface of asteroids that he thought they might crash. Right now they were directly underneath one of the marauders. Ben looked up and could see the belly of the ship literally feet away and in front of them was a laser cannon, but as it was fixed it was no threat to them. The other ship was behind them, but daren't fire in case it hit its comrade. The ship above was trying everything it could to shake them off, but no matter which way they went, or turned, Kardo held them in position.

"Well, I'm glad you came along!" Ben said as the ship above did a complete role, but which Kardo managed to mirror.

"Thanks, I've got to say given the circumstances, I'm rather enjoying this. Oh dear hang on," he yelled.

The marauder was heading for a large asteroid that had a huge peak jutting out of the side of it. If they hit that it would be curtains for sure.

"Kardo there!" Ben shouted.

"Where?"

"At the base, there's a huge arch."

"Seen it well spotted."

It was hard to see at that distance, and Kardo switched on their forward lights as they peeled away from the marauder and headed in a steep dive towards the arch. As they did, it bought them out in the open and the other marauder opened fire on them. All around were streaks of light from their cannon which was hitting the surface, sending up rock and dust as they exploded on the surface and around the arch.

Eventually they made it to the arch and shot through it, coming out the other side and Kardo pulled them in to a steep climb. The ship that they had been hiding under was heading in their direction and firing at them, but Kardo managed to evade this and headed back out into space again.

"Ben see if you can see that asteroid the cargo ship was hiding next to."

Ben worked on his sensors and eventually picked it up. "It's about two hundred kilometers away."

"Let's head there then. Those two behind us won't take too long to catch us again. And I think they won't be happy when they do. Call your friend again and find out where they are, before our luck runs out."

With that they headed towards a small cluster of asteroids with the other two ships only about ten kilometers behind and closing.

.....

The Huntsman was flying through the asteroid belt as fast as it could and with such precision. Max knew he would never have been able to do it.

They were strapped in tight as they weaved in and out of obstacles, their powerful lights picking them out as if they were snowflakes caught in light. How they never hit anything, who only knew. Now and then they skimmed surfaces. They all just sat there and watched as if they were on a roller coaster ride.

"How far are we now?" Max asked.

"Well they are moving around all over the place, but we should be there within five minutes," Sarana replied.

Max activated the headsup display for the laser cannons, while Hope checked to make sure all the systems were working, and they had full power.

Sarana was monitoring the sensor controls, watching as Ben and Kardo were weaving in and out trying to shake off their pursuers. She then noticed another ship entering the area, and after checking told everyone that the Carpathian ship was now close by.

"Those guys never give up, do they? I bet it's that one called Nino Bassi. I guess they are looking for the freighter too. Let Ben know and we need to find that freighter, ask him if he knows where it is?"

Max could now pick out in the distance the glow of the engines from the ships chasing Ben.

"Ben, you have other company coming up on your right, it should be visible soon. It's a Carpathian ship. We think it's looking for the cargo ship as well, do you know where it is?"

"We are heading there now. How far away are you? Those ships chasing us are too close for comfort."

"Hang on Ben I'm opening fire on your two companions now."

Max fired the cannons at both ships. Although he knew he wouldn't damage them because of the distance, it should be enough to put a fright up them for now.

One of them veered off to the left and came round to attack them.

"Huntsman peel away and head for the Carpathian ship, Hope send a missile in the direction of that pirate ship heading our way."

"Will do," she replied and sent one on its way.

The Carpathian ship looked in a bit of a state. It looked badly damaged and dented in places where it had obviously taken a beating. Max added to this and opened fire on it. It responded back and hit them as they flew over the top of it. The marauder that they had fired a missile at also opened fire on the Carpathian ship, which in turn fired back. The pirate ship and the Carpathian ship were now locked into a battle, so they headed off towards the other one still chasing Ben and catching it up, they fired on it.

"Dad where are you?" Max called.

"We are high above you. We have all ships on our monitors including the one hiding, and the Dreadnaught which has just entered the fray. It has opened fire on both the Carpathian ship and the pirate ship catching them completely by surprise."

"Good that gives us time to help Ben, Ben can you hear me?"

"Loud and clear, can you get that ship off our back?"

"We are going after it now."

With that the other ship appeared in Max's sights, as it swung round an asteroid in pursuit of the space car, all the time firing at it. They were gaining on it fast and opened fire. The shots hit, but the shields were holding on. They now returned fire on the Huntsman forcing them to peel off and try and come up beside them. The car now had a smoke trail coming from it as it turned around another asteroid and disappeared.

317

"Dad, can you see where they went?" Max called.

"They are slowing down and are nearing the cargo ship, which has just shot at them, and is powering up ready to make a run. Pull back and go over the top of the asteroid, we are on way to take on that pirate ship, go and help Ben."

As they pulled away, the huge shape of the freighter appeared and opened fire on the marauder. As the marauder returned fire, the freighter got one of its huge wings under it and literally flipped it into a spin.

Max and the girls watched this as they headed over the top of the asteroid and came down above the cargo ship. The car looked in a bad way, Max opened fire on the cargo ship, while Hope and Sarana opened the rear hatch.

"Huntsman get us between them both we need to get that car on board before it's too late."

With that they came in between the two ships and took the fire from the pirate ship; Max fired back.

"Kardo get your car on board now!" Max ordered.

"Will do, see you in a minute and thanks."

They were now stationary. The pirate's freighter started to build up speed and pull away from them. Just then the Carpathian ship appeared and started firing at the pirates as it tried to pull alongside the cargo ship. They seemed determined to dock with it and steal the cargo. Max heard the alarm to say that the rear was secure, and within a minute he was joined on the bridge by the others. He turned round to see the blackened faces of Ben and Kardo. He stood up and gave Ben a hug and looked at Kardo and said thanks for looking after his friend.

"Right let's see if we can capture that ship," he said taking his seat as he again tried to target the Carpathian ship.

The Dreadnaught also now appeared in view and opened fire on the Carpathian ship with such a volley of shots that it immediately disabled it and left it floating there on fire.

"Max we are being contacted by the Dreadnaught," Sarana said.

"Put him on."

A face appeared, the man had short grey hair and a mid-brown skin, he also a smile spread across his face.

"My name is Sino, Well done. The captain of the Ajax told me about you guys. I'll take it from here. There are some tanks on the way to help me. These folk will be arrested and face trial and no thanks to you, the cargo has been recovered."

As he said that they saw ten tanks appear and surround the two ships.

"Go back to your parent's ship and await orders," came the final transmission.

After they had docked in to one of the cargo bays, and been reunited with their parents, Max was sitting with his friends after they had all cleaned up and got a change of clothes. Squala had also joined them, and they were all talking about their adventure, but more importantly what they should do with Squala. If the Treaty got hold of him, they would never see him again.

Kardo now also felt part of this little team and was joining in with ideas.

As they were talking Ben's and Steve's Dads appeared in the room and everyone went quiet as they stood there looking at them.

"I have just spoken with the captain of the Ajax. They have got in custody the leader of the pirates, Black, his sidekick Rolfe and sixty of his team. On top of that they have a Carpathian called Nino Bassi and his crew. The rest of them fled back to their system." Ben's Dad then walked over to look out of the window at the asteroid belt. He turned round and continued. "The Carpathians high command had contacted the Treaty and denied any knowledge of what he was up to. Obviously they don't believe them as they were quick to tell them this. The cargo that was stolen from us is now safe. It was as you all thought on the freighter. Bainbridge sends his regards to you all and thanks your tenacity in rescuing us and putting an end to the pirates' reign of terror in this region. However, he is sending a boarding party to take Squala and your ship away for further examination."

Hope walked over to Squala and spoke, "They can't do that he has helped us and been a friend. If we let them do that, we will betray him."

Everyone now stood protectively around him, including Kardo, who said, "I agree with her. He defected from his people to help them. Also, they made a promise to return the ship they borrowed."

"We know that," Steve's Dad said, then looked at Kardo. "They also want you to return with them. You could be jeopardizing your career if you have any part, or any knowledge of what we are going to do and don't tell them."

As he said this everyone looked at him and they all said as one voice, "What are you going to do?" Just then the doors opened, and Max's Mum came in.

"We are going to look after him. Squala told me that he can shrink down to a transport mode, so I'm going to hide him in our cabin. Your father, with your help is going to hide the Huntsman as you call it. Squala, you need to come with me now." And with that they left.

"Now we need to move fast before this boarding party arrives."

Chapter Twenty-Two

The return to Trieg.

Max had been back at school now for a month. The excitement of their adventure and all the exposure to the news channels, now seemed like a faded memory, however he had one more thing to do and sitting here in his room waiting was driving him mad, but as always, he had to be patient. They had all agreed to wait till things had settled down.

They were sure Bainbridge hadn't bought their story that Squala had run off with their ship during the battle. The Treaty was far too keen to get their hands on Squala, and they in turn weren't going to let them, no matter what the cost.

Fortunately for them, in the heat of the battle the only person who could have seen anything was the captain of the Dreadnaught, and he was on record saying that he saw nothing because he'd had his hands full. Little did everyone know that Max's Dad and Sino went back a long way.

They had all been interviewed by the security police to find out what had happened to their ship, and where they had got it. They all said the same thing... that they'd stolen it from a planet called Kalin. Squala must have taken it and escaped.

They had eventually left them alone, but their search had dug up nothing. Kardo had told Max that they were frustrated, but he thought that Bainbridge was secretly happy. Kardo had also got a bravery award for his part in the battle and had been promoted to a first officer on a tank squadron based on the Ajax.

Everyone was happy for him because he had not only looked after Ben but had loosely confirmed their story about the ship disappearing during the battle.

However, they were all looking in the wrong place, the one place they would never dream of looking... his Dad's freighter... both Squala and the Huntsman had been concealed there away from prying eyes.

.....

Max's communicator vibrated; it was Steve's Dad.

"Max, good to hear your voice. Believe it or not I am visiting Jupiter 2 on a last-minute job." Hearing his voice bought a huge grin to Max's face.

"Knowing you are on half term for a couple of days, I wondered if you and Hope might like to join me on a trip." Even through the communicator you could hear the laughter in his voice.

"Wow, I wasn't expecting to hear from you," Max replied excitedly. "Is Steve with you?"

"Yes, so is Sarana, they are both keen to see you. I have you booked on the 10 o'clock shuttle so you had better get your skates on."

"Leaving now, see you soon!" With that he grabbed his coat and ran to the tram station, calling Hope on the way, knowing full well that she would be ready and waiting. He had to be quick as the timing was crucial. The corridors were packed with people going about their daily tasks. He went as quickly as he could and got to the platform just as Hope arrived.

Their journey to the space station was uneventful. No sooner had they arrived, than they saw Steve hovering above everybody in his chair, waving at them.

"Hi, you two, been looking forward to seeing you."

"Yep, me too, what's the plan?" Max asked looking around the crowd that had started to thin out. He couldn't see anyone following them, but he was conscious of the cameras.

"Well Dad's got the new cruiser up in the flight deck and once we get there, we will be off."

"Excellent, where are we going, do you know?" Hope asked with a smile on her face.

Steve looked down at her as they moved through the crowd towards the elevator to take them to the flight deck. "I believe we are off to Venus, but I'm not sure," he replied.

They got to the flight deck, and Max was pleased to see the cruiser was exactly like the one they had crashed on Treig, only it was now grey in color.

.....

They embarked and after saying their hellos, took their seats on the bridge as they made their way out of the hangar, got clearance for the space highway, and headed for Venus. The space highway was busy in places, and they had to slow down near Earth for a bit before the final leg of the journey.

As they slowed down on the approach the planet started to grow bigger. All you could see was the grey cloud mass of the planet. No one lived there but the planet was robotically mined, and the ore transported up to huge processing stations in orbit around the planet.

As they approached one such station, they saw the Vanquish. They had let Max name the freighter, and he named it after the ship in his dreams. He felt it was a fitting name given the likeness to his dreams and what had occurred. It had been repaired at the repair facility on Titan, headed up by Sarana's

Dad. Her parents, along with Hope's were already on board, along with Ben and his parents.

The Vanquish was underneath a huge shoot leading out of the side of the facility. The shoot was pumping ore into the huge bays in one of the wings. They came in under the ship and entered the shuttle bay underneath.

After disembarking they made their way to the bridge where everyone else was waiting for them.

"Any troubles Pat?"

"None whatsoever, got a bit held up around Earth, but that's about it."

"Ok as we have discussed, once loaded up we shall head off to this Nebula where this planet is hidden. Thanks to Ovrie." He looked at Sarana's Dad. "We should be able to mask our trail once through the gateway, and if we have any other problems Senator Wiseman will give us additional cover.

"Tuc," he said, looking at Ben's Dad, "will be going with Max and Steve to the planet, and before you two say anything that is final. We don't want anything else happening. Pat will follow in the cruiser as back up should we need it; Sandy are we ready to go?"

"Yep."

"Let's go then."

And with that the Vanquish powered up and went on its way.

.....

The journey to the Nebula was uneventful and Max, Steve, Squala and Tuc were now heading into the red cloud, with Pat following behind. The Huntsman had already contacted Nyxam to tell him of their return and as the planet came into view, they were met by two more ships that were identical to the Huntsman. They went through the atmosphere and landed back in the hangar from which they had set out so long ago.

As they disembarked, they were met by half a dozen discs that led them to a huge room, which as expected, was empty.

"I am pleased that you have honored your word Max and Steve. Who are the others with you?"

"This is Tuc a parent of a friend of ours who helped us rescue our parents. The other one is an android from a planet called Carpathia. He has also helped us. But he can't go back to his people now as he fought against them."

"I can see this from the log from your ship, which I believe you named the Huntsman. I am pleased that you rescued your families. But why have you brought him here?"

Steve piped up. "He needs somewhere safe to stay, so he won't come to any harm, and we thought that you would help us on this."

"His life is in danger, not only from his own people but also ours who want to do experiments on him," Max added.

"I see, again I will contact the elders. I will speak with you shortly."

"I would never have believed it, if I hadn't seen it with my own eyes," Tuc said shaking his head in bewilderment.

Max and Steve just looked at each other while Squala stood silently behind.

"Don't worry Squala," Steve added.

"I'm not, what will be will be."

After a while Nyxam replied that the elders were happy for this. He also told them that the elders were now thinking of getting their people motivated to try and rebuild their home world again. It was partly due to them, that they felt there was good to be had after all.

After they said their goodbyes to Squala and promised him they would stay in touch, they headed back to the Huntsman who took them all back to the Sagaris. Once docked, Max and Steve thanked the ship for everything and stood there silently as it departed.

Max's parents had laid on a party for the friends and families as a final closure to the whole adventure as they headed back to the solar system and for the friends, back to school.

Chapter Twenty-Three

The Prison Planet Pluto

Black and Rolfe were sitting in their cell. The room was small and dark, and through the small window they could see out over the icy surface of the planet; every now and then a small, automated drone would fly past looking for any attempts at escape. The winds were howling, and even through the thick walls you could hear it. Just the thought of it sent shivers down people's spines. Without proper equipment no one could survive out there. It amazed Black they even had drones patrolling. He and his crewmates had been sentenced to life imprisonment. They had learned that they had been outsmarted by a bunch of school kids, and one of them had seen him on the Jupiter 2, and the LA service stations. He had also learned that the Carpathian Nino Bassi had been sent to a remote mining colony by his superiors as punishment. It bought a smile to his face that the kids had also ruined the Carpathian. To Black that wasn't far enough as he was convinced that, given the chance, Bassi would come after them.

"Well Sir, this place is freezing. Do you have any plan at all?" Rolfe said shivering.

"None at the moment my friend, but as always, an opportunity will arise, and when it does, we'll take it. I want to hunt those kids down and teach them a lesson for ruining me, you wait and see," he said, putting an arm around his trusted aid and looking out of the window with an evil grin across his face.

The End

Coming soon! The next adventures of Max and friends:
Max and the Galactic Slave Trader

For updates please follow the group **The Space Adventures of Max and his Friends** on Facebook.

Printed in Great Britain
by Amazon

38202577R00192

Above: Roman cavalry soldier at Segedunum Museum.

Right: Danger, Romans at work.

Original Roman bathhouse at Gainers Terrace.

Bathhouse reconstruction, 1999.

and there is some evidence that women had lived in the fort at some time in later years. Apart from providing housing, a number of traders and businesses would have been present in the town to serve the needs of the soldiers and the local population. People would have ran and worked in inns and taverns, shops, workshops, bathhouses and brothels and would have employed butchers, leather workers, blacksmiths, carpenters, as well as farmers. To provide food, many fields outside the fort to the north have been found that would have supplied crops and livestock for the soldiers, their horses, as well as the many residents in the town.

Gateway reconstruction at Arbeia Fort.

Arbeia Roman Fort Barrack building reconstructions.

Reconstructed Commanding Officer's House and Barracks at Arbeia.

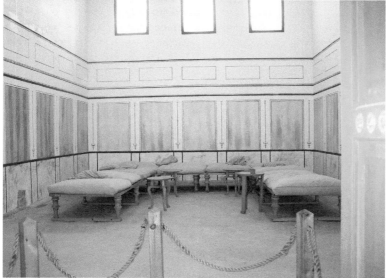

The dining room inside the Commanding Officer's House at Arbeia.

Segedunum was occupied until around 410 when Roman rule ceased in Britain. It is likely that people continued living in and around the fort for a number of years, but as the garrison had left the buildings would not have been maintained and people would have gradually moved out to seek a living elsewhere. In addition attacks from the Picts to the north and from the river by the Angles and Saxons may have led to new settlements being built inland. The famous antiquarian John Collingwood Bruce in his book on the Roman wall in 1867 (third edition) suggested that according to legend a plague desolated the original town that had been built out of the ruins on the site of the camp and terrified residents left for shelter elsewhere.

SIXTH TO ELEVENTH CENTURIES

After the Roman fort and town were abandoned small settlements developed around Wallsend Green and at Willington as the centres for farming communities.

A number of individual dwellings may well have scattered across the district, which later developed into farmhouses. The land in Wallsend and Willington was over time donated to the church. Originally the monks of St Cuthbert administered it from Jarrow where the famous Venerable Bede was based from 673 to 735. It is thought there may have been a ferry between Wallsend and Jarrow near to where the present pedestrian tunnel is today.

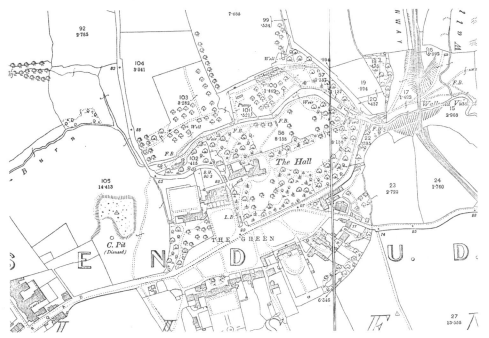

Wallsend in 1897. (Ordnance Survey)

The monks of Jarrow oversaw Wallsend and Willington until the Norman Conquest in 1066. After that the Normans laid waste to much of northern England but the area must have been populated again by the mid-1100s as Holy Cross Church was built around AD 1150 to serve both the villages of Wallsend and Willington.

Wallsend Village Green looking west.

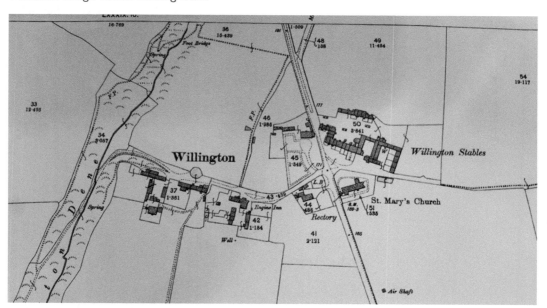

Willington village, 1895. (Ordnance Survey)

Willington stables at Willington village, *c.* early 1900s.

The Wallsend to Jarrow ferry was originally founded by the monks of Jarrow.

Holy Cross Church, *c.* 1900.

TWELFTH TO SEVENTEENTH CENTURIES

The land at Wallsend and Willington was eventually taken over by the monks of Durham, who administered it from Jarrow, and the townships of Wallsend and Willington became part of the manor of Westoe. Agriculture was the main form of occupation with a hierarchy of workers employed on the land ultimately paying dues to the lord of the manor. The lower classes of surfs or agricultural labourers were tied to work only for the lord on his land on an annual basis and if they left they could be hunted down and returned to work on the manor. Wallsend and Willington shared a mill and all grain had to be ground there. In 1354 the Black Death killed nine people in Wallsend and seven in Willington.

Wallsend and Willington continued as farming communities. Individual farms in Willington village were set around an oval-shaped village green with a pond at either end. It was about 5.5 acres in size with farmhouses and buildings of the West Farm and Middle Farm on the south side and those of the Willington Farm on the north side. The village smithy was between the West and Middle farms.

Other farms in Willington included North Farm; Willington Out Farm (also known as Greenchesters or Moor Gate as it was near a gate on the Shire Moor); Halfway House Farm (Rose Inn) that was on the main road between Newcastle and North Shields just to the east of the present Rose Inn; and the Willington Low or East Farm.

In Wallsend there were the Rising Sun Farm and High Farm in the northern part of Wallsend and the farms around the Green cultivated the southern areas. A village pump was established in Wallsend Dene below Holy Cross Church to serve both villages. To the north of the townships in 1464 was an area of common land called the Threap Moor that separated Wallsend from Shiremoor and Long Benton. By 1539 Wallsend was divided into seven farms and Willington had eight.

Wallsend village started to attract wealthy merchants from Newcastle to develop mansions on the Green. The riverside at Willington was referred to as Howdon and William Richardson in his book suggests that the name came from 'how', meaning 'enclosure', and 'dun', meaning 'a sandhill'. It was here where the Howdon Burn met the River Tyne that the industry of salt pans developed in the fourteenth century, being first recorded in writing in 1539. A community developed around the salt pans known as Howdon Panns, owned by the Anderson family from Newcastle. The salt pans continued to operate until around 1789 when tax increases and other sources of salt were found. Salt pans were large metal discs or pans filled with

Wallsend Village Green looking east.

Engine Inn on the south side of Willington Village Green.

Moor Gate Farm or Greenchesters, c. 1930.

THE OLD ROSE INN, WILLINGTON-on-TYNE. — F. W. CORNER 1911 —

Old Rose Inn,
Church Bank, on
the turnpike road
between Newcastle
and Tynemouth.

East Farm, Wallsend,
on High Street East,
pre-1930s.

seawater or brine that were suspended over a coal fire and once the water evaporated it left sediment of salt that could be collected and then the process was repeated again. South Shields, Cullercoats and Seaton Sluice also had a number of salt pans at this time. The first reference to coal mining was in 1581 in Willington when Robert Dudley leased land from Elizabeth I for twenty-one years at 100 shillings and in 1665 Sir Francis Anderson got a lease from Newcastle Corporation to dump ballast from coal-carrying ships on land at Willington that later became Willington Quay.

Other industries were built up around this settlement including shipbuilding industries. Glassmaking also developed in the area around 1600 when families of Huguenots such as the Henzells and Tyzachs arrived in Britain from France after being driven out by religious persecution. They chose the location as many materials were available in the area such as sand (from ship ballast) and coal, as well as having an available workforce. The works concentrated on making broad glass to be used in making windows and works were set up close to the river where they could be exported to London and European markets. The works eventually became outdated and production was transferred to Lemmington in Newcastle around 1780.

EIGHTEENTH CENTURY

Agriculture was still dominant and Wallsend Green continued to attract Newcastle merchants to develop country houses. Howdon Panns developed into an industrial complex as salt panns and glass production continued until the 1780's and were complemented by other industries including shipbuilding and chemical industries which developed westwards on reclaimed land to form Willington Quay.

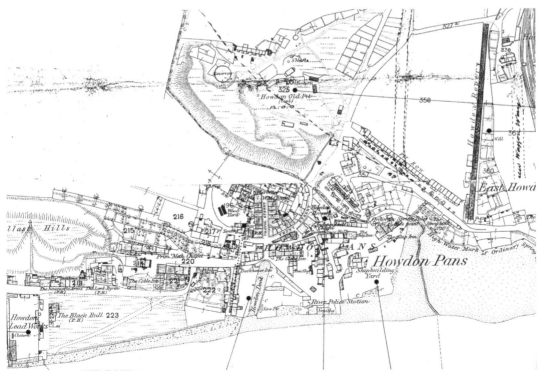

Howdon Panns, 1855. (Ordnance Survey)

SHIPBUILDING

The Hurry family from Great Yarmouth established shipbuilding at Howdon in the early 1770s to the west of the glasshouses and salt pans. A large dock was constructed together with slipways and soon Howdon became an important shipbuilder for the navy and many famous 'Wooden Walls of England' were constructed here. The dock was quite extensive for their day and consisted of a double dry dock, building slips for four vessels, a 500-foot-long river-facing quay, a ropery and sail-making lofts and warehouses. The ropery is easily identified on early plans of Howdon Panns as it is a long thin building extending northward on the north-east edge of the village. Examples of the ships built at Howdon include His Majesty's Frigate *Syren*, which had twenty-eight guns, and *Argo*, a forty-four-gun battleship that was at the time the largest vessel to be constructed on the Tyne. This set the scene for later shipbuilding records to be broken at Wallsend. In these early days of shipbuilding the entire ship – including masts, ropes, sails, etc. – was constructed on or near the site. At this time the Hurry family developed all these ancillary industries but later the ropeworks became an independent business taken over by the appropriately named Knott family. Following Nelson and Collingwood's success in the Battle of Trafalgar in 1805 new orders for warships declined and the Hurry shipbuilding business found itself in financial difficulties and ceased trading in 1806. No buyer could be found and the business was sold off in parts with shipbuilding and repairing continuing until the mid-nineteenth century when the dock silted up and suffered from mining subsidence. The Hurry family also had their own fishing and whaling fleet that regularly visited the Greenland fisheries and blubber boiling houses were established on the northern bank of Howdon Burn.

COAL MINING

In the later years, when steam engines were developed, deeper coal mines could be sunk and mines were sunk at Howdon, outside Wallsend's boundary (1799), Wallsend (1778), Willington (1772) and Bigges Main (1784) with communities growing up around them.

Willington Colliery was the first to be developed when coal was reached in 1775 in the High Main Seam (6 feet 4 inches thick) at the Engine Pit close to Middle Engine Lane and to where the public house Walls End is now. The original partners were William Gibson, town clerk of Newcastle, Mathew Bell and William Bell, later known as 'Bell & Browns'. Although

Willington Colliery, 1840s. It opened in 1775.

Wallsend A Pit, 1844.
It opened in 1781.

AIR SHAFT OF "A" PIT, WALLSEND. SUNK 1777.
THE HOUSE ON THE RIGHT WAS THE RESIDENCE OF THE LATE MR. JOHN BUDDLE

the coal was of the highest quality the pit suffered a lot from flooding and to overcome this problem an expensive but effective solution was arrived at. They built a long tunnel known as the 'Tyne Level Drift' that was 2,030 yards long and led from the pit to the River Tyne at Willington Gut. It served Willington and later Bigges Main collieries for many years. In addition, as good ventilation was required, a number of individual shafts were sunk across the district from 1776 when the Edward Pit was opened on the site of the present car park of the Jolly Bowman pub to 1806 when the Willington Low Pit was opened south of Archer Street near Willington Terrace. During this time the following pits were opened: Milbank Pit, in the present Police Station car park on Middle Engine Lane; Belle Pit, in Hadrian Park; Bigge Pit, north-east of Hadrian Park First School; Bewicke Pit, north of Broomfield Avenue; and the Craster Pit, east of Hotspur Road.

William and John Chapman of Wallsend Colliery commenced digging a shaft in 1778 but they ran out of money in 1781 and their banker, William Russell, took over the site. Soon after this they reached the High Main Seam (6 feet 6 inches thick and 666 feet deep), which quickly got a reputation as the best coal in Britain and made Mr Russell a very rich man, making over £1,000 per week, a fortune in those days.

He then proceeded to buy Brancepeth Castle and estates in Durham in 1796 for £75,000 where he lived in luxury and did little for the workmen who provided his wealth. As the deep mines needed good ventilation it was necessary to open numerous individual pit shafts all over the district to exploit the coal. At Wallsend the A and B pits (1781) were close to Segedunum Roman Fort, C Pit or Gas Pit (1786) was close to Wallsend Green in Wallsend Park, D Pit (1786) was situated on the present golf course close to Wallsend Burn, E (1791) and F pits (1802) were close to present Coast Road on the north side not far from Millfield Avenue and Chicken Road respectively and G Pit or Church Pit (1802) was close to St Peter's Church, west of Hadrian Metro station.

Bigges Main Colliery was worked by the Benton Colliery owners and the first shaft was sunk in 1784 at the Powder Monkey hill close to the present railway to the west of the Powder Monkey pub. A further shaft known as the George Pit was situated to the north-west of the supermarket on Wiltshire Drive, and another shaft known as the William Pit was situated outside Wallsend in Little Benton to the west of the George Pit but connected to it by a waggonway. The first shaft at Bigges Main village was sunk in 1789 north of the Wallsend Golf Club house.

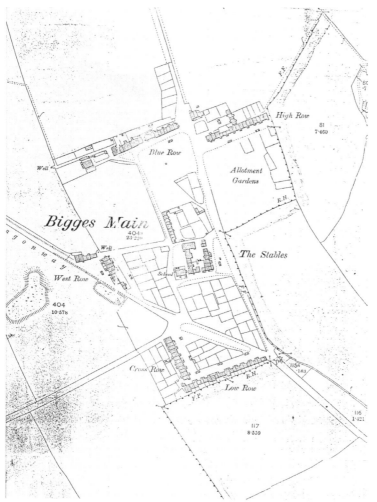

Bigges Main in 1897.
(Ordnance Survey)

Killingworth
Waggonway
wooden viaduct
and village pumps at
Wallsend Dene.

Churchill Street, formerly Copperas Lane, passing through Willington village, looking south, *c.* 1913.

A major change to the appearance of the whole district was the building of timber waggonways all over Tyneside to transport coal from collieries both within Wallsend and beyond to the River Tyne.

A number of timber waggonways were built across Wallsend to serve these mines and included (1) the Gosforth Engine Waggonway, dating from 1740 or earlier and built on the line of the later Coxlodge Waggonway dating from 1808, which passed through Bigges Main and led to Benton Way; (2) the Killingworth Waggonway in 1765, which passed through High Willington and down to Willington Quay to the east of Willington Gut; (3) the Willington Waggonway, which was built in 1776 from Willington Colliery and parallel to the Killingworth Waggonway; (4) the Willington Waggonway loop through Bigges Main and extended to Benton Way of 1785 (and the earliest standard gauge railway yet discovered); (5) the Wallsend Colliery waggonway of 1780 that extended east from the A and B pits along the line of Buddle Street and Hadrian Road, with a link up the line of Park Road from C Pit in Wallsend Park (which was linked to the D, E and F pits), to the Wallsend Staithes at Davy Bank; and (6) part of the famous Killingworth Waggonway on which George Stephenson experimented with his locomotives was built in 1830 as a diversion from the original line to terminate at Davy Bank, involving building an extensive wooden viaduct over Wallsend Burn close to Crow Bank.

Before 1749 the main road through Wallsend to North Shields went through Wallsend Green and over Wallsend Burn by means of a ford. The road was described as being in such bad condition that it was a danger to travellers. A new turnpike road was opened in 1749 on the line of the present Wallsend High Street, Church Bank, Rosehill Road and Tynemouth Road and originally a toll had to pay. One of the original toll gate cottages (later called Firtrees cottage) that collected tolls was situated on Tynemouth Road close to the present to A19 Tyne Tunnel approach road until the 1930s.

Close to Willington Mill on Ropery Way was a terrace of housing known as Keelman's Row, which suggests that a community of keelmen must have lived in this area and operated keels to carry coal and other goods along the river to ships waiting close to the river mouth. A large number of keelmen lived on the east side of Newcastle in the Sandgate area where they built the Keelmen's Hospital in 1701.

Firtrees Cottage, the original toll house on Tynemouth Road, near the present A1, looking east, c. 1920s.

Keelman's Row, Willington Quay, c. 1931. It was demolished in 1932.

The Willington Ropery was established in 1789, adjoining Willington Gut to the west of Willington Quay, by William Chapman, a former merchant ship captain turned businessman from Whitby. His sons inherited the business in 1793 and Edward Chapman ran the business and lived nearby and was also responsible for some useful inventions in rope making, which were patented.

NINETEENTH CENTURY

During this century Wallsend was transformed from a collection of small rural villages into a centre for new industries based on the extended shores of the River Tyne. The population in 1801 was 3,120, doubled to 6,715 by 1861 and by 1901 it had risen to almost 29,000.

COAL MINING

Coal mining developed rapidly in the first half of the century and Wallsend coal was so popular in London and other markets that all other local collieries called their coal 'Walls End' coal in order to get the highest prices. Wallsend, Willington and Bigges Main collieries continued to produce great quantities of coal in the early years of the century until the High Main Seam was exhausted and lower seams such as the Low Main Seam, The Bensham Seam, Beaumont and the Brockwell Seam were deeper and more difficult to work.

John Buddle, known as the 'King of the Coal Trade' was the manager of Wallsend Colliery from 1806 to 1843. He took over when his father, the previous manager and former school teacher, also called John Buddle, died. He was the foremost mining expert of his day and lived close to the pit shafts in a house built on the site of Segedunum Roman Fort. He was constantly working on improvements both underground and above ground and he invented a number of standing engines and the steam locomotive called the *Steam Elephant* in 1815. When the future Russian Tsar Nicholas visited the north of England in 1815 he asked if he could visit a colliery. He came to Wallsend and John Buddle arranged to have 'pit clothes' provided for him and his aides, but when the tsar looked down the pit he exclaimed: 'Ah! My God it is the mouth of Hell, none but a madman would venture in to it.'

He refused to go down but his assistants were all instructed to go down and report back to him. John Buddle was one of the founder members of the Society for the Prevention of Accidents in Coal Mines in 1813. Sir Humphrey Davy invented his safety lamp after experimenting at the Wallsend and Hebburn collieries, working closely with John Buddle, and later all miners used the Davy Lamp in the pit. Despite all the miners having the lamps and John Buddle introducing the most advanced ventilation system ever seen in a coal mine, Wallsend Colliery suffered the worst recorded pit disaster in 1835 when on the 18 June an explosion underground led to the loss of the lives of 102 men and boys. This disaster was

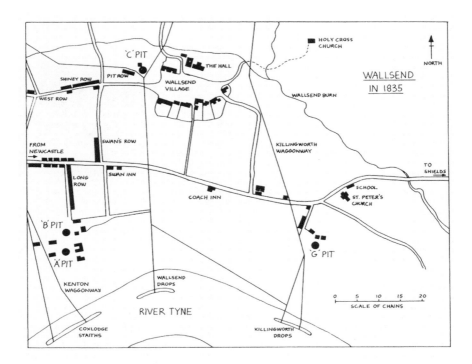

Wallsend in 1835.

Carville Shore, 1830, with Wallsend Drops in the distance.

Wallsend Colliery
G Pit or Church Pit
in 1844.

only fourteen years after an earlier disaster at the same pit had claimed fifty-two lives. Most of the miners are buried in St Peter's churchyard. The loss of life in mining accidents was a common occurrence and only significant events were recorded including the first incident on 21 October 1782 when John Johnson was killed by gas. Other recorded explosions took place when miners were using candles and the sparks from a flint mill to gain some light. Three lives were lost on 6 November 1784; two lives lost on 12 December 1784; one life lost on 9 June 1785; two lives lost on 4 December 1785; six lives lost on 6 April 1786; seven lives lost on 4 October 1790; thirteen lives lost on 25 September 1803; and eleven lives were lost on 19 December 1838. Conditions for workers in the mines were appalling, with no safety clothes or equipment provided in the early days, and children went down the mine from as young as seven years old and all were expected to work for twelve hours a day for six days a week in the pitch black. Miners, including children, descended the mine holding onto ropes and chains that were also used to lift the coals back out in baskets or 'corves'. One local poet recalled two brothers falling to their deaths after the youngest lost his hold and his brother tried to catch him. The miners themselves had to sign a bond each year that tied them to that colliery for the year, with severe penalties if they left during the year to work elsewhere. They lived in very basic overcrowded mining cottages rented from the colliery owners and if they were injured and could not work they could be evicted and if they were killed their widow and family would also be evicted.

Willington Colliery did not have as many accidents as at Wallsend but also had a number of fatalities over the years: on 3 December 1829, four lives were lost; on 20 September 1831, seven lives were lost; and on 30 March 1840 one life was lost but two men and five boys were badly burnt. The worst accident happened on 19 April 1841 at the Bigge Pit when thirty-two men and boys were killed and only three escaped alive. The cause of the accident was a young boy who during his twelve-hour shift in the pitch black had deserted his position, where he had to open and close a trap door to let waggons carrying coal through, to go and play with other boys. Richard Cooper, a trapper boy aged only nine and who died that day, was blamed for the disaster.

Willington Colliery
Edward Pit, c. 1933. It
was sunk in 1776 and
closed in 1930.

Bigges Main village.

No disasters are recorded for the Bigges Main Colliery but five deaths have been recorded by Durham Mining Museum between 1839 and 1864 including three Summerson brothers who were killed on 29 December 1839. John and William were aged sixty and Robert was fifty-eight.

The Bigges Main Colliery was based on what is now Wallsend Golf Course and a sizeable settlement grew up around the pit head that had its own shops, chapel and pub (The Masons Arms, which survived into the 1960s).

Flooding was a constant threat to the collieries in Wallsend and in 1823 a new pumping engine was built at Friars Goose in Gateshead that was paid for by local colliery owners including Wallsend, Willington, Tyne Main, Heaton, Walker and Felling. The consortium of coal owners continued to pay for these pumping engines until 1851 when coal production was less profitable and all the main collieries were flooded out, leading to the closure of Wallsend in 1854, Willington in 1856 and Bigges Main in 1857. Coal mining in the Wallsend area ceased until the later years of the century as coal owners tried to overcome the flooding problems. In 1866 a new shaft was dug beside the G Pit known as the H Pit and the latest Cornish pumps were set up to pump out water, commencing in 1867. In 1891 the Wallsend & Hebburn

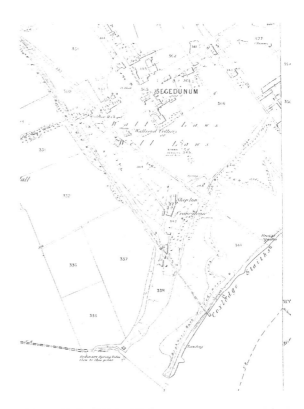

Wallsend Carville Shore, 1858.
(Ordnance Survey)

George Stephenson's Cottage with
Ballast Hill, Willington Quay, 1803.

Coal Company was formed and set up another pump in 1894 and it took three years before the first coals were raised at the H Pit in 1897 from the Yard Seam, then in 1898 from the Low Main Seam and in 1901 from the Bensham Seam.

The waggonways developed further and Wallsend Drops were built to enable full waggons of coal to be discharged directly into the holds of waiting ships moored at the purpose-built staithes.

Ships coming back from London and other destinations had to load up with ballast on the return journey to make the ships stable and this ballast was then deposited on the banks of the Tyne to form massive ballast hills. George Stephenson was employed to look after the engine at the ballast hill in Willington Quay in 1802 and his son Robert was born in the cottage they lived in at the foot of the ballast hill in 1803.

George moved to Killingworth Colliery in 1804 to work on the colliery engine before designing his own. George and Robert both became famous railway engineers and bridge builders. George Stephenson worked closely with William Losh, a senior partner in Losh & Bell Ironworks in Walker who lived at Point Pleasant House in Wallsend, close to where Stephenson had lived, and they designed a new metal rail called the' Losh Rail' in 1819 that was used on the Killingworth Waggonway. The development of waggonways, locomotives and improved staithes and coal drops led to a great drop in work for keelmen on the Tyne, and violent strikes took place in 1809, 1819 and 1822. The end was in sight for keelmen and this would have affected those living in Keelman's Row on Ropery Lane, although the majority lived in Newcastle.

Howdon Panns and Willington Quay continued as the main centre for industry in Wallsend in the early years of the nineteenth century. The salt pans, glassworks and early shipbuilding

Drops and Spouts at Wallsend,
By T. H. Hair 1844.

Above: Wallsend Drops, 1844.

Left: Willington Viaduct with Keelman's Row to the right.

declined but new industries developed on the reclaimed land on the riverside. This was made by using ships ballast to extend the shore, from 1665, by the Anderson family from Newcastle, who leased the land from Newcastle Corporation. Benjamin Brunton from Newcastle bought land in the old township of Howdon and established the Howdon Brewery in 1802 to the east of Front Street, adjoining Howdon Burn.

Willington Quay in 1897. (Ordnance Survey)

Shipwright's Arms, Howdon Panns, *c.* 1920s.

Howdon Panns from Norman Terrace and Cycle Parade, 1909.

Ballast Hill, Willington Quay, from Church Street, Howdon.

The brewery is clearly marked on the first Ordnance Survey map of the area dated 1855. Interestingly many public houses are named in such a small area including The Ship Inn, The Globe Inn, The Dockhouse Inn, The Coble Inn, The Black Bull, The Lord Byron, The Newcastle Arms on the Howdon Panns side of Howdon Burn and The Jenny Inn and The Duke of Wellington on the East Howdon side. To balance this there is a Temperance Hall beside the brewery and a number of chapels as well as a river police station. Other workplaces identified include a shipbuilding yard close to Howdon Burn, Howdon Ropery, at least three smithies (blacksmiths), Howdon Dock, a wood yard and Howdon Lead Works. Further west beyond the ballast hills, in 1855 Willington Quay was developing on land that was reclaimed from the river using the ballast. A ship-repairing yard was built to the rear of The Ship Hotel on Potter Street around 1835 and was called the Willington Slipway.

It was founded by Thompson Smith and later became Messrs Thomas Adamson & Son from 1851 to 1857 when they also built tug boats. William Cleland, the manager of Palmers Shipbuilding Yard, took over the yard in 1866 and in 1872 it was renamed William Cleland & Co. Ltd. William Cleland died in 1876 but the company continued as ship repairers into the next century.

Potter Street,
Willington Quay,
c. 1913.

Willington Mill
overlooking
Willington Gut.

In 1806 the Willington Mill was built adjoining Willington Gut. It was built by George Unthank, who was later joined by Joseph Proctor in 1829 and was later referred to as Proctor's Mill. It was the first steam-driven mill to be built in the north of England and was built on a grand scale with seven stories and seven sets of grinding stones. A large house was also built beside it adjoining Willington Gut. The mill buildings later formed part of Haggies Ropeworks and the Willington Mill itself became one of the most haunted buildings in England, so much so it has had a book written about it.

The Willington Ropery continued to expand during this century and Edward Chapman became sole owner in 1820 when his brother left the business and in 1829 Washington Potts became a partner and built Low Willington House opposite the works. Around 1840 Mr Potts sold the business to Robert Hood Haggie, who was a member of the Haggies Ropeworks family from Gateshead and who moved into Low Willington House. Mr Joseph Proctor of Willington Mill and Robert Hood Haggie built a school on the site for children of both works. On 3 June 1873 there was a major fire at the ropeworks that also nearly burnt down the railway viaduct, which was being converted from timber to cast iron. The factory was rebuilt with modern equipment and the company continued successfully for the rest of the century.

Howdon station was originally called 'Howdon for Jarrow'. The footbridge is now at Goathland in North Yorkshire.

Howdon & Jarrow Ferry. 4042

Howdon to Jarrow paddle ferry before 1921.

In 1839 the first railway line was opened from Newcastle to North Shields and followed the line of the present Metro through Wallsend with stations built at Wallsend (but called Carville as the area was then known) to serve Wallsend and at Howdon to serve Willington, Willington Quay, Howdon Panns and Jarrow. In addition a new direct road Howdon Lane was constructed to link with the ferry to Jarrow, who did not get a direct rail link until 1872.

A magnificent seven-arched viaduct was built over the Wallsend Burn, designed by John and Benjamin Green (who designed the Theatre Royal and Greys Monument in Newcastle). It was built in wood originally but replaced with iron later in the century.

The Riverside Railway line was opened in 1879 (part of it from Neptune Bank to Davy Bank now forms part of Hadrian's Way, the long distance walkway and cycleway) to serve riverside industries along the Tyne. There were three new stations built in Wallsend at Carville, Point Pleasant and Willington Quay. At this time the former Carville station was renamed Wallsend station.

From the mid-century the River Tyne Improvement Commission undertook the task of dredging the River Tyne to improve navigation and allow larger vessels to sail up to Newcastle and beyond. The river's main channel was deepened and narrowed and a lot of land was reclaimed, often using ballast from the ballast hills, and this made large tracts of land close to the river available for new industries to develop.

Carville station on Riverside Railway in 1969. It was closed in 1973.

Tyne View Terrace, Willington Quay, looking east, *c.* 1913.

Howdon Road looking west, *c.* 1915.

River Police vessel at Howdon Panns.

At Howdon, as the original township was still subject to flooding on a regular basis, the existing docks and quays had suffered from silting and subsidence from coal mining and many buildings were poorly built and outdated, a radical solution was proposed. During the 1860s a vast reclamation project took place involving the removal of the ballast from the ballast hills to bury the ancient town of Howdon under 6 feet of material. Howdon Burn was put in a culvert and a decision was taken to extend this plateau out into the River Tyne to form a new dock at Howdon. Part of the land was retained by the River Tyne Improvement Commission and the remainder was used for shipbuilding.

CHEMICAL AND LEAD INDUSTRIES

Lead making commenced in 1847 on land owned by Newcastle Corporation that had been recently reclaimed to the west of Tyne Street. The Cookson family, who already had an established lead works at Hayhole (east of Howdon), took over the firm and gradually developed into other products including antimony and Venetian red in new works on adjoining land in 1864. The manufacture of Venetian red was abandoned in 1890 to concentrate on antimony by the Cookson firm, which later became the Anzon Works. The company built a large chimney on top of the ballast hill to disperse fumes and they built what looked like a railway bridge over Stephenson Street to carry the flue from the factory to the chimney. This was a major landmark in the area for many years, eventually being demolished in the mid-1900s. In the late 1800s housing for workers was built to the north of the ballast hill and west of Howdon Panns village and named Norman Street and George Street after directors Norman and George Cookson.

The Wallsend area attracted a number of chemical companies and a copperas works (copperas is a sulphate of iron) developed close to Willington Colliery on the site of the present Rosehill Tavern, which was previously occupied by (High) Willington House. Copperas Lane was the name of the lane that became Churchill Street after St Mary's Church was built. In 1818 the copperas works were sold to Bell & Brown, the colliery owners, and at that time was situated on the north side of Willington House and had two large copperas houses, a

Willington
Quay Parade,
Stephenson Street.

Cookson's bridge
over Stephenson
Street carrying flue to
chimney on Ballast Hill,
c. 1913.

Tyne General Ferry, *c.* 1908.

dwelling house, a yard and large copperas beds. Copperas was used for making ink as well as tanning leather and dying. On the riverside a number of chemical companies were established following the closure of the local mines in the middle of the century. The companies utilised available material such as salt, chalk (from ballast), coal and sulphur to create alkali, which in turn could produce soda crystals for washing products, bleaching powder and other by-products. Two men living in Wallsend were responsible for establishing the chemical business: William Losh and John Allen. This led to a considerable blight to the climate of the town, killing many trees, and later in the century many of these companies relocated to Teesside as that river was better suited to developing the chemical industry over a much larger area. William Losh, who lived at Point Pleasant House in Wallsend, studied chemistry in Paris and he introduced Le Blanc's process for creating alkali into his Walker works in 1821. John Allen, who lived originally in John Buddle's old house, Wallsend House, and later moved to the Red House on Wallsend Green (and had the Allen Memorial Church named after him), started working as a chemist in South Shields. In 1828 he set up a factory using the Le Blanc process at Heworth. He then built a new works in Wallsend in 1847 to the east of the site of the future Swan Hunters yard near the present petrol station. The company was called John & William Allen and soon flourished. He built houses for his workers on the High Street between Station Road and Sycamore Street. In 1862 John Glover built a second chemical works in Wallsend known as Carville Chemical Works, which was located to the east of Allen's on the site later occupied by Parson's Marine Turbine Company and now Oceana Business Park. John Glover from Newcastle started work as a plumber and later worked in a chemical factory in Felling. He was the inventor of the Glover Tower, which was very successful, but he did not patent it and lost out on much wealth. He built Glover's Row (the first flats to be built in Wallsend) to house his workers on a site between High Street East and the Metro line west of Waggonway. A third company was set up by John Lomas in 1871 to the south-west of Point Pleasant House and was known as Messrs John Lomas & Co. A severe fire destroyed the works in 1877 and over 300 men lost their jobs as a result. Owing to advances in chemical production elsewhere in the country, notably in Cheshire and later on Teesside, the chemical industry in Wallsend had almost ceased by 1883 when the Wallsend Chemical Company was formed to try to revive the industry. This was unsuccessful and the site was closed and dismantled before Swan & Hunter took over the site in 1894.

SHIPBUILDING

Shipbuilding first developed at Willington Quay and later extended along the riverside to replace the chemical works in Wallsend. Early companies included Palmers and Clelland's in Willington Quay and Schlesinger Davis and Coulson, Cook & Co. in Wallsend. Later Swan & Hunter took over the Wallsend yards and expanded.

As land was reclaimed from the river in Willington Quay new shipyards appeared to the west of Cookson's and the Tyne Cement Works. In 1849 John Coutts moved from an earlier shipyard in Walker to set up a new one, Coutts & Parkinson, at Willington Quay to build iron ships. They launched the first ship in 1851 named *Thomas Hamlin* (at 1,350 tons) and extended the yard westward in 1852. The yard was not a success and was eventually taken over in 1859 by Messrs Palmer Bros. Charles Mark Palmer and his brother George had been shipbuilders in Jarrow since 1852 and were looking to extend their business, launching their first vessel *Port Mulgrave* in 1860. They employed William Cleland to manage the shipyard and initially did very well. In 1863 Charles M. Palmer arranged a special launch day when four vessels were launched at the same time from opposite yards (two from Willington and two from Jarrow).

Riverside at
Howdon and
Willington Quay,
c. 1930s.

Palmer Street and Mark Street were built for their workers in Willington Quay. The Palmers had also bought the ironworks and coke ovens at Wallsend in 1855 and also built houses for the workers (north of the present Hadrian Road, now occupied by factories), calling two streets Palmer and Mark then naming the others First to Seventh Street. In 1865 Charles M. Palmer sold the company to investors but remained chairman. Soon after, the ironworks and coke ovens were closed and William Cleland left the company in 1867 to set up his own company in Willington Quay.

A ship-repairing yard was built to the rear of The Ship Hotel on Potter Street in around 1835 and was called the Willington Slipway. It was founded by Thompson Smith and later became Messrs Thomas Adamson & Son from 1851 to 1857 when they also built tug boats. William Cleland, the manager of Palmers Shipbuilding Yard, took over the yard in 1866 and in 1872 it was renamed William Cleland & Co. Ltd. William Cleland died in 1876 but the company continued as ship repairers into the next century.

In 1876 William John Bone, who had managed an earlier failed shipbuilders on the site in Willington Quay to the east of Willington Slipway, set up the Tyne Iron Shipbuilding Co. Ltd. It was a successful company that had built up a good reputation by the end of the century.

In 1900 the Northumberland Shipbuilding Company Ltd, established in 1898, extended its works into the Howdon area over the culverted Howdon Burn.

The first shipbuilders In Wallsend were Schlesinger, Davis & Co., who set up in 1863 on the riverside below the fort of Segedunum. Albert Schlesinger trained at Stephenson's engine works in Newcastle and Frederick Davis worked in Charles Mitchell's shipyard in Walker. At first they built sailing ships, then progressed to steamships and bought housing in nearby Clyde Street for their workers. The company was successful until 1884 when a depression in shipbuilding occurred. The company never fully recovered and closed in 1893. The site was later taken over by Swan & Hunter in 1897.

Coulson, Cook & Co. was founded in 1871 at St Peter's in Walker by John Coulson, a former manager at Chas. Mitchell's yard in Walker, and Richard Cook, the brother-in-law of Charles Mitchell. It was established as an offshoot to Mitchell's yard in Walker, who could not build all their orders for iron steamers.

They moved to Wallsend in 1873 to expand the business on a site to the east of the shipyard of Schlesinger, Davis & Co. The company did well until they built their thirteenth ship and got into financial difficulties. Charles Mitchell had to buy the business. He then put another brother-in-law in charge, Charles Sheridan Swan, who had been the managing director of Wallsend Slipway Co. Ltd. The company was renamed C. S. Swan & Co. and was

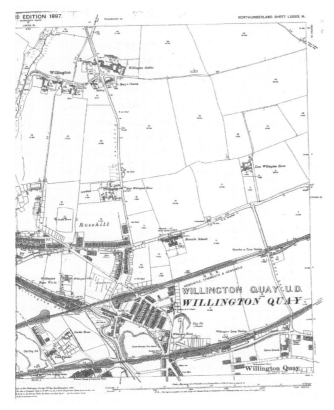

Willington and Willington
Quay in 1897. (Ordnance Survey)

a modest company employing 717 men on a 7-acre site with a 270-foot river frontage and building 8,532 tons of shipping. In 1880 disaster struck the company when Charles Sheridan Swan was returning from a business trip to Russia when he fell overboard from the steamer he was travelling on between Calais and Dover and was killed when he hit one of the paddles. Mr Mitchell persuaded George Burton Hunter to leave his Sunderland shipyard S. P. Austin & Hunter and set up in partnership with the widow of Charles to form C. S. Swan & Hunter in 1880, of which he became the managing partner. Shipbuilding saw an upsurge from 1880 and the company soon required additional space, so in 1883 they bought 16 acres of land formerly occupied by the chemical company owned by Messrs J. & W. Allen to become the east shipyard. In 1884–85 the first steel vessels were built at Wallsend, namely SS *Burrumbeet* and SS *Corangamite*, for an Australian company. By 1893 they were the largest Tyne shipbuilder, constructing nine vessels with a tonnage of 31,088 tons. In 1895 the company became a limited company, C. S. Swan & Hunter Ltd, with G. B. Hunter as its head and Charles Sheridan Swan Jnr as one of the directors. The business expanded further in 1897 when they bought the lease of the former shipyard of Schlesinger, Davis & Co. The additional 7-acre site was used initially to build floating dry docks.

Tyne Pontoons & Dry Docks was set up by Wigham Richardson in 1880 as a ship repair business, with two pontoons or submersible floating docks that could be used to raise vessels for repairs. It occupied the site adjoining Swan Hunters to the west of Benton Way, which in turn bounded the Neptune Yard in Walker.

MARINE ENGINEERING

The major marine engine-building company of Wallsend Slipway developed on reclaimed land to the west of Willington Gut. Wallsend Slipway Co. opened in 1871 near to the Gut. It started life as a ship repair yard with two slipways, each 1,000 feet long and built to repair ships for established shipbuilders including Mitchell & Co. of Walker.

Charles Mitchell was the first chairman and his brother-in-laws Charles Sheridan Swan and Henry F. Swan, from a prominent Wallsend family, were directors. C. S. Swan was the first managing director and he was married to John Glover's daughter. In 1874 C. S. Swan left to take over a former Wallsend shipyard Coulson, Cook & Co. and he was replaced by William Boyd, who soon developed the successful building of engines and boilers on site as well as ship repair. In 1878 the word 'Engineering' was added to the company name as engine building developed. In 1882 the first triple expansion engines to be built on Tyneside were built here and in 1895 a dry dock, 540 feet long, was opened. In 1895 Andrew Laing joined the company and later took over as general manger and modernised and expanded the company, including taking over the former cement works to the west of the site in 1897.

North East Marine developed the adjoining site, opening in 1882 after setting up in Sunderland as marine engine builders in 1865. NEM also built houses for its workers immediately to the north of its site with a clear hierarchy depending on skills. Unskilled workmen lived in flats on South Terrace, skilled men lived in terraced houses on North View and foremen and management lived in semi-detached villas in Roland Road and Northumberland Villas. The Wallsend works were first known as the Northumberland engine works and the company established itself on Tyneside as shipbuilding yards expanded.

In 1848 a number of coke ovens were built by Mr John Carr at Wallsend Quay at Davy Bank. In 1855 he built two blast furnaces as well, but they were not a success and were taken over by

Wallsend riverside and Willington Gut, 1897. (Ordnance Survey)

WILLINGTON ROPERY AT END OF 18th AND FIRST HALF OF 19th CENTURY.
VIADUCT BUILT IN 1839.

Facsimile of Water Colour Drawing by the celebrated local Artist. T. M. RICHARDSON.

Haggies Ropeworks in front of the Willington Viaduct.

C. M. Palmer & Co., who turned the business around. In 1864 there was a serious explosion at the works, which were closed in 1866. They were reopened by the Royal Greek Iron Company in 1874.

Charles Parsons, the famous inventor of turbine engines, built his *Turbinia* works, called Parsons' Marine Steam Turbine Co. Ltd, at Wallsend in 1897 to develop the steam marine turbine engine. This followed the performance of the *Turbinia* during the Spit Head Naval Review in 1897 when the *Turbinia* demonstrated that she was the fastest vessel in the world at the time. The factory was built on land previously occupied by the Carville Chemical Company and Mason & Barry, copper smelters.

By the end of the century almost all riverside sites had been developed for shipbuilding and coal exports.

Haggies Ropeworks developed alongside Willington Gut and the long narrow ropewalk building, extending from the railway viaduct to Church Bank, became a feature of the landscape for well over 100 years.

Willington Quay also had a gasworks close to Willington Gut, as well as brickworks operated by Addison Potter, who established his fire brickworks at Willington Quay in 1846, which later developed into a cement works. Addison Potter was twice mayor of Newcastle and lived at Heaton Hall. He eventually had Potter Street and Addison Potter School named after him.

Most collieries also had brickworks attached to make use of waste clay materials and many houses in Wallsend were built using bricks emblazoned with the brickworks' name (e.g. Addison Potter, Atlas Wallsend, Wallsend & Hebburn and just Wallsend, examples of which can be seen at Beamish Museum).

St Peter's Church was opened in 1809 and was built to replace the Holy Cross Church that had stood as a ruin since 1797 when the roof was removed for restoration, although this did not take place. The old school house on Wallsend Green was used as a temporary place of Worship. St Peter's Church was extensively rebuilt in the 1890s into its present appearance.

WALLS END CHURCH.
North.^d

Above: St Peter's Church,
as built originally in 1809
before alterations.

Right: Wallsend in 1897.
(Ordnance Survey)

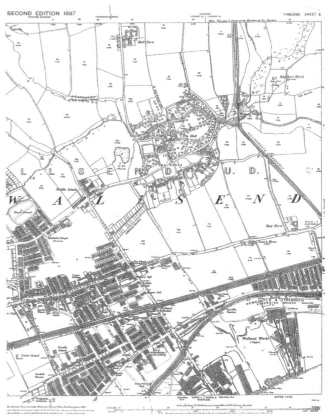

The first school in Wallsend was built on the Green in 1776 on the corner of Crow Bank and three generations of Joseph Mordue were the schoolteachers. They also lived on the site and developed a brewery on Crow Bank (that has given its name to the present Mordue Brewery in North Shields). In 1833 St Peter's School was opened on Church Bank close to the new church. Schools were also provided in Wallsend and Willington Quay by the Methodists and Wallsend Co-operative Society also built a school in Wallsend.

Following the Education Act of 1870 new schools were built to serve Wallsend and Willington, namely the Buddle on Station Road in 1877 and the Bewicke in 1878 on Tynemouth Road These schools complimented the existing Stephenson Memorial School on Stephenson Street, which was built in 1860 in Willington Quay.

The Co-operative Society developed shops in both Wallsend and Willington Quay in the later years of the century and in Wallsend either side of North Road they developed housing with appropriately named streets such as Equitable Street, Mutual Street and Provident Terrace.

Paddock Hall on the right and Bewicke Schools on Tynemouth Road, c. 1913.

CO-OPERATIVE STORES, WILLINGTON QUAY, 1818.

Co-operative Store in Willington Quay.

The Co-op Laundry and Gordon Square on the left in Equitable Street, Wallsend, in 1974.

High Street East, Wallsend, *c.* 1905.

High Street East, Wallsend, looking west close to Station Road, *c.* 1903.

High Street West, Station Road and Neptune Road provided shops, pubs and other buildings, bringing much-needed services and facilities for the rapidly expanding housing sites close to the river, to serve the growing population of shipyard and other workers.

The most impressive building was the Wallsend Café, which was built on the south-west corner of High Street West and Station Road. It was built in 1883 by George Burton Hunter as a café and workers institute, offering technical education and recreational opportunities to workers in a temperance building as a challenge to the many public houses being opened in the town. It was the first building in Wallsend to be lit by electricity and is said to be the building where the first electric switch was invented. John Henry Holmes of Newcastle was one of the first companies to install electricity in buildings but nobody had worked out how to safely turn the supply on and off in individual rooms. This led to John Henry Holmes inventing the electric switch, which was then patented in 1884 and used worldwide. The Wallsend Masonic Hall was also built on Station Road in 1892. An early theatre was also built in Portugal Place called the Theatre Royal, which was close to the early police and fire station built on the corner of High Street West and The Avenue. Pubs built at this time on High Street West included the Queens Head, Anchor Inn and the Duke of York. The Ship Inn, the Dock Hotel, Carville and Commercial pubs were built to the south of the railway line to serve the local community.

Many new places of worship were developed at this time, including St Luke's in 1887. The Carville Methodist Chapel was built in 1906 beside the original Colliery Chapel (built in 1812), the original catholic school-chapel of St Aidan (built in 1866) and St Columba school-chapel (built in 1876).

St Luke's Church opened in 1887.

Churchill Street, Willington, looking north. It was formerly known as Copperas Lane.

TWENTIETH CENTURY

The borough of Wallsend was established in 1910, incorporating Willington, Willington Quay, Howdon and parts of Benton including Bigges Main. In 1974 it became part of North Tyneside Council. The population of Wallsend had risen to 41,000 by 1911 and continued to increase during the century as the town developed more industries and large areas of new housing were built. Wallsend Town Hall was opened in 1908 and local government responsibilities and jobs developed over the century to provide schools, housing, roads and infrastructure as the town expanded northwards from the river. The Town Hall also had a magistrates' court and a fire station attached beside Wallsend Baths.

A new police station was built in Alexandria Street, and Wallsend High Street developed into a major shopping area with a wide range of shops and services to meet the needs of the expanding population.

In 1966 the centre of Wallsend was redeveloped to build the Forum Shopping Centre. Pubs, cinemas, clubs, libraries and sports facilities were built to meet the leisure needs of local people and also provided lots of new jobs as well.

New Rose Inn with Burn Closes Bridge in the background.

Council work lorries
outside the depot
in Warwick Street,
Wallsend, *c.* 1930s.

Wallsend Town Hall,
c. 1910.

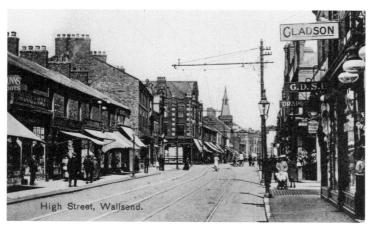

High Street West,
Wallsend, looking east,
c. 1911.

High Street West, Wallsend, looking east, *c.* 1905.

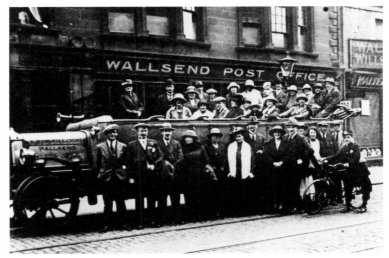

An outing from Wallsend Post Office in a Stockill's charabanc, *c.* 1920s.

Work taking place to build the Forum Shopping Centre in the mid-1960s.

Pearl Cinema, Willington Quay
LSC Acc 13922

Pearl Picture Palace on Potter Street, Willington Quay, after 1914.

Station Road looking south towards the High Street, *c.* 1932.

Right: A 1951 advert for Wallsend Industrial Co-operative Society Ltd.

Below: Woolworth's store on Wallsend High Street in 1988.

In 1926 Sir G. B. Hunter built the Memorial Hall on Frank Street, built as a memorial to all the workers from Swan Hunters who gave their lives in the First World War. In addition health services were provided including a smallpox hospital and an infectious diseases hospital (Hadrian Hospital) – both in the Battle Hill area – as well as maternity hospitals at Willington Quay and the Green and a new clinic on the Green in 1940.

Transport links were improved with regular ferries between Howdon and Jarrow and Wallsend to Felling. Later the opening of the Tyne Tunnels with the pedestrian and cycle tunnel in 1951 and the vehicle tunnel in 1964 replaced the ferries. The Coast Road was upgraded to a dual carriageway in the 1960s and Hadrian Road was built to link Wallsend and Willington Quay in the 1960s and soon after the Riverside Railway closed in 1973. As traditional industries declined new industrial estates were built to provide new employment opportunities.

Wallsend Clinic with Wallsend Hall behind on the Green.

Wallsend Memorial Hall.

Hadrian Hospital, formerly the Infectious Diseases Hospital, Wallsend, 1892–1984.

Wallsend Ferry Landing.

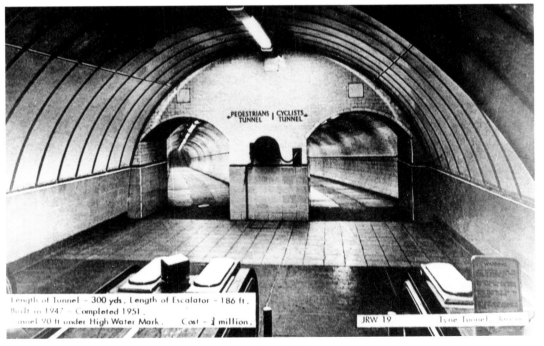

Tyne pedestrian and cycle tunnels opened in 1951.

Tyne pedestrian and cycle tunnels escalators.

The halfway point in the pedestrian tunnel where Northumberland and Durham meet.

Sculptures outside the north entrance of the Tyne pedestrian and cycle tunnels.

COAL MINING

Wallsend Colliery continued to develop after G Pit was reopened, and in 1901 the output of coal was 16,000 tons but the cost of pumping was £16,000 a year.

Many problems with ventilation also occurred as the Bensham and Low Main seams were worked, which necessitated sinking a new shaft near the Rising Sun Farm, commencing in 1906 with coals being drawn up for the first time in 1908. New housing was built for the workers nearby at Rising Sun Cottages. In 1913 the old Edward Pit was reopened and coal drawing commenced again. A second shaft was sunk at Rising Sun, opening in 1915, to improve ventilation and to become independent of G Pit. Electric power superseded steam power both above and below ground soon after for greater efficiency and reduced costs.

The First World War reduced the output as many miners went off to fight, but by 1920 the yearly output from the Wallsend and Willington pits was 524,715 tons. There was a national strike in 1921 but in 1922 the three pits produced 874,592 tons. In August 1925 five men were killed in an explosion at the Edward Pit. In 1934 the shaft at Rising Sun was deepened to reach the Brockwell Seam and a new coal preparation plant was built, as well as pit head baths around 1937. In 1947 the coal mines were nationalised and the Rising Sun received a great amount of investment including a major reconstruction costing £2.9 million.

In 1960 a third shaft was sunk down to the Beaumont Seam to improve access and ventilation. A 115-foot-high winding tower was constructed and underground improvements took place. It was estimated that the coal reserves would last for sixty years from the newly modernised pit. Production in 1964 reached 650,000 tons a year with 1,750 men employed. Over the next few years adverse geological conditions as well as drainage problems resulted in major production difficulties and the colliery closed as a result in April 1969, with over

Train derailment in Wallsend in 1905 beside the Church Pit.

Wallsend Colliery G Pit shaft, 1908.

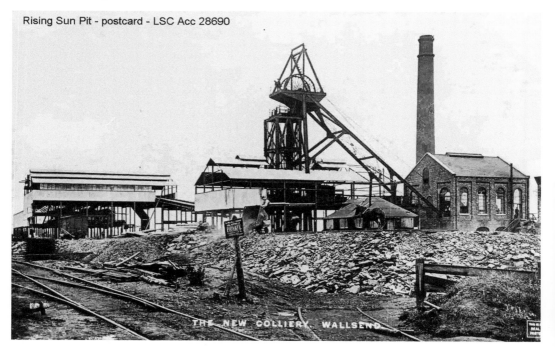

Rising Sun Colliery, *c.* 1920s.

Railway leading to Rising Sun Colliery.

Rising Sun Colliery No. 3 shaft and waste heap.

Rising Sun Colliery No. 3 shaft opened in 1962.

Managers and senior staff at Rising Sun Colliery, 1960s.

1,500 men losing their jobs. The winding tower was demolished in 1970 and the former pit heap was reclaimed to form the Rising Sun Country Park. The last miner to leave the pit was Albert Evans on 25 April 1969. There were no more major mining disasters but in his book *Wallsend Best* Ron Curran records that there were up to forty-seven individual fatalities at the pit. The men died from explosions, stone falls, shot blasting (using explosives), accidents with machines and one man was killed by a lump of ice falling down the shaft. The last man killed in the Rising Sun Colliery was George Fatkin on 10 February 1969, only two months before the pit closed. Today in Wallsend all obvious traces of mining have disappeared but many legacies can still be found including the Rising Sun Country Park, waggonways throughout Wallsend and streets built on former waggonways such as Park Road and Portugal Place, former colliery housing at Rising Sun Cottages and in the Diamond Street area, the Miners' Hall on Station Road and the Barking Dog miners recreation ground, and the Buddle schools and street names such as Buddle Street.

SHIPBUILDING

Wallsend became world famous for shipbuilding during this century based on a number of factors. C. S. Swan & Hunter Ltd had successfully built two liners for Cunard in 1901 and 1902, the *Ivernia* and the *Carpathia* (famous for rescuing survivors from the Titanic), which had their engines supplied by Wallsend Slipway, who had strong links to the company. Charles Parsons in Newcastle had invented the steam turbine engine that had been successfully used in the *Turbinia* and set up his Turbinia Marine Turbine Works at Wallsend. The British government were determined to regain their dominance on the seas by building a faster ship than the Germans and were prepared to invest in developing such ships.

In 1903 C. S. Swan & Hunter Ltd and Wigham Richardson & Co. Ltd, the nearby shipyard in Walker, combined to form Swan, Hunter & Wigham Richardson Ltd to build a new liner for the Cunard Line. They also bought the Tyne Dry Docks Co. Ltd that adjoined Swan Hunters yard to give the company a continuous river frontage of 1,400 yards and a site of around 80 acres, half of which was in Wallsend. The directors included George B. Hunter, Wigham Richardson and Charles John Denham Christie. They won the order to build RMS *Mauretania*, which was part funded by the government to ensure that Britain could build a faster ship than Germany as at that time the Germans had the fastest ships in the world including the *Deutschland* and the *Kaiser Wilhelm II*, which were capable of 23 knots. To build the ship a larger berth had to be built and this involved digging out the former steep bank leading down to the river. During these works they discovered the branch wall of Hadrian's Wall as it descended down the hill from the Roman fort of Segedunum and into the river. The remains were carefully recorded by local antiquarians then lifted and transported to Wallsend Park where they were rebuilt into a slope as a visitor attraction. (Interestingly the stones were returned to the site when the Roman museum opened in 2000.)

In addition a massive weatherproof shelter was built over the berth to enable continuous work to take place on the ship. The keel was laid in 1904 and the ship itself was launched in 1906. It then moved downriver to Wallsend Slipway, who fitted the turbine engines and the ship left Tyneside in 1907 to head to Liverpool. RMS *Mauretania* went on to be the fastest ship to cross the Atlantic from Liverpool to New York for the next twenty-two years, recording an average speed of 26 knots. During the First World War it was used as a hospital ship and it continued as a liner until 1935 when it paid a last visit to the Tyne on the way to be broken up for scrap in Scotland.

Launch of *Mauretania*, 1906.

Mauretania at North Shields, 1907. (Tyne & Wear Archives and Museums)

Mauretania and *Turbinia*, 1907. (Tyne & Wear Archives & Museums)

Howdon Band supporting locked-out shipyard workers in 1910.

Swan Hunter dry dock blacksmiths, 1914.

Dinner hour at Swan Hunters, *c.* 1914.

George V visits Swan Hunters during the First World War.

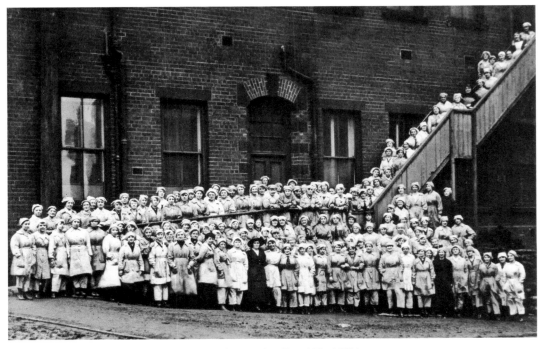

Female workers at Swan Hunters during the First World War.

BRASS FOUNDRY DEPARTMENT—SEPARATING BRASS FROM ASHES

Female workers in the brass foundry department at Swan Hunters.

A 1951 advert for Swan
Hunter & Wigham
Richardson, Ltd.

18 Dec 1920

S.S. Meduana After the Fire. Swan Hunters Wallsend

3

Two men were killed during a fire on the SS *Meduana* that led to the ship keeling over in 1920.

Men and women shipbuilders at Swan Hunters during the Second World War.

Following the success of the RMS *Mauretania* Swan & Hunter became world famous and orders flowed in for all sorts of vessels, and during both world wars they built countless ships for the navy, a tradition that continued until the end of the shipyard. They built hundreds of ships apart from a wide range of naval vessels and many other types of craft including floating docks, liners, tankers, super tankers, ferries, cable-laying ships, icebreakers, floating cranes, etc. The most famous and notable ships included the following: HMS *Anson* in 1942 (battleship with a pub named after it); HMS *Arc Royal* in 1981 (aircraft carrier launched by the Queen Mother and flagship of the British Navy); HMS *Illustrious* in 1978 (aircraft carrier launched by Princess Margaret); *Esso Northumbria* in 1969 (the largest oil tanker in the world and first of eight to be launched at Wallsend. The others were *Esso Hibernia, Texaco Great Britain, London Lion, World Unicorn, Windsor Lion, Tyne Pride* and *Everett F. Wells*); *Sir Galahad* in 1988 (a replacement ship for one lost in the Falklands War); *James Clark Ross* in 1990 (research ship); HMS *Richmond* in 1993 (the last complete ship to be launched by the old Swan Hunter company before closure); *Pride of The Tyne* in 1993 Tyne ferry and the last vessel launched by the old Swan Hunter company); and *Lyme Bay* (the last ship to leave Swan Hunters but it had to be completed in Scotland).

C. S. Swan Hunter & Wigham Richardson Ltd merged with Smith's Dock in 1966 and became the Swan Hunter Group. In 1967 the company took over Clelands Shipbuilding Company and John Readhead & Sons. In 1968 it inherited the Walker Naval Yard and the Hebburn yard of Hawthorn Leslie and in 1973 took over the Palmers dock in Hebburn.

In 1977 the shipbuilding industry was nationalised and became part of British Shipbuilders. It was then privatised in 1987 and closed the Neptune yard in 1988. In 1993 the company, which still employed 2,400 workers, suffered a financial crisis and the receivers were brought in to break up the company. The last ship to be completed by the old company under the receiver was the HMS *Richmond* in 1994. Thousands of workers lost their jobs. Jaap Kroese, a Dutch millionaire, bought the Swan Hunter site in Wallsend in 1994.

The Queen visits Wallsend Town Hall in 1954.

The Esso Northumbria overlooking local houses.

World Unicorn shortly before its launch.

The Atlantic Conveyor at Swan
Hunters overlooking Segedunum Fort.

The *Recorder* cable-laying ship is ready
to be launched at Swan Hunters, 1954.

HMS *Illustrious* moored at Royal Quays.

Swan Hunters beyond Segedunum Roman Fort.

WALLSEND SLIPWAY

The company continued to prosper under Andrew Laing, who became general manager and a director of the company in 1903, and William Boyd stepped back to pursue his political interests and was Wallsend's first mayor in 1901 and first alderman in 1906. In 1903 the company were closely linked with C. S. Swan & Hunter and from 1905 they built steam turbine engines for them including for the famous *Mauretania*. In 1910 it built the famous giant electric crane, capable of lifting 180 tons, which dominated the skyline for most of the century.

The company was very busy before and during the First World War and when over 800 men joined the forces they employed 220 girls to work in the factory doing a wide range of tasks. The company suffered when there was a slump in shipbuilding but the Second World War kept the yard occupied for many years. The company continued to operate until the late 1980s when it was closed as a result of a decline in demand and the crane was dismantled in 1989. The yard was taken over by Howard Doris offshore company, who filled in the large graving dock to enable it to build massive oil and gas rigs. AMEC later took over the yard.

Wallsend Slipway from the air.

The paddle tug is seen in front of the Wallsend Slipway crane.

A 1951 advert for Wallsend Slipway & Engineering Co. Ltd.

Drawbridge over Willington Gut, *c.* 1913.

Wallsend Slipway workers inside part of a turbine for *Mauretania*, *c.* 1906.

Mauretania propeller at Wallsend Slipway. (Tyne & Wear Archives & Museums)

Women workers during the First World War at Wallsend Slipway.

Female workers at Wallsend Slipway. (Tyne & Wear Archives & Museums)

NORTH EAST MARINE

North East Marine continued to expand in the early years of the twentieth century, utilising electricity from the nearby Carville Power Station.

They were the first company in the world to adopt electric power throughout the works and the first to buy electricity in bulk. It also erected the first cantilevered crane on the north-east coast in 1909 that was capable of lifting 150 tons. The company supplied many engines for ships over the years as well as undertaking many other marine related contracts. The company also had similar ups and downs to other marine engineering businesses and did well during the wars. The company closed in the 1980s and the site was taken over by Press Offshore, then AMEC to build offshore rigs for the gas and oil industry. The NEM crane was controversially demolished in the early 1990s after it was first granted listed building status and then de-listed following a public inquiry.

North East Marine crane was erected in 1909.

Workers at North East Marine constructing crane in 1909.

North East Marine Engineering Co. from Hebburn.

TYNE DRY DOCKS CO. LTD

Ship repair remained an important business in Wallsend after Tyne Pontoons & Dry Docks was bought up by Swan & Hunter, continuing to repair ships and other vessels until it closed at the same time as the main company.

LAMBIE BOATBUILDERS

Robert and David Lambie set up a boatbuilding yard at Davy Bank in 1892 building many smaller vessels including, from 1958, boats built from fibreglass including a number of ocean-going yachts. The firm continued until 1972 when it was taken over by Ryton Marine who built the Tyne ferry *Freda Cunningham* there before going into liquidation in 1973 with the yard then being taken over by William Brothers Offshore in 1974.

CLELAND'S

Clelland's in Willington Quay had a very successful business in building smaller or coastal vessels until 1967 when it was taken over by Swan Hunter. It continued in business until 1984 when the yard was taken over by AMEC to build oil rigs.

Ready to launch the *Bashubar* at Cleland's, 1957.

The *Fairwood* following its launch at Cleland's, 1961.

NORTHUMBERLAND SHIPBUILDING COMPANY LTD

During the First World War the company built a large number of ships and launched thirteen in one year. The company prospered until the 1920s when the shipbuilding industry went into decline. It went out of business in 1924.

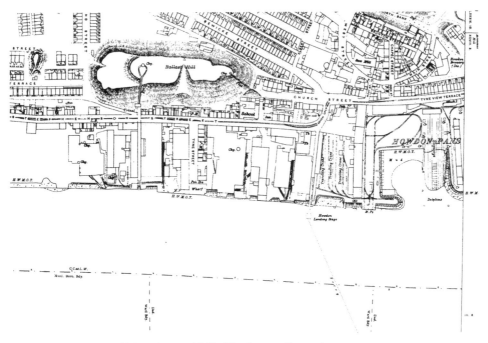

Willington Quay and Howdon in 1913. (Ordnance Survey)

ELTRINGHAM'S LTD

The company was established in 1912 on land previously occupied by Palmers shipyard and the cement works of Addison Potter. It was initially called Jos. T. Eltringham & Co. Ltd and was a second shipyard for the company from South Shields established in 1846. George Renwick, MP for Newcastle, was one of the promoters. The new yard was opened in 1914 and a large number of war vessels were built. In 1919 it became Eltringham's Ltd. The company closed in 1922.

In 1930 all the main surviving shipbuilders in Britain formed a company called the National Shipbuilders Securities Ltd. This company was set up to buy up redundant shipyards and remove all shipbuilding equipment to ensure they would not be used for shipbuilding again. The former sites of the Northumberland Shipbuilding Co. and Eltringham's Ltd were bought up by this company and cleared.

During both world wars many women were employed in the shipyards and related industries to backfill for the vast number of men who volunteered to fight in the wars. They made a massive contribution to the war effort but when men returned after the war they were obliged to give up such roles in many cases.

R. HOOD HAGGIE & SON LTD

The ropeworks at Willington Quay continued to prosper throughout the century and its landmark ropewalk building beside Willington Gut was still in use until the 1980s when it was demolished. The company consolidated its premises south of the Willington Viaduct and the famous haunted Willington Mill was converted into a canteen and offices.

Hemp being delivered to Haggies Ropeworks, Willington Quay, 1935.

Steel wire-making machines inside Haggies Ropeworks.

The ropeworks employed a large number of female staff who were known locally as 'Haggies Angels'. In 1959 Haggies became part of the British Ropes Group (established in 1924). In 1976 the company was renamed Bridon Ltd and had its headquarters in Newcastle. In 1973 the Willington Quay factory produced 19,330 tonnes of wire rope, totalling 6,800 miles in length. In 1977 the company employed 850 people on the Willington Quay site. The company still exists and is now called Bridon International Ltd, Willington Quay, and is part of a larger international company Bridon-Bekaert (The Rope Group), who claim to be world-leading specialists in the manufacture of wire and rope.

CARVILLE POWER STATION

Carville (A) Power Station, the largest in Britain at the time, was built in Wallsend to the east of Swan Hunters in 1904.

It replaced an earlier power station built on Neptune Bank, on the site later taken over by Thermal Syndicate, which quickly needed to be upgraded to meet demand. The original power station was opened in 1901 and was developed by the Newcastle-upon-Tyne Electric Supply Company (NESCo) using new technology developed by Mertz and McLellan, a newly

Newcastle-upon-Tyne Electric Supply Co., Ltd., *Interior of Generating Station*
Carville Power Station, 1904.

Carville Power Station, Wallsend, opened in 1904 and was the largest power station in Britain.

Soldiers at Carville Power Station during the General Strike in 1926.

established company in Newcastle. This company were the first in the world to offer three-phase electricity generated by Parson's steam turbines, which were the largest in the world at the time. This type of electricity was ideal for industry. NESCo led the world in power development for over thirty years, leading to the establishment of the National Grid. The success of the turbines led Cunard to specify the use of turbines in *Mauretania*.

Carville Power Station also used turbine generators built by C. A. Parsons & Co. and was built by NESCo to supply power for the developing shipbuilding industry, other industries and also to electrify the railways and trams. Thermal Syndicate and Castner Kellner set up in Wallsend as a direct result of having available cheap electricity. In 1916 the power station was doubled in size by building Carville B Power Station and it was considered to be the 'first major generating station in the world'. Carville A operated until 1932 and Carville B until the early 1950s. The turbine hall of Carville B survives and is occupied by Pipe Coil Technology Ltd.

TYNESIDE TRAMWAYS AND TRAMROADS CO.

Major tram depot Tyneside Tramways and Tramroads Co. was established on Neptune Road in 1902, next door to the Neptune Power Station, and remained there until 1964. The first trams travelled to North Shields from Wallsend and in the same year they followed the old line of the waggonway through Bigges Main to connect Wallsend to South Gosforth. The chairman was John Theodore Merz, who was also vice-chairman of the Newcastle upon Tyne Electric Supply Company who built the power station.

COACH OPEN, WILLINGTON QUAY, 1908.

Coach Open, Willington Quay, *c.* 1914.

CASTNER KELLNER CO.

In 1906 Castner Kellner Co., formerly known as the Aluminium Co., were attracted to a site in Wallsend from Oldbury near Birmingham by the availability of cheap electricity provided by the Carville Power Station. Hamilton Castner was an American who worked with Austrian Karl Kellner to develop their method of electrolysis. The company had moved from producing aluminium to making sodium and sodium peroxide and opened a factory on the banks of the river to the east of Davy Bank, which was later extended in 1912. In 1920 the company was taken over by Brunner, Mond & Co. and they operated until 1929 in Wallsend and then moved to Billingham on Teesside and later became part of ICI (Imperial Chemicals Industries Ltd).

THERMAL SYNDICATE

Thermal Syndicate was set up in 1903 as a direct result of the building of the Neptune Power Station at Wallsend. Richard Paget, who was interested in developing the use of fused silica, met Charles Mertz and William McLellan to discuss proposals and then persuaded Lord Armstrong and Mertz & McLellan to set up the company. They appointed Dr Frank Bottomly, who already worked for Mertz & McLellan to head up the company using a wooden hut beside the Neptune Power Station to carry out research. After some time Dr Bottomly was successful in fusing the silica by passing heavy electric currents through carbon rods to produce vitreous silica products that had a wide range of uses in the chemical industry as they were acid and heat resistant. The company was then formally

Thermal Syndicate factory buildings, seen from beside the Neptune Pub, over the Riverside Railway.

set up as Thermal Syndicate Ltd. With no competition in early years, the company soon opened a London office in 1907 and further offices in Brussels and New York were opened in 1910 to sell their products, which were trademarked Vitreosil. The company continued to expand and Wallsend was its world headquarters. The site itself was developed on Neptune Road, with new buildings being built. The former offices of the Gas Board Neptune House were taken over as their head office in 1960s until new offices were built on the east of the site in 1980. A new Fused Magnesia Plant was built at Benton Square in 1965 and this was well known in the area for having very loud explosions taking place as part of the process, so much so that road signs were erected outside the plant warning of potential explosions. In 1988 the company was bought by the Saint-Gobain Group but retained its name until the end of the century.

MONITOR SAFETY DEVICES

Charles Leslie Stokoe opened a factory on Kings Road, adjoining the Coast Road, in the 1920s or 1930s to manufacture safety devices. The advert on the wall of the factory read: 'Monitor Safety Devices C.L. Stokoe Patents'. He was an inventor who specialised in designing a range of safety devices to measure the flow of liquids, thermostats, pressure alarms and other indicators, all of which he patented then manufactured successfully in Wallsend for many years. The factory was demolished in the 1990s and housing was built on the site.

"MONITOR"

PATENT SAFETY DEVICES LTD.

WE MANUFACTURE FOR EXPORT TO ALL PARTS OF THE WORLD THE FOLLOWING UNITS FOR SAFEGUARDING MARINE AND LAND POWER PLANT :-

FLOW METERS.
PRESSURE ALARMS.
FLOAT ALARMS.
THERMOSTATS.
INDICATOR PANELS.
MINE FAN REVOLUTION INDICATORS.
ELECTRICALLY OPERATED VALVES.
BOILER WATER LEVEL INDICATORS.
ETC.

Regd. Trade Mark **"MONITOR."**   C. L. STOKOE PATENTS.

"Monitor" Works,   Kings Road,   Wallsend - on - Tyne.
TEL:- WALLSEND 63831.

A 1951 advert for Monitor works, Wallsend.

VICTOR PRODUCTS

Reg Mann set up Victor Products in 1929, specialising in the design and sale of mining equipment, and it became a public company in 1955. It was originally based on North View, opposite St Peter's Church, and went on to occupy a large site bounded by the Metro line and Limekiln Road. In 1958 he was awarded a CBE for his contribution to industry and following his death a charitable fund was set up in his name – R. W. Mann Fund – which still gives grants to local organisations. The company is now located on the Port of Tyne land at Tyne Dock, South Shields, and claims to be the world leader in the manufacture of electrical connectors for the global coal-mining industry with facilities in Europe, the United States and South Africa. The original factory was demolished in the 1990s and is now occupied by housing.

NORTH EAST ELECTRICITY BOARD

The North East Electricity Board (NEEB) set up a meter testing station in Wallsend on Kings Road, south of the Coast Road and opposite Monitor Engineering, in the 1960s. It served the North East, servicing and testing electric metres as well as being a base for meter readers to operate from. The buildings were demolished and redeveloped for housing in the 1990s.

GASWORKS, HOWDON LANE

In 1908 new gasworks were built on Howdon Lane to the south of the present Metro line and Howdon station, replacing the original gasworks that were close to the River Tyne and Willington Gut in Willington Quay. The works were absorbed into the Newcastle & Gateshead Gas Company in 1925. The two massive storage tanks, the later one built in 1931, close to the railway were major landmarks in Howdon for most of the century and the site covered a large area, extending southwards to the former Riverside Railway and Willington Quay Station. Much of the former site has now been replaced by housing.

GEORGE ANGUS

A new factory was built north of the Coast Road on the outskirts of Wallsend in 1956 by the long-established Newcastle firm of George Angus & Co. Ltd. It specialised in the manufacture of rubber seals for a wide range of industrial uses. In 1968 the firm merged with Dunlop Ltd to form the Dunlop Angus Industrial Group. The company continued on this site until the 1990s, when it was renamed Freudenberg. They relocated to New York and the site was taken over by B&Q and other uses.

M. W. SWINBURNE & SONS BRASS WORKS

Mark William Swinburne from Newcastle set up a brass foundry and works with his son Charles on the site of the former Gair's Ropery, on the corner of Park Road and Hadrian Road, south of the railway line. The company specialised in brass works for ships and marine engines. Mark William Swinburne was Mayor of Wallsend in 1911–12. Charles took over the business in 1912 but the pressures of work led to him committing suicide in 1922, walking in front of a train at Heaton station. The business continued to be successful until the 1980s when it was closed and the land was taken over by J. M. Keith for storage purposes. Later the Energy Academy, a college for renewable energy, part of Newcastle College was built on the site.

BRIMM'S

Brimm's Plant Hire had a storage yard on the south side of Hadrian Road, west of Point Pleasant Terrace and east of the fire station, for many years before it was replaced by housing in recent years.

SHEPHERD OFFSHORE

Shepherds Offshore have purchased a number of sites in Wallsend in recent years to complement their businesses in Walker. Some are used for storage purposes and others have been developed. During a recent development at Benton Way in 2013 the remains of the timber Willington Waggonway were discovered (*see* mining section).

WILLIAM PRESS

William Press was one of the first companies to develop riverside sites in Wallsend to build structures for the offshore oil and gas industries. They took over the former sites of the Tyne Improvement Commission and Northumberland Shipbuilding Co. in 1975. They built many modules for offshore drilling rigs including the largest to be built in the world at one time, weighing over 200 tons. A lot of former shipyard workers were employed in the industry. The company later became AMEC in 1981.

AMEC

AMEC was a specialist company set up to build giant offshore platforms for the oil and gas industries. In the mid-1980s they occupied riverside sites at Willington Quay and later took over the former North East Marine site using the offices as their headquarters.

Oil rigs being built on the riverside beside Willington Gut.

WILLIAM LEECH HOUSE BUILDERS

The well-known builder Sir William Leech built some of his company's first houses in Wallsend in the 1930s on the Kings Road estate, north of the Coast Road. The company expanded nationally and built many more houses in north Wallsend. It became part of the Beazer Group in the 1980s, which was later taken over by Bellway's, another North East company.

PAMETRADA

The site of the Turbinia Works in Davy Bank became Pametrada, a research establishment, in 1944. It researched improvements to turbines used by the Admiralty and merchant ships. It later merged with the British Shipbuilding Research Association in 1962 and some years later merged again with the National Maritime Institute to form British Maritime Technology in

A 1951 advert for Parsons Turbines.

The Queen Mother visits Pametrada in Wallsend, 1956.

1985. The former site of the Wallsend Research Station is now the site of Oceana Business Park and the Pametrada Art Centre occupies part of the site.

SWALES

Swales Timber Yard occupied the site to the east of the gasworks on Howdon Lane and south of the railway line at Howdon station for many years. New industries are now based on the site.

WALLSEND HERITAGE CENTRE & ROMAN FORT EXCAVATIONS

The first museum in Wallsend was opened in 1986 in a former office building opposite the present Segedunum Roman Museum and was known as Wallsend Heritage Centre. It celebrated both the Roman and industrial heritage of the town near to where Segedunum Roman Fort had been rediscovered.

A major archaeological exercise was undertaken from 1975 to 1986. After the excavations were completed the outline of the fort was marked out by decorative paving and certain buildings were marked out on the surface. New Housing on Wooley Street was built beyond and overlooking the fort to the north. To the west of the fort and north of Buddle Street the former Carville Methodist Church, Colliery Chapel and Sunday school were demolished and a 30-metre-long replica Roman wall was built as a tourist attraction linked to the museum.

Excavations north of Buddle Street in 1975, seen from Simpson's Hotel.

Excavations on Buddle Street in 1975, with Simpson's Hotel on the right.

Simpson's Hotel on Buddle Street, Wallsend, closed in 1981.

INDUSTRIAL ESTATES

From the 1950s to the 1980s a number of purpose-built industrial estates were developed on various sites in Wallsend to provide small factories for new businesses. Some of these were built on vacant land and others on former colliery or housing sites. These sites included Oak Grove (with W. B. Kerr's coaches and an ambulance station), Maurice Road, Gerald Street, Point Pleasant, and Hadrian Road (with the bus depot, J. M. Keith, and City Electrical Factors) in Wallsend. There was also a small industrial area on the south side of Wallsend Green where the former 'Stadium' roller-skating rink had been converted into a number of industrial uses including motor car manufacture and storage uses.

The buildings were used as government offices and training workshops after the Second World War and the 'Dole Office' was based here for many years, together with other businesses including Stockhill's Removals Company. Other industrial estates were built at Bewicke Road and Stephenson Street (where a new plywood factory, Tyne Plywood Ltd, was built and other factories were used by Status Kitchens and the Carpet Warehouse). Nearby was the depot for Marsden Freight Services, Campbell & Isherwood Ltd, Tyne Gangway Co. Ltd, D.E.V. Engineering, Houseman Hegro and other smaller businesses. On the riverside former shipyards were used by Barrier Surface Treatments and Cookson's Antimony Works.

The former Stephenson Memorial Schools on Stephenson Street, opened in 1860, were demolished after a new school was built beside Howdon station and the site used for industry. Another industrial estate was developed at Norman Terrace (with J&J Fashions) in Willington Quay. The former settlement known as Howdon Panns was completely lost in the 1960s when the Tyne vehicle tunnel was built and then opened by the Queen in 1964.

The stadium building on
Wallsend Green in 1985.

Wallsend Motor Company,
High Street.

Inside the laboratories at Cookson's Antimony Works, Willington Quay, *c.* 1963.

In the 1970s a new technical college was built to the north of the Coast Road in Battle Hill to provide training for the local workforce. The South-East Northumberland Training College, or SENTEC as it was known locally, offered a wide range of vocational training courses. It is now called Tyne Metropolitan College.

TWENTY-FIRST CENTURY

In 2000 Swan Hunters was awarded a contract to build two Royal Fleet Auxiliary vessels: the *Largs Bay* was completed in 2006 but the second ship, the *Lyme Bay*, was not completed on Tyneside and had to be floated up to Glasgow for completion later that year. In 2007 the cranes and its floating dock were sold to a company in India and in 2008 they were dismantled and taken to India in the floating dock. From 2008 the company continued to operate as ship designers with around 200 staff and when Jaap Kroese died in 2016 the number of staff was around forty. In 2016 Gerard Kroese relaunched the company to offer design advice and provide equipment for the offshore renewables and subsea oil and gas energy markets and had a staff of twenty-seven in 2017.

North Tyneside Council bought the Swan Hunter shipyard in the early 2010s and have invested in improvements to the site including new vehicular access to attract future industries. In recent years Swan Hunters yard has been the base for the TV series *Vera* with the former office doubling as the police station. Part of the office buildings have now been converted into the 'Centre for Innovation' to attract new businesses.

The former Wallsend Slipway site was used to build the famous Millennium Bridge and was floated down the Tyne, carried by an enormous floating crane, on 20 November 2000.

The same yard has recently been used for building massive bases for offshore wind turbines. Cleland's shipyard site now houses a waste transfer and recycling station. Many of the former shipbuilding sites in Wallsend and Walker have been bought by Shepherd's Offshore, a logistics and property company providing services to the offshore industry.

On Davy Bank S.M.D. (Soil Mechanics Dynamics) is now a pioneering company developing undersea robotic craft. This company is situated close to many new businesses based in the Oceana Business Park, which occupies the site of the former Turbinia Works, Pametrada and Carville Power Station sites.

In 2000 Thermal Syndicate changed its name to Saint-Gobain Quartz Plc and in 2006 celebrated its centenary. The company on the site is now known as Heraeus Quartz UK and is the world's largest integrated quartz glass producer with eight production facilities worldwide. Quartz glass made in Wallsend is used in computer equipment, optical fibres and laser technology.

Smulders is an international steel construction company who took over the former Wallsend Slipway site in recent years and in 2018 built a number of massive bases for wind turbines that dominated the skyline of Wallsend for many months.

A giant crane carries the Wallsend-built Millennium Bridge to Newcastle in 2000.

Giant bases for wind turbines built on the riverside at Wallsend.

A view over Willington Gut of the wind turbine bases under construction.

Wallsend Town Hall Business Centre is the new name for the former Wallsend Town Hall, which was taken over in the early 2010s by a company that have set up a hub to help to establish and provide support and facilities for new businesses. The company have been so successful that the Town Hall is now full of new and expanding firms and the company are now seeking additional premises to extend the business and have identified the former Buddle Arts Centre to convert into business use. The former Wallsend Baths have also recently been converted into a base for an electrical contractor.

In 2000 the new £10 million Segedunum Roman Fort, Baths and Museum, the largest museum on Hadrian's Wall, opened to celebrate the towns Roman and industrial heritage. The main buildings took over the former Swan Hunter Institute buildings and canteen and a new 35-metre viewing tower was built along with a life-sized replica Roman baths complex. The shape of the Roman fort buildings were marked out on site using a combination of original stones and modern materials. The museum is now a major tourist attraction as well as being a major education resource for local schools.

To the north of B&Q, on Middle Engine Lane, Northumbria Police have recently built a new headquarters building close to the Silverlink Retail Park, part of which falls within the original Wallsend boundary. Wallsend continues to adapt to new challenges and work opportunities.

Wallsend Festival stalls in the Forum in 2002.

Buddle Schools and later
Buddle Arts Centre on
Station Road, Wallsend.

Roman soldiers march from
Wallsend Metro station to
Segedunum Fort in 2000.

The former Riverside Railway looking east towards the Ship Inn and Segedunum.

Sentius Tectonicus at Segedunum Roman Fort.

ACKNOWLEDGEMENTS

This book has been written on behalf of Wallsend Local History Society and all proceeds from the royalties will be donated to the My Name'5 Doddy Foundation, who are raising funds to aid research into motor neurone disease. The society was established in 1973 and meets in St Luke's Church Hall, Frank Street, at 7.00 p. m. every second Monday of the month.

I wish to record my special thanks to all who have helped me in the past and especially to those who have been recently active on the committee. The present committee includes Liz Liddle, Dorothy Hall, Elaine Borthwick, Jean Cleathero, Phyll Laws, George Laws, Edmund Hall, Alan Maddison, Barry Martin, Brian Robson and Lennie Fisher. I have used a number of photographs from the society's collection.

I would also like to thank North Tyneside Libraries for the use of a large number of old photographs from their excellent Local Studies Collection. Special thanks are due to Joyce Marti, John Allen and Clare Pepper for their help and expertise. I would also like to thank previous staff from the Local Studies section who have, over many years, built up an invaluable store of local history through their collections and research and have been very helpful to me over the years. They include Eric Hollerton, Alan Hildrew, Diane Leggett and Martyn Hurst. I would like to take this opportunity to encourage anyone who has any old photographs of buildings or scenes in Wallsend to make them available to the Discover Local Studies Library in North Shields Central Library or to Wallsend Local History Society.

My thanks are also due to Tyne & Wear Archives and Museums and in particular to Nick Hodgson and Lizzy Baker for providing images, as well as the staff at Segedunum Roman Fort, Baths and Museum and the Committee of Friends of Segedunum. My thanks also go to the staff at Amberley Publishing including Jenny Stephens and Marcus Pennington.

Finally, I would like to thank my wife Pauline (for reading the manuscript), sons Peter and David, granddaughter Isla, Sue, Wendy, Lucas and Mary and Malcolm, Honor, Christine, Dave, Lawrence, Liz, Susan and Dominic for their encouragement and support.